Murder in Seville

NICK SWEET

CONTENTS

Chapters 1 – 60

MURDER IN SEVILLE

Chapter 1

She was surprised by the sound of footsteps that seemed to have come out of nowhere, and turned to see a man some thirty paces behind her.

Was it the same one as yesterday?

She couldn't be sure. She saw that he was wearing jeans and a casual jacket. But he was too far away for her to be able to make out his face in the murky light.

It was the twilight hour, and the pros and pushers and their johns had all turned in long ago. They had littered the gutters and pavements with used needles, cigarette ends and other testimony of the night's desperate revelries. As for the legal traders that claimed the area in the daytime, they would still be sleeping in their beds.

She told herself there was nothing to worry about.

So if that was the case then why did she have this antsy feeling in her gut?

She turned her head to take another look.

It wasn't the same man…was it?

He had the same loping gait.

Only wasn't the one she thought had been following her yesterday a little taller and leaner?

She couldn't be sure either way.

The man was gaining on her.

She told herself to get a grip. There was no reason to be frightened… Or was there?

She could feel her heart pounding in her chest.

She quickened her step as she passed more warehouses and a café, all still closed. Her breakfast show was due to go live in a couple of hours, and she needed to prepare herself. That meant being briefed by Oscar, her programme manager, on her guest and the things she ought to be talking to him about. It also meant being made up, so she would look her best for the camera. All this stress was the last thing she needed.

She was breathing hard, even though she was used to running on the treadmill and in good condition.

Difference was, she didn't have anybody on her tail when she was at the gym.

Just keep walking – and stop thinking.

The entrance to the studio was just up ahead. She hurried the rest of the way, and breathed a sigh of relief as she went in through the door.

The next moment, she told herself she should have stood her ground. Christ, it wasn't like her to behave like this. As the daughter of a famous bullfighter, she'd been taught right from an early age never to give in to her fears.

She dashed back outside, with the idea of confronting the man… But there was no sign of him or anyone else.

Where the hell had he gone?

If he had climbed into his car and driven off then she would surely have heard him.

Then again, he might be the manager of one of the concerns in the vicinity. If so, then he could just have let himself into whichever building it was he worked at.

But which businesses around here opened this early?

She was hard put to think of any.

Maybe the man was hiding somewhere…

All kinds of possibilities were buzzing around in her head as she went back inside. Maybe she was seeing danger where there wasn't any.

Or was that only what she wanted to believe?

Alvaro in reception said, '*Buenos dias*, Pe,' from behind his desk. 'Is anything the matter?'

She shook her head and took the lift up to the second floor.

Chapter 2

Pe cocked an eyebrow when Oscar told her that the guest she was going to be interviewing on today's show had an even shadier past than the man she interviewed last week, Antonio Costa. She said that she knew Pedro Villalonga was close to General Franco, back in the bad old days of the dictatorship. 'But there's more,' Oscar said, and he dropped a manila file onto her desk. 'Take a look for yourself.'

The long, lean body was lying face down on the bed, naked and spread-eagled, and the ankles and wrists were tied to the bedposts. He'd been gagged and something large…Christ, it was a sawn-off *bull's horn* that had been rammed up his ass.

The victim was male, blond, and appeared to be somewhere around the age of sixty. Inspector Jefe Luis Velázquez felt the body: it was still warm. The bedspread was covered in blood, and some of it had dripped onto the parquet flooring.

Seeing a pair of trousers hanging over the back of an upright chair by the dressing table, Velázquez slipped on his rubber gloves and went through the pockets. He found a bunch of keys and a brown leather wallet. Inside it were the victim's ID, driving licence, and a card to show the man was a registered veterinarian.

And there was a sheet of paper with some writing on it on the bedside table. Velázquez picked it up, and saw that the writing had been typed in what looked like the Times New Roman font.

HELLO, INSPECTOR JEFE VELÁZQUEZ. I'M SO GLAD YOU COULD COME. I JUST THOUGHT I SHOULD WARN YOU TO KEEP AN EYE ON THAT LOVELY WIFE OF YOURS. JUST THINK OF ALL THOSE PEOPLE OUT THERE THAT WATCH HER BREAKFAST SHOW. SHE SEEMS SO EXPOSED TO THE PUBLIC, IF YOU KNOW WHAT I MEAN. IT WOULD BE AN AWFUL PITY IF YOU WEREN'T AROUND TO TAKE GOOD CARE OF HER.

LEAVE THIS CASE WELL ALONE, FOR YOUR LOVELY WIFE'S SAKE.

Velázquez folded the sheet of paper and slipped it into his pocket. He glanced in the mirror on the dressing table. He saw a tall figure that had somehow stayed lean, despite his penchant for red wine and fried food. He was thirty-seven, but the dark bags under his eyes made him look older. He really should try to get more sleep and go to the gym. He might take a leaf out of Subinspector Gajardo's book and dress better, too. The navy polo shirt he had on was badly creased. Ditto his black chinos. He looked like a swarthy athlete gone to seed. His craggy face was filled with anger and indignation. He saw fear there, as well. The cragginess and the anger and indignation were an old story. But the fear was something new.

What did the killer know about Pe?

No sooner had he asked himself this than he realized the stupidity of the question. Practically everyone in Spain knew who Pe was, now that she had her own television show.

He made an effort to pull himself together. The killer wanted to make this personal, that much was clear. But Velázquez had a job to do, and he wasn't about to let anyone prevent him from doing it.

Going through the drawers in the dressing table, he found a small, personal phone book and documents pertaining to the victim's car insurance. He saw that the man had owned a Porsche and made a note of the registration number.

He opened the small phone book and flicked through the pages. He found entries for the Maestranza bullring in Seville, and a ranch belonging to the Gutiérrez family. Old Gutiérrez was known to be one of the movers and shakers in the region. Velázquez had read a fair bit about the man in the local newspapers over the years. So he knew that Gutiérrez and his people had been staunch supporters of the Franco regime back in the day. And it was only after the new constitution was written that they had begun singing the praises of democracy and the rights of ordinary working people. But talk was cheap and Velázquez knew bullshit when he came across it.

He slipped the small phone book into his pocket, along with the victim's car keys, ID and other cards. Voices rose from below, followed by footsteps on the stairs. Moments later,

4

Velázquez's number two, José Gajardo, came in through the open door. He was sporting a new light-blue summer suit that fitted his lean frame perfectly. '*Jees-sus.* What a mess.' Gajardo came over to the bed to take a closer look. 'Who called the murder in, boss?'

'The girl that comes in to clean up.' Velázquez heard more voices drifting up from below, followed by heavy footsteps, and Judge Miguel Bautista entered the room. A stocky figure in a beige linen suit, he sounded slightly out of breath as he came over to the bed.

The Judge was here to make a preliminary inspection. Velázquez's job was to persuade him there was enough evidence to take the case to court, and he knew from past experience how stubborn the man could be.

Bautista shook his head in disgust. 'All we need in this heat.' He mopped his brow with a handkerchief and looked at Velázquez. 'I assume all the relevant people have been notified?'

Velázquez assured the Judge that they had. Just then, the Médico Forense, Manolo Hernandez, came hurrying in. Following on his heels were a photographer the Inspector Jefe didn't recognize and David Morales, a fingerprint man Velázquez had known for years.

Hernandez set down his briefcase on the night table and looked at the body. 'Boy, what a way to go.' He took out a thermometer. 'A huge thing like that would've ripped through the lining of the alimentary canal and penetrated the large and small intestines.'

Velázquez watched as the doctor lodged his thermometer between the victim's buttocks, so that it was held in position by the bull's horn. 'It could well have punctured the stomach and even the liver, too.' The doctor was taking things out of his case. 'He'd have bled to death very quickly.' He glanced at Velázquez. 'Now you're going to ask me to tell you the time of death.'

'You're a mind reader.'

'There's no way I can be exact, as you know,' Hernandez said, continuing to go about his work.

5

'How about if you take a look in your crystal ball?'

The doctor was holding the thermometer up to the light. 'I'd say somewhere between one and five hours ago, going by the body temperature.' He looked at the Inspector Jefe and shrugged. 'Sorry I can't be more precise than that, Luis, but I never did have much in the way of supernatural powers.'

'Thanks, Manolo – it's better than nothing.'

Velázquez looked at his wristwatch: the time was now 06:43, so the murder must have taken place at some point between around 01.43 and 05.43. That was assuming the doctor's off-the-record estimate of the time of death was not wildly off the mark.

He turned to his number two and jerked his head, to signal that he wanted a word with him in private. Then he left the room, and Gajardo followed him out and down the stairs.

'What's up, boss?'

'I found this.' Velázquez reached into his pocket and brought out the victim's ID card. 'I need you to take some copies of it. I'll see you and the rest of the team back at the Jefatura for a briefing when I've finished here.'

The Subinspector glanced at the photo then went out.

Velázquez took a look around downstairs. Oak beams ran across the high ceiling and there were prints of paintings on the whitewashed walls. He recognised Goya's *Los fusilamientos del 3 de mayo*. Expensive-looking Turkish rugs covered the polished wooden boards, and yesterday's edition of *El Pais* lay open on the pinewood coffee table. The shelves were crammed with books, and the big grey eye of the television screen gazed out at the room from its stand in the corner. All in all, it seemed like rather a nice place to live. But it wasn't necessarily such a nice place to end up dying.

Down in the street, Velázquez found the victim's Porsche parked just a little way along from the entrance to the block. He opened the door with the keys he'd taken from the crime scene, and went through the glove compartment. He looked under the seats and then in the boot. All he found was a map of Spain, a box of tools, a spare tyre, and a packet of mints.

He locked the car, and went back to the building, reentering it just as Judge Bautista reached the bottom of the stairs. The Judge fixed him with a dour expression and said if the *modus operandi* was anything to go by, they were almost certainly looking for a jealous lover on this one. Bautista smoothed down his grizzled beard. 'It shouldn't be too hard to find out who the man was involved with, Inspector Jefe,' he said. 'But you'll need to give me something that'll stick this time.'

'We'll be working round the clock.'

'You'd better be. Screw up again and people will start to wonder if it's more than just a run of bad luck you've been having.'

While nobody would have guessed it from the expression in his hawk-like eyes, Velázquez felt like telling the man where to go. But he could hardly do that.

Besides, he realized the truth of the Judge's words.

'I'm finished here,' Bautista said. 'Let me know as soon as you've got something, Inspector Jefe.' And with that he went out.

Velázquez went back up to the bedroom, where the fingerprint expert was going over the bedframe with a small brush. The Inspector Jefe took out the note that was left by the killer and unfolded it. 'This was left on the night table,' he said. 'I need you to go over it for prints as a matter of priority, David.'

The fingerprint expert read the note.

'As you can see,' Velázquez said, 'the killer's trying to put the frighteners on. I'd like to keep this between you and me. The last thing I want is for my wife to find out.'

Chapter 3

'Look at this.' Inspector Jefe Luis Velázquez was handing out to the members of his team the copies Gajardo had made. 'It's taken from the victim's ID card,' he said. 'The cleaning girl found him dead on the bed at his house on Calle Alhondiga early this morning. He was skewered by a bull's horn.'

A silence fell over the room. Agente Jorge Serrano, a freckled, ginger-haired Madrileño, was the first to break it. 'What do we know so far, boss?'

'He was a qualified vet, and we can see from his ID that his name was Arjan Gelens...fifty-eight years old, and he was Dutch...born in Rotterdam. Although he was a naturalized Spanish subject, so he must've been living here for at least ten years.'

Agente Sara Pérez, a beautiful young brunette who, like Jorge, was from Madrid originally, asked about the time of death. The Inspector Jefe told her what he knew. He mopped the sweat from his brow with his handkerchief. 'Sara, Jorge and Javi, I need you to get over to Calle Alhondiga and show people the photo of the victim. Talk to the man's neighbours, and people that work in the shops, bars and cafés in the vicinity. We need to hear from anyone who saw or heard anything, as well as anyone who can give us any information at all on Gelens. There must be people who knew the man, and can tell us where he hung out and who he did it with...anything at all... And don't forget, it's a particularly vicious and dangerous killer we're after, so we'll all be working long hours on this one. We need to catch him fast, in case he's planning to get up to any more mischief. ' He clapped his hands. 'Come on, let's get going.'

The three officers filed out.

'What about me, boss?' Gajardo asked.

'I need you to go and find the cleaning girl, Monica Pacheco, and bring her in, José.' Velázquez took out his notebook, found the relevant page, and handed it to the Subinspector. 'Here's her number and address,' he said. 'And check to see if she's got a criminal record, too.'

Gajardo made a note of the woman's details then went out.

No sooner had Velázquez found himself alone in the office than the telephone on his desk rang. It was the fingerprint man. He had searched the note for prints and come up with *nada*. 'The guy must've worn gloves, Luis,' he said. 'I'm still working at the crime scene, and I'll let you know if I come across any prints that match what we've got on record.'

'Thanks, David.' Velázquez hung up. He glanced at his watch: it was coming up to half-past eight. That meant Pe's breakfast show would already have started. The note the killer left at the crime scene had unnerved the Inspector Jefe. It was because of this that he felt a sudden urge to see his wife's face, just so he'd know she was all right. It was ironic, he thought, that Pe had been talking – only in private and with him, so far – of giving up her job as a television presenter and trying to make a career for herself as a bullfighter. He had no doubt that she was serious about it. She had been practising with bulls in private for some time now, under the expert guidance of a professional. Presenting her television show was boring, she said. She wanted to do 'real work', something with a hint of danger about it. She'd always been crazy about bullfighting, ever since she was a little kid. He supposed it was in her blood, because her father had been a great *torero* in his day.

Naturally Velázquez hated the idea of Pe changing career. Not because he didn't want her to be happy, but because he knew the risks bullfighters ran.

And now *this*…

He went out to the café on the corner, and sure enough, Pe's programme was showing on the television behind the counter. He thought how beautiful his wife was, with her lovely eyes that seemed to radiate intelligence and her perfect bone structure. He was very proud of her.

He parked himself on a stool, and turned his attention to what was happening on the screen. Pe was interviewing Pedro Villalonga, the cabinet minister. The man was a total hypocrite, and Pe was ripping into him and making the guy squirm in his seat. How was it, she asked him, that he had managed to effect such a total turnaround in his political thinking in such a short space of time? Villalonga acted like he didn't understand the question. 'From being a fascist when you were a key player in General Franco's dictatorship to the proponent of democracy you purport to be today, I mean?' The politician argued that he had merely adapted to the changes that he saw taking place all around him. It was perfectly permissible and even normal, he said, for a man to change his mind about things over time.

Having satisfied himself that Pe was okay, Velázquez dropped some coins onto the counter and said, '*Hasta luego*' before he made for the door. But before he reached it, he heard his wife say evidence had come to light that would appear to confirm Villalonga's having been in sympathy with the Nazis' genocidal aims. That stopped Velázquez in his tracks. He turned to look at the screen in time to see his wife open the file on her lap. He heard her tell her guest that her team had unearthed a number of memos bearing the minister's signature.

As he listened to Pe reading one of the memos, Velázquez realized that this was some heavy shit she had on Pedro Villalonga. She was giving today's guest an even harder ride than she had given Antonio Costa on last Friday's show. A *much* harder ride, in fact. When all was said and done, she only asked Costa about rumours that were circulating to the effect that he was involved in corrupt activities. But she didn't have any hard evidence against the man.

Today was different.

The memo Pe had just read aloud, for millions of viewers to hear, was something else. It offered proof – assuming the document could be authenticated – that as a young man Villalonga was instrumental in ordering the deportation of Jews from Spain to Vichy France during the Second World War. Pe paused before adding the killer blow – that these poor Jews would then have been handed over to the Nazis.

Villalonga must have known when he wrote the memo that he was sending those Jews to the concentration camps.

Velázquez was mightily impressed with the work his wife was doing here. Her timing and delivery were cool and professional, as ever. But he was also more than a little worried, because

Pedro Villalonga was a rich and powerful man. If people attacked someone like him then they needed to realize there would be consequences.

Pe turned her head to look at the camera. Her expression had changed. She looked worried – alarmed, even. She said she was sorry but they were going to have to cut the programme short.

Hearing this, Velázquez broke out in a cold sweat. Something was clearly very wrong at the studio.

What if Arjan Gelens's killer had now gone after Pe, as he threatened to do in the note he left at the crime scene?

Velázquez dashed out to his car and set off. He drove with his foot on the floor and the siren blaring, as he weaved his way through the rush-hour traffic.

Before he got anywhere near the studio, he found the road was blocked by squad cars and the surrounding area had been cordoned off. Then he saw Pe, standing with a group of others on the pavement. He pulled over, then climbed out of his car and hurried up to her. 'Thank God you're all right,' he said.

'Luis.' She looked surprised. 'What on earth are you doing here?'

'I heard there was some kind of trouble at the studio and I got worried.' He looked around. 'What exactly's going on here, anyway?'

'There's been a bomb threat,' she said. 'All we know for sure is there hasn't been any explosion – not yet, anyway.'

'Jesus Christ.' He puffed out his cheeks.

'We're hoping that it's just a hoax and we'll be able to go back on air soon,' Pe said. 'We'll have to wait until we've been given the okay first, naturally.' She raised a hand to shield her eyes from the sun as she looked over at the entrance to the building. 'Hopefully they'll be able to tell us something before too long.'

Velázquez looked at his wife long and hard. He loved her like crazy, and couldn't bear the thought of anything happening to her.

'Anyway, I'm quite safe, so I'm afraid you made a pointless journey.' She gave him the kind of smile that could make a man's day or break his heart.

He asked her who had answered the phone when the man that

11

made the bomb threat called. That would be Alvaro, who worked in reception. She turned and pointed to a grey-haired man in his fifties, short and with a potbelly.

Velázquez went and talked to the man. He learned from him that the caller hadn't said much – just that everyone should get out of the building right away because a bomb was set to go off. Then the caller hung up. Even so, Alvaro was able to tell from the few words the caller uttered that he had a local accent.

Velázquez figured that should narrow the search down to about half a million people in the province.

He headed off towards the building. A uniform barred his path, and he showed the man his ID. 'It's only the bomb disposal people that are allowed in there, sir.'

'I have reason to believe this incident may be linked to a murder I'm investigating,' Velázquez said. 'Now if you'll get out of my path...'

The uniform stood aside and Velázquez carried on his way. Once inside the building, he had the bomb disposal people wanting to know who he was. He showed his ID to the head of the unit, a man of compact build with receding black hair, and told him the same thing he had told the uniform outside.

The man nodded, and told him he and his officers were still searching to see if there was a bomb on the premises. Velázquez said in that case, he would take a look around.

His emotions were getting the better of him and all kinds of ideas were going through his mind. What if it had been Arjan Gelens's killer who made the bomb threat? In that case, it might just be a hoax the man had pulled to enable him to get close to Pe. The guy might even have sneaked into the empty building, and be lying in wait for when she returned. Anything was possible.

Velázquez took out his Sig Sauer 226 9mm combat pistol, just in case, and set about searching the building.

He didn't find anyone on the premises that shouldn't be there.

He checked again with the bomb disposal men. They still hadn't found any bomb, but would keep looking until they were completely sure the building and the immediate vicinity were safe.

He went behind the reception desk, picked up the telephone and dialed the number for directory enquiries. A woman answered and he told her who he was and where he was calling from. There had been a bomb threat, he said, so he needed to know where the last call to the studio was made from.

The woman put him on hold. Velázquez stood there, tapping his foot and hoping to Christ the bomb threat wasn't for real and that he wasn't about to get blown up.

The woman came back on the line and told him that the call had been made from a telephone kiosk nearby on Calle Coral. All that told Velázquez was that there was no way he'd be able to discover the caller's identity.

He thanked the woman and hung up, then went out and rejoined Pe. She seemed a little surprised that he was still here. Didn't he have a killer to catch? Something in her tone told him she suspected he was worrying about her. He knew only too well how she resented it when she felt he was being overprotective. Or was he reading too much into her manner and just imagining all this?

Either way, he realized it was no good allowing his fears for his wife's safety to get the better of him. He would only succeed in ruffling her feathers that way. Besides, he had already done what he came here to do, which was to establish that she wasn't in any imminent danger. 'I'll catch you later, then, Pe.' He planted a kiss on her cheek. 'God, you smell *nice.*'

'So I should,' she said. 'This perfume's what I got from you for my birthday.'

Chapter 4

Back at the Jefatura on Calle Blas Infante, Inspector Jefe Velázquez consulted the victim's personal phone book. He found the entry for the Maestranza bullring and dialed the number. A gruff masculine voice answered. Velázquez explained why he was calling, and learned from the man on the other end of the line that Arjan Gelens had been on a retainer to look after the bulls. The man knew Gelens 'to say hello to' but that was all.

Once he had hung up, Velázquez was about to call the Gutiérrez ranch, but then decided it might be better to take a drive down there. Sometimes you could learn more from questioning people face to face.

Mateo Vidal called downstairs to say he had checked Arjan Gelens out, and no, the man didn't have any previous. 'I hope Pe's keeping well,' Vidal said. 'Ana's a real fan of her show, never misses it.' Velázquez said he'd pass the message on when he got home then hung up.

He carried on working his way through the numbers in the victim's personal phone book. He called Gelens's doctor and dentist, as well as a plumber and an electrician who had done some work for him. They were all sad to hear the bad news, but none of them saw any way they could possibly be of assistance.

He was about to dial the next number when Gajardo called to say he had the cleaning girl, Monica Pacheco, downstairs. 'Oh, and I checked to see if she's got any previous, boss,' he said. 'She hasn't.'

A posse of reporters showed up and Pe figured it was time to make herself scarce, so she hurried off to a nearby café with Pili. They sat at a table and had just been served with their order when Oscar came in. He looked tall, slim and elegant in his jeans and T-shirt, but a little flustered. He went up to the counter and told the waiter what he wanted, before he came over and joined them. 'Pity about the timing of this bloody bomb scare, Pe,' he said. 'You had Pedro Villalonga on toast there.'

Pili ran a hand through her peroxide-blonde bob. 'I'll say,' she said, 'you had him squirming in his chair like the rotten worm he is.'

The door opened and three men dressed in blue overalls came in.

Pe took a bite of her toasted baguette. 'So what's the state of play?'

Oscar shrugged. 'Matter of having to wait and see, I'm afraid.' The waiter came over with his coffee and roll. 'It's probably some lonely nut job with nothing better to do than waste everyone's time.' He tasted his coffee. 'I only wish they'd chosen Canal Five to try this nonsense with, instead of us,' he said. 'At least that would've given the useless sods something interesting to talk about instead of the bullshit they normally run.'

The door opened, and a man wearing chinos and a denim jacket came in. Instead of ordering anything he went over to the three men in blue overalls and said something to them. One of the workmen said something in reply, then the man turned and made for the door.

As she watched him go out, Pe felt the tiny hairs on the back of her neck stand on end. Without stopping to think, she got up and went out after the man and followed him along the pavement. She was almost sure he was the man she'd reckoned might have been tailing her earlier.

When she reached the corner, she saw him getting into a car that was parked on the other side of the street. She ran towards the car. '*Wait!*' she called. '*Stop!*' She was waving her arms, but he started up the engine and drove off.

She ran after the car a little way, but it accelerated then turned the corner and disappeared out of sight.

She wondered whether the man had seen or heard her. It was impossible to tell.

She returned to the café and asked the workmen who the man in the black leather jacket was. They didn't know. He had just asked if there were any restaurants near here, one of the men said.

She went and sat down, and Pili asked her if anything was wrong. She shook her head. 'You looked like you were in a mad hurry to catch up with that man,' Pili said. 'Who was he?'

Before Pe could think of a reply the door opened and Miguel Sainz, a reporter she knew, came in. He was of medium height and build, and wore jeans, trainers and a striped shirt. He spotted her and came over, then said hello and asked if there was anything she could tell him about what was happening here. Pe shrugged and said they were waiting to hear some news from the bomb disposal men. Maybe he should go and ask them.

The reporter drew up a chair and sat down. 'So there's been a bomb threat?'

She nodded and sipped her coffee.

'Have they found a bomb?'

'Your guess is as good as mine.'

'You accused Pedro Villalonga of being a Nazi sympathiser on today's show.' He ran a hand through his brown mop of hair. 'Is there anything else you would like to share with my newspaper's readers on the subject?'

'If they were watching the show then they would've heard everything I have to say about it for the time being,' she said. 'If we decide to run another show on any of this then we'll make it known through the appropriate channels beforehand. So my advice is that you and your readers should watch this space.'

'Did the way you brought the show to an abrupt end have anything to do with Villalonga and what you said to him in the interview?'

'That's enough for now,' Oscar said. 'Pe's told you everything she knows, and you can see she's been shaken up by all this. How about you let us have our breakfast in peace, huh?'

Inspector Jefe Velázquez went down to Incident Room 2, to talk to the victim's cleaning lady, Monica Pacheco. She turned out to be an attractive woman of twenty-six, with long black hair and a dark tan. José Gajardo, immaculately dressed as ever in a grey linen suit and white silk shirt, had been sitting with her.

Velázquez sat at the desk and told the woman who he was. 'My colleague here, Subinspector Gajardo, will already have introduced himself, I'm sure.'

She gave Velázquez a surly look. 'I asked him for some cigarettes ages ago, and he still ain't got me them yet.'

The Inspector Jefe looked at his number two. 'Perhaps you could see to it, José.'

Gajardo got up and went out.

Velázquez gave the girl what he hoped was an avuncular smile. 'So how about if we start with you telling me what you saw and did from the time you arrived at the victim's place this morning.'

'Ain't much to tell other than what I already said to the officer when I called.'

'I'd like to hear it all again anyway.'

She brushed something from the denim skirt she was wearing. 'Like I told him, I got there at around ten-to-six – '

'Bit of a funny time to start work, isn't it?' he said. 'I've never heard of anyone having a girl come to clean up for them at such an early hour.'

She shrugged. 'It's what he wanted.'

Gajardo came back in, and looked at the girl. 'I hope you like Ducados.'

She took the two cigarettes from the Subinspector's outstretched hand. 'These taste like shit,' she said. 'I normally smoke Camels.'

Gajardo shrugged. 'It's all there was.'

Velázquez said, 'You were talking me through what happened from the time you arrived at the house, Monica.'

'I just went there to clean up.'

'Did you see anyone at the house when you arrived, or anyone leaving?'

'No.'

'And why did Arjan want you to start so early in the morning?'

'He said he'd be working through the night, and he asked me if I could make an early start so as to be finished by ten a.m.'

'What was supposed to be happening at ten?'

'He said he hoped to be back by then, and that he would want to catch up on some sleep. He didn't want me around waking him up.'

'Had he asked you to start work that early before?'

'Sometimes…if he had to go to see to an animal during the night. He offered to pay me extra for the inconvenience, so it was fine with me.'

'So you got to the house, and then what happened?'

'I went into the bedroom and saw him lying there like that.'

'What time was this?'

'A few minutes after I got there.'

'Did you touch the body?'

'No, it was obvious he was dead…wasn't no way nobody was gonna survive being skewered on a bull's horn like that.'

Velázquez nodded. 'Must've been quite a shock for you.'

'I'll say.'

'Have you any idea who killed him?'

'No.'

'Did he have any enemies?'

'I've no idea.'

Velázquez made a note in his pad. 'Tell us about Arjan.'

'I never really knew the man.'

'But you saw him and spoke to him from time to time,' Velázquez said. 'What was your general impression?'

She shrugged. 'He was like any other guy in lots of ways.'

'Flirted with you, did he?'

'No, I don't mean like that.'

'What, then?'

'He made a lot of mess and needed a woman to come and clean up after him.'

'What else?'

'You do know he was gay, I suppose?'

'Did he have a partner or any boyfriends?'

'The only one I met was Klaus.'

'Describe this man, Klaus, for us.'

Gajardo came into the gents' as the Inspector Jefe was washing his face at the sink. 'D'you reckon the victim's being gay might've had anything to do with it, boss?'

'Could well do,' Velázquez said. 'It's hard to think of anything much more phallic the killer could've used as a murder weapon than a bull's horn.'

'Just what I was thinking.' The Subinspector zipped up his trousers. 'With any luck, we'll find the boyfriend pronto and get him in for questioning.'

The two men walked up the corridor together, and Velázquez was about to take the lift but then he thought better of it. There was always the chance he might find himself sharing it with his immediate superior, Comisario Alonso. And he needed that like a kick in the ass right now. The Comisario would almost certainly buttonhole him and want to know whether he had any suspects. The man worried far too much about keeping the Mayor and the city's other bigwigs happy for Velázquez's liking. Seeing that justice was done seemed to be somewhere near the bottom of his list of priorities.

Gajardo asked why they were taking the stairs. 'Not on a health kick, are we?'

'You could call it that.'

With his short legs, the Subinspector was struggling to keep up with Velázquez's long strides that took in three steps at a time. 'So what's our next move, boss?'

Velázquez stopped and turned to look at his number two. 'Go over to Calle Alhondiga and see how the others are getting on,' he said. 'Tell them all to be here by twelve for another briefing.'

Back up in the office, Velázquez sat at his desk and picked up the phone. He got a man on the line who worked for an organization that oversaw vets working in the region. He learned from the man that Arjan Gelens first registered as a veterinarian in Spain in 1965 – although it was always possible he could have worked in the country before that in some other capacity.

19

He thanked the man for his time and hung up, then turned his attention to the next number on his list. He saw that the vet had written the initials ADLT by the side of it. He dialed the number and found himself speaking to a woman who said she didn't know any Arjan Gelens. Velázquez said that was odd because her number was in the man's personal phone book.

In that case it would be her husband Alfonso that he wanted to talk to. But what was this all about? Velázquez asked if her husband had a surname. He did and it was 'de la Torre'. He was a famous bullfighter. Perhaps the Inspector Jefe had heard of him? Velázquez knew who Alfonso de la Torre was all right. He asked the woman where her husband could be found, and she said he practised with the bulls at the Gutiérrez ranch at this hour every day. He thanked the woman for her time and hung up.

The next number got Velázquez through to an Estela López. She ran a yoga class that Gelens had attended on and off during the previous eighteen months or so. She told him that the man had suffered with pains in his lower back, and found that doing yoga helped ease the pain.

Velázquez asked her what else she could tell him, and learned that Gelens had been the reserved type. 'The sort you can see in class,' she said, 'and never have a clue what they are thinking, or what sort of lives they lead.'

That was a great help.

Chapter 5

Inspector Jefe Velázquez kicked off the briefing by reading from his notebook the description that Monica Pacheco had given him of the victim's German boyfriend.

'So it's a gay German called Klaus we're looking for,' Jorge Serrano said. 'I tried to write down what you just said, boss, but I'm having trouble keeping up.'

'He stands at one eighty-two or thereabouts...skinny build...has his red hair done in a feather cut. He dresses like David Bowie's Ziggy Stardust. You know, sheer mesh top and glittery trousers.'

'Age?' Agente Sara Pérez asked.

'Fortyish.'

'Bit old for it, isn't he? I mean, even up in Madrid where they've got the *Movida* going on, nobody dresses like that at *forty*...do they?'

Oficial Javier Moreno, a pale young man of slight build and pale complexion, said, 'Well this guy does.'

Jorge Serrano reached into the pocket of his blue *guayabera* for his lighter. 'But we don't have any evidence pointing to this Klaus guy's involvement in the murder yet, do we?'

Velázquez shook his head. 'He wasn't at the apartment when Monica Pacheco arrived to clean up.' The Inspector Jefe ran a hand through his thick black hair. 'Jorge and José, get out there and do the rounds. Start with the gay bars,' he said. 'Sara and Javier, I need you to go back over to Calle Alhondiga and keep plugging away there.'

He asked if anyone had any questions or suggestions.

Javi Merino said the way he saw it, the victim had most probably picked a guy up in one of the local bars then taken the man home and let him tie him to the bed. 'And by the time he realizes what a mistake he's made, it's too late...'

Velázquez said it was far too early to be jumping to any rash conclusions. 'Just get out there and do your stuff. And let me know if you turn up anything.'

The gates of the bullring were closed when Velázquez pulled up outside. He climbed out of his Alfa Romeo and took a look around. Finding that nothing much seemed to be going on at this hour, he figured he'd call back another time.

He climbed back in behind the wheel of his car and set off once more. Minutes later, he crossed the river, then headed south and picked up the motorway. It wasn't long before he had left the city behind and was passing fields full of olive trees and cereal crops. The breeze smelt of the dry land as it washed over him and tossed his hair. In the distance, to the south, he could see the mountains spread out against the horizon and baking under the afternoon sun. He moved into the middle lane and cruised at a steady 120 kph.

Seeing the ranch up ahead, he drove as far as the gate then reached out through the window and pushed the buzzer on the security gantry. A voice asked him to identify himself and he did so. The iron gates opened and a big, imposing white villa came into view.

He drove inside and pulled up in the gravel parking area, between a Land Rover and a red Lamborghini. And as he climbed out of his Alfa Romeo, a man appeared from one of the side buildings and approached him. The man was of lean build and medium height, and was wearing jeans and cowboy boots. He asked how he could be of assistance. Only from the way he said it, it was clear he was really asking Velázquez what he was doing here.

Velázquez introduced himself and held out his ID. The man looked at it and adjusted the rim on his Stetson. He wondered if the Inspector Jefe was here on account of a *torero* that had been put in hospital by a bull reared on this ranch. Velázquez wondered whether the man was joking. If so then he was far too deadpan to let it show.

He asked the man his name, and learned that it was Roberto Rios. The man said that he worked here as a ranch hand. Velázquez wondered if he knew a vet by the name of Arjan Gelens. Rios said he sure did. Matter of fact, they were expecting him here at the ranch first thing this morning, because they had a heifer that was about to calve anytime soon. But the man didn't show. They'd tried calling his number several times, but nobody picked up. It was strange, because the vet was normally very reliable. If he was ever sick in the past then he always called to explain, and would arrange for someone to come in his place. But not this time.

Velázquez said, 'He was in no state to make a phone call.'

'What…do you mean something's happened to him?'

'He's been murdered.'

Rios's eyes narrowed into crevices. He ran a hand over his craggy face, then through his receding brown hair. He wondered who in hell would want to murder a *vet*. He said it didn't make sense. He wished he could be of greater help. He really did. But with the exception of exchanging a few brief words about the bulls and heifers on the ranch, he had never really spoken to the man.

Velázquez wondered if he might be able to take a look around while he was here. Rios said sure, he'd be only too happy to give him a tour of the place. He asked Velázquez if he liked the bullfights. Velázquez said that he did. Rios took him over to a miniature ring, where a man was working through some moves with a bull.

They leaned on the split-rail fence and watched. The bullfighter was of slender build, slightly less than medium height, and dressed in a black T-shirt and matching tracksuit bottoms. Rios said the man they were watching was Alfonso de la Torre. He might have heard the name? Velázquez nodded.

The *torero* dealt the bull a *veronica*, then turned and looked over at them. The ranch hand called out, to warn him to watch his back. Sure enough, the bull was about to charge again, but the *torero* was ready for him. He skipped aside at the last moment, to let the animal go harmlessly past. Then he came and let himself out through the gate.

Up close, Alfonso de la Torre was a strikingly handsome young man, tanned and with his thick wavy black hair tied back in a ponytail. Velázquez introduced himself then held out his ID. The *torero* glanced at it. 'Has something happened I don't know about?'

'You know the vet?' Roberto Rios said. 'Arjan?'

'What about him?'

'He's been murdered.'

'*Que*?' Alfonso looked stunned.

Velázquez asked him if he had known the victim very well. The bullfighter said no, only from seeing him about the ranch. The Inspector Jefe explained that he was looking for a German by the name of Klaus. 'He dresses extravagantly…like Ziggy Stardust, if you know who that is. He was a close friend of the victim.'

Alfonso de la Torre shrugged. 'Sorry, I wish I could help.'

'In that case,' Velázquez said, 'how come your number is in the man's personal phone book?'

'That would be in case he needed to talk to me about the bulls.'

'When was the last time you talked to him?'

'Two or three weeks ago, I think. But it was just a few words – a heifer had delivered a calf.'

Velázquez gave the bullfighter his card. 'I'd appreciate it if you'd call me on this number if anything else occurs to you.'

Alfonso de la Torre looked at the card and said he would ask around.

Velázquez told Roberto Rios he needed to talk to the owner of the ranch, and they headed back to the house in silence. When they reached the building, the ranch hand asked Velázquez to wait outside for a moment. Then the man went on in through the open front door, which was covered by a bead curtain.

Rios reemerged moments later and said the owner had been called away at short notice. Velázquez said he would come by to talk to the man another time, then turned and made his way back to his car.

The vehicle was hot as an oven inside, and he struggled to get any air into his lungs until he'd got the windows down. Once he was out on the road, he put his foot down and found himself driving on automatic pilot.

It wasn't long before he found himself worrying about Pe. He became angry with himself for behaving, or at least thinking, 'like a rookie'. The killer would be laughing up his sleeve if he knew Velázquez's thoughts. And all because of a little note the man had left at the crime scene.

Not only that, but Pe would be furious if she knew how he was worrying about her like this.

That was all easy to say, but what if something were to happen to her?

He knew that he would never forgive himself.

Chapter 6

When Velázquez reached the city, he stopped by a telephone kiosk to call the studio. Alvaro, who worked the reception desk, picked up. The Inspector Jefe learned from him that the bomb threat turned out to be a hoax. He also learned that Pe had left a while ago.

Velázquez thanked him and hung up. Next he called home and Pe picked up. 'How are you doing?'

'Did you see it on the news?'

'No, I just spoke to Alvaro at the studio,' he said. 'Are you all right?'

'Yes…why shouldn't I be?'

A part of him wanted to warn her to double-lock the door to the flat and stay at home until he got back, but he bit his tongue. She asked him how the investigation was going. 'Early days,' he said. 'I'll see you later.'

She had been about to ask when she could expect him to return home, but he hung up before she could do so.

Pe stretched out on the sofa with a mug of coffee, and began to watch a film. It turned out to be a thriller in which a woman was being stalked. The theme of the film was a little too close to home for her liking, so she stopped watching. She closed her eyes and dropped off to sleep.

She woke up some time later. She glanced at her watch and saw that she must have slept for a couple of hours or so.

She was feeling sweaty and restless, so she decided to take a shower.

She felt good with the arrows of hot water raining down onto her naked flesh. Then she thought she heard a noise coming from somewhere in the flat, and figured Luis must have come home. Now he was investigating this latest murder, she never knew when to expect him. She called to him but he didn't reply.

Perhaps the noise made by the water cascading from the showerhead had drowned out her voice. She turned the taps off and called to him again. Still he didn't reply, and she felt nervous all of a sudden.

What if it wasn't Luis she heard, but the man that had been following her?

She put on her terry cloth bathrobe, and went out into the hallway. 'Hello?' she called. 'Luis? Is that you?'

No answer.

Figuring Luis had maybe come home exhausted and gone straight to bed, she cracked the door to the bedroom. She peered in – but there was nobody in there.

She set off down the hallway, her bare feet leaving their prints on the cold tiles. She hadn't gone far before she heard voices coming from the television in the living room. But hadn't she turned it off before she got into the shower?

Or was she mistaken?

She couldn't be totally sure.

Maybe an intruder broke in and turned it on.

Maybe he was somewhere in the flat.

Maybe he was waiting for the right moment to pounce on her.

She told herself she was being paranoid.

What would Luis say if he knew the way she was thinking right now?

He would wonder if she were losing her mind.

Her heart pounded, as she looked about for something to use as a weapon. She rushed into the kitchen, opened the drawer under the sink, and found the bread knife.

She held it up and looked at it like she had never seen a knife before. And as she did so, she wondered if she had it in her to use it.

She went back out into the hallway, holding the bread knife up.

She hated the idea of stabbing someone…but she found the thought of being attacked, and perhaps raped or even murdered, far more abhorrent.

She checked the door to the flat, to see if it had been forced. It hadn't. But that might not necessarily mean anything. She had heard Luis talk of how some professional burglars used special master keys that enabled them to break in practically

27

anywhere. Or else they poured some substance into the lock that quickly solidified into the shape of a key.

She crept along the hallway, like a cat stalking its prey. She kicked open the door to the smaller of the two bathrooms, then dashed in. She was holding the knife up, ready to defend herself with it if need be…but there was nobody in there.

Then she saw that some books were lying on the parquet floor.

She felt sure that she had left everything ship shape and Bristol fashion when she tidied up the day before. Although it was always possible that the books could simply have fallen from the shelf.

Or perhaps Luis had come in here and knocked them over without noticing last night.

Or maybe there was an intruder in the flat, and *he* had knocked them over…

She went back along the hallway and crossed the living room to the far end. She peered through the glass door that opened onto the balcony…and found that there was nobody there, either.

She told herself she had looked everywhere in the flat, and could now rest assured that nobody had broken in.

Unless the intruder had moved about, and somehow managed to conceal himself in one of the rooms after she had left it.

She figured there was little chance of this having happened, but made another quick tour of the flat anyway, just to make sure.

She breathed a big sigh of relief once she had finally satisfied herself she was alone in the flat.

She went out onto the balcony and looked down at the street. People were going about their business, totally oblivious of her and her concerns. She told herself off for having been so paranoid earlier, and went back into the living room.

Just then the telephone rang. She hurried over to the stand in the hallway and picked it up. It was a journalist wanting to ask 'Inspector Velázquez' some questions about the murder he was currently investigating. She told the man this was a private number. He had no right to call her husband at home.

She hung up.

She went into the kitchen and found the brandy. She poured herself a large measure and took a gulp.

She felt the brandy burn as it went down.

The telephone rang again.

She wondered whether or not to go and answer it. It was probably the reporter calling again…although it might be Luis.

She picked up and said, '*Hola*,' but there was no reply.

She could hear the caller breathing down the line.

'Who is this?'

The line went dead.

She stood there, looking at the receiver like it was some poisonous snake.

She pulled the plug out of the wall.

She finished what was left in her glass and gave herself a refill.

When he arrived at the Jefatura, Velázquez saw there were a number of reporters waiting for him on the front steps. Screw talking to those vultures for a game of soldiers. He drove down into the car park, and took the lift up to the office.

He had just sat at his desk when his telephone rang. It was Gajardo, calling to say he had tracked their man down. The German had been performing with his band in a bar on the Alameda de Hercules. Velázquez told the Subinspector to bring him in for questioning, and hung up. Then he booked Incident Room 1. After that, he made some calls, to check out more of the numbers in the victim's personal phone book.

From the description Monica Pacheco had given him, Velázquez was expecting this man Klaus to be something of an extravagant figure, and in this he wasn't wrong. In his skintight bodysuit and with his flaming red hair done in a feather cut, the man turned out to be every inch the wannabe rock star. But he was a little old to be a *wannabe* anything, from what Velázquez could see.

The Inspector Jefe introduced himself, then kicked off by

asking the man his full name, and ascertained that it was Klaus Bloem. Next, he asked him how he would describe his relationship with Arjan Gelens.

'I can't really see as I would.'

'But I have reason to believe you and Gelens were close.'

'First, I want to know what this is all about.'

'We'll get to that in good time,' Velázquez said. 'But to begin with, I need you to tell me about your relationship with Gelens.'

'This is fucking *unreal*.' Bloem shook his head. 'You pull me out of the middle of a gig and drag me here, then start asking me dumbass questions.' He held his arms out in a gesture of appeal to some invisible third party. 'How about you stop this bullshit and just tell me whether Arjan's in some kind of trouble?'

Velázquez exchanged glances with Gajardo, and the Subinspector looked at Bloem. 'I'm afraid,' he said, 'that Arjan Gelens has been murdered.'

Klaus Bloem's face froze in an expression of horror, then he buried his face in his hands and began to sob.

The man was either the greatest talent lost to the cinema since Orson Welles fell out of favor with the Hollywood studio bosses, or he was really cut up. Velázquez said he was sorry.

Bloem dropped his hands from his face. 'Are you *really*?'

'Would you like a glass of water?'

When Bloem failed to reply, Velázquez said, 'We'll take five, then.'

Chapter 7

Back in Incident Room 1, minutes later, Velázquez asked Klaus Bloem if he would like to postpone the interview.

Bloem dried his eyes and cheeks with the back of his hand. No, he wanted to do everything he could to help the Inspector Jefe catch the bastard that killed the man he loved.

So Velázquez resumed his questioning. He learned that Bloem and Gelens were lovers but that they lived apart. Bloem said he had rented a room in a modest apartment on Calle Correduria, in the Old Quarter. He didn't have a telephone, which explained why his name and number didn't appear in the little book Velázquez had found at the crime scene. He scraped together a living by performing with his band and teaching private classes. He gave guitar lessons and also taught a little German.

Given that Bloem earned so little, the Inspector Jefe inferred Gelens had always been the one to pick up the tab when they went out. When he heard Velázquez say that, Bloem told him he didn't care for his tone.

Bloem reminded the Inspector Jefe that he was here trying to help them with their enquiries, so he could do without the bitchy comments.

He said that he had loved the victim and swore that he was not the killer. If *that* was what the Inspector Jefe was thinking then he was barking up the wrong tree.

'So who killed him?' Velázquez drummed his fingers on the desk. 'Because someone really had it in for him.'

'I have no idea.' Bloem ran a hand through his red feather cut. 'Unless it was something to do with the bulls he was paid to take care of.'

'Explain what you mean by that.'

'Arjan came to believe that someone was interfering with them when a bullfighter complained to him after one of the *corridas*.'

'What's the name of the bullfighter?'

'Arjan didn't say. All he told me was that the man had come to him in the strictest confidence, and said he strongly suspected that the bulls he'd fought that night were doped. He also said he reckoned that their horns had been shaved down,' Bloem said. 'The question was, where along the chain it'd happened and who did it.'

'But as the man whose job it was to take care of the bulls at the Gutiérrez ranch and the Maestranza, surely Arjan should've known what was happening to them better than anyone?'

'It was impossible for any one person to be able to keep an eye on all of the bulls twenty-four hours a day, seven days a week – especially seeing as they would start life on the ranch and then be sent out to different bullrings up and down the country when their time came.'

'So what did Arjan do about it?'

'He took blood samples from some of the bulls at both the Gutiérrez ranch and the Maestranza, and sent them off to one of the labs in Seville for analysis.'

'Which lab would this be?'

'He didn't say.'

'Have you got anything else you can tell us that we ought to know?'

Bloem shook his head. 'Nothing springs to mind.'

'In that case you're free to go now, Klaus,' Velázquez said. 'But don't leave town.'

'I can assure you I had no plans to.' Bloem got up and went out.

Chapter 8

Velázquez and Gajardo went upstairs to the office, where it was cool for a change because the air conditioner had finally been fixed. The Inspector Jefe gazed out the window. It was still sunny, despite the fact that it was coming up to 8.25 p.m. The river was a metallic grey in this light, while the bridge was crammed with traffic and pedestrians. Looking out over it all, you had the pleasant feeling of watching a city preparing for the evening.

He turned to Gajardo. 'We need to chase up those samples, José,' he said. 'Get hold of Serrano and tell him that's his job.'

The Inspector Jefe's telephone rang. It was Mateo Vidal, calling to let him know that he'd looked into the backgrounds of the three people who checked out of the Bristol, the hotel near to the crime scene, the morning Arjan Gelens's body was found. 'But none of them had any previous.' Velázquez thanked Mateo for the update then hung up.

No sooner had he done so than the phone began to ring again. '*Hola*?'

'Velázquez?' He recognized the familiar sound of his superior's gruff voice. 'Comisario Alonso here. I need to speak to you.'

The Inspector Jefe's heart sank.

The Comisario was standing by the window when Velázquez entered. The man gestured towards the vacant chair across from his desk. Velázquez sat on it. The Comisario turned and said, 'So there's been yet another murder, Inspector Jefe.'

'It's been a busy year.'

Comisario Alonso sat in his leather swivel chair. 'You haven't been your usual self lately, Velázquez,' he said, and ran a hand over his shiny, egg-shaped head. 'Only to be expected, I suppose, after losing your father like that. It can take a while to come to terms.'

Velázquez's eyes narrowed, as he wondered where his boss was leading with all this.

'Which is why,' the Comisario said, 'I want you to see the police psych.'

'There's no need for that, boss – '

'As your superior officer, it's my job to take decisions of this sort.' Comisario Alonso brushed some lint off the front of his jacket.

'But I'm *fine*, I tell you.'

'Look, all you have to do's show up at her office and talk to her.' The man swiveled on his chair. 'Answer a few questions and that's it. Just routine.'

'Right now though, Comisario, I just don't have the time.'

'*Make* the time.'

'What about the murder investigation?'

'What *investigation*?' The Comisario shrugged. 'I went down and watched you and Gajardo interview the victim's boyfriend through the one-way window. This is an open-and-shut case if I've ever seen one…and what's more, Judge Bautista agrees with me.'

The Inspector Jefe didn't say anything.

'Damn it, Velázquez…it's obviously this man Bloem that did it. The victim clearly cheated on his boyfriend, and the German killed him in a fit of jealous rage.'

'But that's mere supposition at this stage.'

'Her office is up on the top floor.' Comisario Alonso didn't seem to have heard what Velázquez said.

The Inspector Jefe wondered what his boss was up to? Was the man planning on trying to make out he had gone loopy, so he could take him off the case and have the murder pinned on Klaus Bloem?

'But can't it at least wait until after I've made an arrest, Comisario?'

'If you insist on keeping the investigation open a while longer, then you have the right to do so. But let me tell you, every *reasonable* person thinks you should charge this man Bloem now and have done with the matter.' Comisario Alonso shrugged his broad shoulders. 'So far as the psychologist goes, it's just a matter of delegating any jobs that need doing while you're in with her.'

Velázquez sighed, realizing there was no point in arguing.

'The Mayor's not happy,' the Comisario said. 'I had him on the phone a little while ago. He wanted to know how it is that my officers can't seem to keep a lid on things.' He brought his balled fist crashing down onto the desk, making his mug jump so that coffee splashed over the varnished mahogany. 'Damn it, man…do you realize what effect murders like this and the ones we had earlier in the year are having on the reputation of this city and the tourist industry?'

Chapter 9

Velázquez buttonholed José Gajardo on the stairs. He asked him if he'd yet managed to get a printout of all the calls made from the victim's home telephone in the four days leading up to the murder. The Subinspector said that was the next job on his list.

Velázquez told him about how the Comisario wanted him to see the police psych. 'But keep it under your hat, won't you?'

'Did you just say something, boss? I think I suffered a bout of temporary deafness.'

Velázquez woke up in the middle of the night feeling awful. He'd had a nightmare that filled him with panic. He got up, pulled on a dressing gown, then padded out to the living room.

He began pacing up and down.

He wondered about Klaus Bloem. The man had clearly been in love with the victim. That much was clear. But the question was, had he killed him?

Comisario Alonso was clearly all for arresting the man.

But Comisario Alonso was talking out of his ass, as usual.

Not because Klaus Bloom was necessarily innocent, but because the Comisario wanted him arrested for all the wrong reasons.

Velázquez went into the kitchen and found the Scotch, next to the wine rack. There was enough left for a large one. He took a tumbler down from the shelf and emptied the contents of the bottle into it.

He untied the knot on a small rubbish bag that had been left on the kitchen floor, ready to be thrown out. No sooner had he dropped the empty bottle into it, than he saw something that stopped him in his tracks: a bit of empty packaging with HOME PREGNANCY KIT written on it…

Pe drove into work and slotted her car into the parking bay

reserved for her. There was only one other car in the lot, an old Fiat that she knew belonged to Alvaro who worked in reception.

She killed the headlights and felt spooked for a moment as she sat there in virtual darkness. She climbed out of the car, before she locked it and set off for the entrance to the studio. It was only a matter of some thirty metres, but the times when she had reckoned she was being followed were playing on her mind now. Christ, she told herself, Papa would be ashamed of you if he knew how nervous you are. 'And you say you want to be a bullfighter?' he'd say.

But no, this was different. Matching your professional skill against a bull was one thing. And feeling that you were being followed in the dark and possibly at risk of being attacked by a man who would be stronger than you and possibly armed, was something quite different.

She figured she had every right to feel anxious, and breathed a sigh of relief as she went in through the door. She said *buenos dias* to Alvaro in reception. He greeted her in turn and told her she was the first in after himself.

She took the lift up and entered the office, then went on through the door at the end into the small partitioned area where the filing cabinets were kept. After the way her interview with Pedro Villalonga had been cut short, she was determined not to miss the chance to make use of the file she had on the man. The stuff in there was pure journalistic dynamite, and she had come into work even earlier than usual today to give herself some extra time to study it.

She slipped her key into the lock and thought she heard someone at her back, on the other side of the partition. She turned abruptly, but it was impossible to see through the frosted glass. 'Hello?' she called. 'Pili, is that you? Oscar?'

There was no reply and a shiver of fear ran through her.

She scolded herself for getting the willies like this. She turned the key in the lock and had just opened the drawer when she heard footsteps behind her.

There was no doubt about it this time: *there was definitely somebody there.*

She made to turn her head, but before she could do so a gloved

37

hand took hold of her neck. The hand held her in an iron grip. She tried to scream but then the man's other hand came up to cover her mouth.

He rammed her into the filing cabinet, so that the drawer she had opened slammed shut with the weight of her body. She tried to turn but the man's grip was like a vice. She was struggling to get air into her lungs. She felt like she was going to pass out…and then something hard hit her on the back of the head.

And that was the last thing she knew for a time.

When Pe came round, there was smoke everywhere. She coughed and sputtered as she struggled to her knees. She saw flames licking up the walls. The man who attacked her must have set the place on fire.

She had to get out of here.

She clambered to her feet, then held her hand over her mouth and ran out onto the landing. She considered taking the lift down, but then figured that was the *last* thing she should do in a fire.

There were flames on the stairs, but she jumped through them the way a dog goes through a hoop…and fell as she landed, banging her head against the wall. Dazed, she picked herself up and continued to make her way down the stairs until she came to a wall of fire.

It was no good. There was no way out. She was about to be burned alive.

At that moment, she heard a voice call out to her. She called back, and then she heard the sound of a fire extinguisher…then water started pumping up the stairs. The flames died down enough for one of the firemen to dash up to where she was standing. He lifted her onto his back and hurried back down with her, through the smoke and flames.

She was coughing and spluttering and barely knew where she was, and then she passed out.

Chapter 10

When Pe came round, she was in the back of an ambulance. Oscar was looking down at her. 'You're going to be okay,' he told her.

'There was a man in the office,' she said. 'He attacked me and hit me on the back of the head.'

'He was after the file with the memos.'

'Is everyone safe?'

Oscar nodded. 'You were the only person in the building apart from Alvaro,' he said. 'He smelt smoke and called the fire services. Then he went upstairs to try to get you out, but the fire was already too fierce for him to be able to rescue you. I got there just as the firemen pulled up. Luckily they didn't have far to come, and arrived in time to save the day.'

'Did they get the man who did it?'

'No, he got away I'm afraid.'

'It has to be the same person that made the bomb threat,' Pe said. 'What about the file?'

'Unfortunately that's gone…and the whole damn office with it.'

The police psych was sitting at her desk when Velázquez entered her office. A redhead in her mid-thirties, she was wearing a dress with a floral print and a professional smile. 'Hi,' she said. 'I'm Ana Pelayo.' She stood up and offered him her hand. Velázquez gave it a tentative shake. 'Glad you could make it.'

They both sat down. She kicked off by asking Velázquez where he was from and made small talk for a while to break the ice. Then she asked him how he had been feeling lately.

'Just fine.' He presented her with a smile the way soldiers in days of old would hold up a shield in battle.

'I've been reading your file.'

'I hope it didn't send you to sleep?'

'Not at all,' she said. 'You've had a rough year, losing your father so suddenly like that. And you had a string of difficult investigations straight afterwards.'

He nodded.

'It can't have been easy for you?'

'No, "easy" isn't the word I'd use.'

She smiled and tamped her pencil on the desk. 'How are things at home?'

'We're doing okay.'

'Your boss seems to think your behaviour's changed of late.' She twirled her pencil. 'Would you agree?'

'No.'

Were this shrink and the Comisario out to paint him as a madman?

Velázquez could imagine how they might have worked it between them. Comisario Alonso could have offered to put in a good word for her with her superiors, if only she were to do him a favor in return and write up a report on Velázquez saying he was mentally unfit to serve…

Ana Pelayo leaned back in her chair. 'How does Pe feel about your work?'

He shrugged. 'She knows I'm committed to what I do.'

'And what about the fact that she's become something of a celebrity these days?' She fixed him with an up-from-under look. 'Can't be easy, living with a woman whose every move's fodder for the gossip columns?'

'We get along okay.'

'How do you feel about being referred to as "her husband the homicide detective" in the gossip columns? Does that make you feel small and undervalued?'

'I certainly don't welcome attention from the media,' he conceded. 'But being relatively famous has become a fact of life for Pe, just as dealing with criminals is for me.'

Ana Pelayo nodded. 'Maybe that's something we can talk about in our next session.'

When Velázquez returned to his desk, Gajardo told him he

had just finished going through the inventory of calls to and from the victim's phone. The Inspector Jefe cocked an eyebrow. 'And?'

'Guess who called him the day before he was killed, boss.'

'Don't tell me it was our friend Ziggy Stardust?'

'You got it in one. Ziggy called him three times that same day. And who do you think Gelens called?'

'What is this, twenty bloody questions?'

'Only Alfonso de la Torre of all people,' Gajardo answered his own question. 'It happens he was on the phone to him for just over half an hour.'

'I can see you've been busy, José,' Velázquez said. 'I think we'll have to talk to Señor de la Torre again.' He looked over at Pérez. 'Go and pick Klaus Bloem up and bring him in here, Sara. And hold him until I get back.' He turned his head to look at Merino. 'You can go with her, Javi.'

Moments later, Jorge Serrano came hurrying in. 'Have you seen the news, boss?'

'What's happened?'

'The studio where your wife works was set on fire.'

Velázquez's blood turned cold. 'Is Pe okay?'

'I'm sorry but that's all I heard.'

Velázquez called the studio. Nobody picked up. He called home. Nobody picked up there, either. He dashed out of the office and took the lift down to the car park, jumped into his Alfa Romeo and set off with his foot on the floor and the siren going. He drove through the heavy traffic like his was the only car on the road. The other drivers either had to make way or get hit. They made way.

When he arrived at the studio, the place was one big ball of fire. Beside himself with panic, he spotted Pe's makeup artist, Pili, standing with a small group of people. He dashed over to her and asked where Pe was. She told him Pe had been taken to the Hospital Virgen del Rocio in an ambulance.

He ran back to his car, jumped in, and drove at breakneck speed to the hospital. He pulled up outside the front steps and ran into the building. He found Pe lying in a bed in the Emergency ward. She was hooked up to a saline drip and looked tired.

She smiled when she saw who it was, and assured Velázquez she was all right.

He breathed a sigh of relief. 'But what happened?'

'He hit me on the head, and set the place on fire before leaving me for dead. I was lucky to get out of there.'

'Did you get a look at the guy?'

'No…he came at me from behind and took me by surprise,' she said. 'Whoever it was, he was obviously after the memos.'

Velázquez felt tears of rage and sympathy welling up inside him. He kissed his wife on the forehead, and promised her that he would get whoever had done this and make them pay.

Seeing how emotional he was getting, and how hard he was trying not to let his feelings show, Pe told him she would be fine once she'd had a cup of coffee.

Sometimes a woman had to act like she was strong, even when she didn't feel it. She knew how Luis wanted to be able to protect her. She knew, too, how terrible he must be feeling right now because he had not been able to do so. And knowing this, something in her wanted to mother him – even *now*, of all times, when she was the one that was in a bad way.

She realized that he was blaming himself for what happened. But she knew that nobody could possibly be to blame other than the bastard that attacked her and the person or persons he was working for, assuming that he had not acted independently.

But if she could see the truth of this, Velázquez obviously couldn't. He hated himself, as Pe had so rightly intuited, for failing to be there for her in her moment of need.

And just as he blamed and loathed himself, so he loved and admired Pe for her gutsy approach to life.

It broke his heart to see her like this, being so brave.

He went and found a pay phone and called Gajardo's number at the Jefatura. The Subinspector picked up and Velázquez told him what had happened. 'I need you to arrange for Pe to be kept under armed guard for the rest of her stay in the hospital, José,' he said. 'Have you got that?'

'Sure, boss. I'll take care of it straightaway.'

They hung up. Velázquez returned to his wife's bedside in the

Emergency ward, and had one of the nurses bring them some coffee.

Then he waited for the armed guard to arrive, before he gave Pe a kiss and headed off.

Pe sat up in her hospital bed, reliving the nightmare that she had been forced to endure. She recalled the whole terrifying episode down to the last detail.

She felt utterly powerless, and yet she knew that this was just what her assailant wanted her to feel.

If she allowed herself to fall into a pit of depression now then she would be playing right into the bastard's hands.

No, the way to approach this was to fight it. And that meant continuing to do her job and go about her life like nothing had happened.

She wondered whether she had the strength to do that, and told herself that she had no alternative. When bad shit happened, you could either give in or stand up and fight.

And Pe might be a lot of things but she knew she was no quitter.

Chapter 11

Velázquez was driving over Triana Bridge some ten minutes later. The sun had just gone down and the lights from the bars and restaurants along the dock were shimmering on the surface of the water. But the Inspector Jefe was in no mood to concern himself with such matters, because he was taken up with the lyrics of the David Bowie song he had playing on the cassette player.

Klaus Bloem clearly modelled himself on Ziggy Stardust, so Velázquez figured listening to some of Bowie's stage persona's songs might help him to understand his suspect a little better.

He drove in this way, with his mind off somewhere weird and wonderful with Ziggy Stardust, until he found himself slotting his car into a space outside the Forensics building on Avenida del Dr. Fedriani. As he ran up the front steps, he became conscious of the sound of trumpets or cornets, playing in the distance. They were practising for Holy Week.

He went in through the glass doors of the big nondescript building, and took the lift down to the basement. Upon entering the lab, he found the stocky form of his friend, Juan Gómez, dissecting the body.

The place smelt of formaldehyde, and Velázquez fought the queasy sensation that invariably assailed him when he came here. '*Hola*, Juan,' he said. 'So what have you got?'

'Not a lot, I'm afraid.' The pathologist shrugged. 'The cause of death was having the sharp end of a bull's horn thrust up his anus. It ruptured the wall of the alimentary canal, passing through the small and large intestines and into the stomach. The victim would've bled to death in next to no time.'

None of which was anything Velázquez didn't already know. 'And?'

'The bruising and hemorrhaging at the back of the head suggests the victim was struck by a heavy blunt instrument.'

Velázquez figured the killer must have knocked Gelens out first before he killed him. He turned to leave. 'Let me know if you turn up anything else, Juan.'

'Don't I always?' Gómez said. 'And be sure to give my favorite chat show host my love, won't you?'

Some reporters blocked Velázquez's path on his way out. They wanted to know what progress he was making on the investigation. He said he had nothing to tell them at the current time, but when he did have a statement to make he would be sure to let them know.

One of the reporters pushed a microphone in his face and asked him if he was close to making an arrest.

'No comment.'

'Could you at least tell our viewers whether the victim's boyfriend is your number one suspect?' the man said. 'And if so then why haven't you already charged him?'

'All I can tell you is that no arrests have been made as yet,' Velázquez said. 'And now if you'll excuse me, I have work to do.'

He shat in the milk as he hurried back to his car. Those fucking reporters were scum. He despised them almost as much as he did Comisario Alonso.

He drove back to the Jefatura, to pick up Gajardo, and then they headed off out of the city.

There was no sign of Alfonso de la Torre, when Velázquez and Gajardo arrived at the Gutiérrez ranch. Roberto Rios was there, though, and he told them the bullfighter had just left. They would probably find him at his house, out past Villablanca.

They resumed their journey and soon came to Villablanca, another of the 'white villages' of the region. Velázquez drove at a slow crawl into the middle of the *pueblo,* then he saw a group of old guys sitting outside a bar up ahead. He pulled over and called to them, then explained that he was looking for the *torero* Alfonso de la Torre's place. One of the men said he knew where it was and gave the Inspector Jefe directions. If by any chance Velázquez failed to find it, the man said, he'd just have to stop and ask someone. Practically everyone from around here knew where Alfonso de la Torre lived, the *torera* being something of a local legend.

Velázquez thanked the man before he headed back out of the village, then rejoined the road they'd been on earlier. It was just a matter of heading for Argonales and taking the second left, he told Gajardo. After that they'd have to keep their eyes peeled.

Minutes later, they saw what they were looking for. The bullfighter's place was an attractive, whitewashed villa set back a little from the road. The property was enclosed by a well-tended garden and surrounded by farmland. In the distance, the village of Villablanca spread itself against the hillside white as an egg in a frying pan.

Velázquez pushed the button on the security gantry. Moments later, a woman's voice said, '*Hola?*'. The Inspector Jefe quickly identified himself and explained that he needed to speak to Señor de la Torre.

The gates opened and they drove inside and pulled up in the pebble forecourt, then climbed out of the car. Velàzquez took a look at the house's façade. Two dormer windows jutted out from the pitched roof, and there were three more double windows downstairs. The two detectives walked up the short path that led to the door. Gajardo said it was the kind of place he might buy – if he won the lottery. Looking in through one of the downstairs windows, Velázquez saw a figure move. He pushed the bell and moments later a tall, attractive brunette came and opened the door. She was in her mid-to-late-twenties, and wore slim-fitting Levi's and a top with BOSTON UNIVERSITY printed on it.

'You would be Señora de la Torre, Alfonso's wife, I assume?'

'That's right.'

Velázquez held up his ID and the woman let them in. 'Alfonso's pottering about in the back garden.'

They entered into a large room done in the open-plan style. The whitewashed walls were adorned with photographs of Alfonso in action in a number of different *corridas*. There were also three large oil paintings that looked as though they must have been specially commissioned. Long, thick beams ran the length of the room under the high ceiling, and the sunlight came crashing in through the windows.

Señora de la Torre told Velázquez she would go and get her

husband. As she was crossing the room, the bullfighter came in through one of the open French doors. He was wearing newish jeans, trainers and a plain navy-blue T-shirt. '*Hola*, Inspector Jefe,' he said. 'This is a surprise.'

Señora de la Torre asked the two officers if they would like something to drink. Velázquez shook his head, and the woman went and busied herself in the kitchen area at the far end of the open expanse.

Alfonso gestured for Velázquez and Gajardo to take a seat, and they perched themselves on the leather sofa. The bullfighter sat in the easy chair, facing them. 'So what is it I can do for you, gentlemen?'

'When I asked you yesterday if you knew Arjan Gelens,' Velázquez began, 'you said only from seeing him about the ranch.'

'That's right,' Alfonso said. 'What's all this about?'

Chapter 12

'We know that you talked to Gelens on the phone the day before he was murdered. We've got a record of the call.'

'The man wanted to talk to me,' the bullfighter said. 'So what?'

'Why didn't you say that when we talked yesterday?'

'I don't know…I guess I forgot about it.'

'Somehow I find that difficult to believe.'

'Besides, it had nothing to do with the case.'

Velázquez told him he would be the judge of that. 'What did you talk about?'

'Nothing much.'

'The call lasted nearly half an hour. That's a long time to talk about "nothing much" to someone you claim not to know.'

Gajardo said, 'Did you know the man was gay?'

'His sexuality was none of my business.'

'That's not an answer to my question.'

Alfonso de la Torre shrugged. 'I guess I never really thought about it.'

'He never mentioned it?'

'No…it's not the sort of thing we talked about.'

'So what *did* you talk about?'

The bullfighter sat still for a moment and looked out the window. Velázquez followed the man's gaze. The garden was all in good order. Small flowers bordered the striped lawn and bougainvillea ran along the hedge, bursting with colour. In the distance, the mountains rested in the heat of the afternoon like a set of jagged dentures. Finally, the bullfighter said, 'This is difficult for me.'

'We can always continue the conversation at the Jefatura if you'd prefer?'

'But surely there's no need for that?'

'That's up to you.' Velázquez shrugged. 'Let's just say you've not yet managed to convince us that you're cooperating – and right now you need to.'

48

Alfonso looked at his wife, who had just come over to where they were sitting to listen in. 'Why don't you tell them what you were talking to the guy about, Alfonso?' she said. 'That way you might save everyone a lot of hassle, yourself included.'

Gajardo looked at Señora de la Torre. 'I take it Alfonso's told you what the conversation was about?'

'No, but I'm sure it had nothing to do with your investigation.' She looked at her husband. 'What's with all the secrecy, anyway, Alfonso?'

'There's no *secrecy*, Yolanda,' the bullfighter said. 'What would I need to hide?' He gestured with his hands. 'It's nothing really,' he said. 'It's just that…well… – okay then, I'll tell you.' He ran a hand over his face. 'Gelens was a vet, as you know, and he was employed to check on the bulls…to make sure they were being fed properly and generally in good health.'

'Yes, we know all that,' Velázquez said.

The bullfighter leaned forward in his chair. 'It turned out that he was concerned.'

'What about?'

'He seemed to think somebody was shaving the bulls' horns and that they were being doped.' He sighed. 'The great bullfighters of the past took really terrible risks. But they were good enough to get away with it – most of the time, anyway. Even so, they got gored occasionally. Some of them even died in the bullring. Take Joselito and Manolete.' He looked at Velázquez. 'And there are of course more recent examples of famous *toreros* losing their lives in the ring – Paquirri, for instance…'

'And nowadays the *toreros* aren't so good, is that it?'

'It wouldn't be true to say there aren't *toreros* who are brave and talented nowadays, because there are. But there aren't many of us.' Alfonso de la Torre's lips curled in an expression of disgust. 'Bullfighting isn't all-in wrestling – it's an art form. It's just like with music. People aren't stupid, Inspector. When they pay a lot of money for a ticket to see some singer perform, they don't want to find whoever it is miming, right? They want the real thing… If the bulls are doped, anyone can work close to the *toro* like the really great *toreros* did. But they'd do it without running anywhere near the same risk of getting hurt or killed…only there's no true value in that.'

'Did Arjan Gelens have proof the bulls were being doped?'

'He said he'd taken blood samples and sent them to a lab to be analysed.'

'Which lab?'

'He didn't say.'

'Did he suspect anyone in particular?'

'That's just it – he wanted me to help him catch whoever it was.'

'So you're saying he didn't know who was doing it?'

'He wasn't sure, but he suspected it might have been one of the Gutiérrez clan,' Alfonso said. 'Or one of the people they have working for them at their ranch. Although it could just as easily have been someone who works at the Maestranza…or someone connected with one or more of the *toreros* that have been on the card there this season.'

'One of the *apoderados*, you mean?' Top bullfighters were represented by *apoderados* the way pop musicians or film stars had agents.

Alfonso de la Torre shrugged. 'Or someone close to them.'

It was true, the top *apoderados* were rich men, so if one of them had gone astray then it was far more likely that he would have paid someone to do his dirty work for him. In other words, if the bulls were being tampered with then the list of possible culprits was practically endless. 'Why do you think Gelens chose to ask *you* of all people to help him?'

'I guess he thought he could trust me.'

'I thought you said you didn't really know each other?'

'No, we didn't, not really – beyond the fact that we'd bump into each other from time to time at the ranch or the Maestranza.'

'Sounds like he was putting a lot of faith in you, if you'd never had much to do with each other,' Velázquez said. 'Calling you like he did, I mean.' The Inspector Jefe leaned forward in his seat. 'Why do you think he did that?'

'That's something you'd have to ask him.'

'Yes, well I'm afraid it's a little late for us to be able to do that.' Velazquez shook his head. 'I'm sorry, but I just don't buy it. How could he possibly have known he could trust you?'

'Look, I don't mean to boast, but everyone in the profession knows me. People pay good money to come and watch me, so I always do my best to make sure they aren't disappointed.' Alfonso seemed embarrassed. It was as if having to blow his own trumpet went against the grain with him. 'Why do you think I've ended up in hospital as often as I have?'

'That still doesn't explain why the vet should've singled you out as the person to open up to about his plans. Not if he didn't know you very well.'

'What I'm saying is, Inspector, I'm prepared to put my life on the line in the bullring, and do so on a regular basis. I respect my art. A man like me doesn't cheat. Not knowingly, anyway. And people realize that. So you could say that my reputation as a bullfighter of integrity goes before me.' He held out his arms in a typically Spanish gesture. 'Does that answer your question?'

'What's your opinion on the matter, then? Do you reckon the bulls were being doped and their horns were being shaved?'

'I really can't say.'

'So you've never had any direct experience of it?'

'Fought against a bull that was drugged or had its horns shaved, you mean?' Alfonso shook his head. 'No, I've never come across it personally. But that's not to say it doesn't happen.'

Chapter 13

Velázquez and Gajardo climbed back into the Alfa Romeo. The leather upholstery was so hot it burned, and the steering wheel was too hot to handle. The Inspector Jefe felt the sweat running down his back. Not that it bothered him. He was accustomed to the heat. It was just something that was *there*. Part of the world he came from. He ignited the engine and buzzed down the windows, before he took a couple of deep breaths. Then he established radio contact with Agente Pérez, and asked her if she and Merino had managed to track down Klaus Bloem yet. '*Si*,' she said. 'We're heading back to the Jefatura with him now. I heard about what happened at the studio where Pe works. I hope she's all right?'

'The studio was burned down and she had a nasty shock,' Velázquez said. 'But she's going to be okay, thank God.' He wiped the sweat from his brow. 'Where was Bloem?'

'Drinking in Ziggy's…it seems like he practically *lives* in the place.'

'Okay, I'm on my way now, Sara,' he said. 'Meanwhile, you can find out if Jorge's managed to trace the samples that Gelens sent out.'

'We must stop doing this,' Klaus Bloem said, when Velázquez entered Incident Room 1. 'People might begin to talk.'

Velázquez pulled out the chair from under the desk and sat on it. 'You know what they say – half the people are always busy talking about the other half.' He cranked out a Judas smile. 'People wouldn't be talking about you unless they thought you'd done something interesting.'

He allowed his words to hang in the air for a moment, like some toxic gas. Then said, '*Have* you?'

'Have I *what*?'

'Done something interesting?'

'Do you always like to engage in repartee of this sort with

52

your suspects, Inspector Jefe?'

'Is that how you see yourself, Klaus – as a *suspect*?'

'It's why I'm here, isn't it?'

'Sounds to me like you've got a guilty conscience.'

'I've had enough of this bull*shit*.' Bloem's upper lip curled in an ugly sneer.

'You called Arjan Gelens three times the day before he was killed.' It was a statement of fact, not a question. 'We've got the phone records.'

'So what?'

'What did you talk to him about?'

'Just chewing the cud.'

'And it took three different calls to do that, did it?'

'I guess it must have.'

'Seems to me like you must have had an awful lot of cud to chew.' Velázquez set the tape rolling, then said the time and date into the microphone. 'The officers present are myself, Inspector Jefe Velázquez, and Subinspector Gajardo. We are at the Jefatura on Calle Blas Infante, in Seville, and are about to interview Klaus Bloem in connection with the murder of his lover, Arjan Gelens.'

The German shook his head in disgust. 'You think I killed Arjan, don't you?'

'*Did* you?'

'You must be sick,' Bloem said. 'How can you really believe I'd kill the man I loved?'

'Have you never heard the phrase 'crime of passion'?'

'You've got it all wrong. It wasn't like that.'

'What *was* it like?'

'I loved Arjan, like I keep telling you. I wouldn't have wanted to hurt him.'

'So what exactly did you talk about in the three telephone conversations you had?'

'I had thousands of conversations with Arjan, and you want me to remember them all?'

'No, just the ones you had the day before he was killed.'

Klaus Bloem dropped his head and ran a hand through his flaming red feather cut. 'I thought I already told you he was worried about the bulls,' he said. 'He suspected that they were being doped and their horns were being shaved.'

'You talked with Arjan for over an hour in total, Klaus, adding up the three conversations. You couldn't have talked about bulls all that time, surely?'

'I never said we did.' Bloem sighed. 'Arjan and I talked about the stuff that friends and lovers normally talk about,' he said. 'You know, what we'd been up to, the things we'd been watching on television – private stuff… I remember telling him about my gig over at Ziggy's.'

'What about it?'

'Just what numbers we played and how it went…the reception we got.'

'Didn't Arjan go to see you play?'

Bloem shook his head. 'He was more the retiring type. Mature, sophisticated – liked a good book or film and a glass of Rioja. A cuddle on the sofa.'

'Different from you, then?' Gajardo said. 'You seem to spend a large part of your time in Ziggy's.'

'Yes, we were opposites.'

'And opposites attract, is that it?'

Bloem nodded. 'In our case that's one cliché that proved to be spot on, Inspector, yes.'

Velázquez tried without much success to get his long legs comfortable under the desk. 'I imagine it must've been a major cause of frustration and perhaps even friction between you at times. You liking to go out to bars, and Arjan always wanting to stay in?'

'No, not really…he knew that he could trust me.'

'So are you saying you were faithful to each other? Or was it an open relationship?'

'We were faithful to each other.'

'In that case, why didn't you live together?'

'Arjan liked to have his own space.'

'Sounds to me like it was neither one thing nor the other.'

'Huh?'

'What I'm saying is, how could you be sure Arjan didn't take lovers behind your back? Or didn't you care if he did?'

'Yes, of course I fucking cared, but I trusted him…and he *didn't*.'

'Look, Klaus, I put it to you that you and Arjan argued about something. Maybe he cheated on you and you saw red. The thing got out of control and you ended up killing him.'

'That's ridiculous.'

'Happens all the time.' Velázquez did his best to look like he empathized with the German. 'If you come clean now then any judge would understand and go easy on you.' He shrugged. 'We're all human, after all. Who hasn't been made to feel jealous at some time in their lives?'

'Stop lying and get it off your chest, Klaus,' Gajardo said. 'You'll feel better afterwards, trust me.'

'I've had enough of this nonsense,' Bloem sneered. 'If you think I killed Arjan then you'd better charge me. Either that or let me go. I'm not saying another word until I've spoken to a lawyer.'

Velázquez hesitated, wondering which way to play this. It occurred to him that he had probably made a hash of the interview. But it was difficult to see how else he might have handled it.

He exchanged glances with Gajardo. 'We're going to take a break,' he said, before he turned off the tape recorder.

He asked Bloem if he needed to use the bathroom or wanted a drink. Bloem shook his head. 'In that case, I need to ask you to wait here for a short while. We'll resume the interview later.'

'This isn't right, Inspector. Can't you just tell me what you plan to do? Are you going to charge me or let me go?'

'Under Spanish law, we can hold a suspect for up to three days without charging him.' Velázquez got to his feet and left the room. Gajardo followed him out.

Jorge Serrano had just finished calling the last of the labs on his list. He glanced over at Velázquez and shook his head, as the Inspector Jefe entered the office. 'There's no record of any blood samples being sent out by Gelens to any of the labs in Seville, boss.'

Chapter 14

'How are we going to play this one, boss?' Gajardo asked.

'That's what I'm trying to decide.' Velázquez ran a finger over his stubbly upper lip. The question was, what might be gained from holding the man? Finally he said, 'It might be better to let him go. That way we can see what he gets up to.'

Gajardo nodded. 'Let him think he's got us beaten...'

Velázquez sent Gajardo out to buy grub. It came in the form of a ham roll *a la catalana* and a bottle of mineral water.

They ate at their desks, and worked as they did so. Velázquez tapped away at the keys of his Olivetti, using two fingers in the plodding fashion that was now second nature to him. He was writing his report. Something he hated to do but which was an essential part of the job. As he typed, his mind began to drift. He found himself wondering about the home pregnancy test kit he'd found in the rubbish bin at home.

It was odd, because they hadn't been trying for a baby.

In fact, they hadn't made love in weeks...months, even. Because he'd been unable to perform.

If all the world really was a stage, as someone famously once said, then Velázquez had forgotten his lines.

Besides, some months back they discussed the possibility of starting a family. Velázquez had been all for the idea. He was thirty-seven, after all. And while at twenty-six Pe still had time on her side, he'd felt nevertheless that the moment was right for both of them.

But Pe surprised him by saying that she had other plans. She told him she had always dreamed of becoming a bullfighter, and she wanted to give it a try before she had children.

Since then they'd hardly made love. And on the few occasions when they had tried to do so, it didn't go very well. For the first time in his life, Velázquez had found himself afflicted by the curse of impotence. So what was this pregnancy test all about?

Was Pe playing away matches?

Just thinking about the possibility made his guts churn.

But why else would she have reason to take a pregnancy test?

Realizing the foolishness of torturing himself in this way, he turned his thoughts to the investigation once more. Having decided he had spent enough time speaking to Klaus Bloom for one day, he sent Merino downstairs to show the man out.

Gajardo asked Velázquez what their next move should be. The Inspector Jefe fixed him with his hawk-like gaze. 'So far all we've got to go on are the versions of events that Klaus Bloem and Alfonso de la Torre have given us.' He shrugged. 'What if one or both of them is lying?'

'That's a point, boss.'

'We need to talk to somebody else who knew the victim, José.'

'Who have you got in mind?'

'We need to find someone.'

Velázquez tracked down Alfonso de la Torre's agent or *apoderado* at his office on Calle Teodosio, a busy street in the Old Quarter. Manuel Bordano was the name printed on the plaque outside, but everyone knew the man as Manolo. He was of middle height and build, and his long, lean face was partially hidden behind the Havana cigar he lit no sooner than the Inspector Jefe had introduced himself.

The man's light-grey linen suit fit him perfectly, and the same degree of professional attentiveness that distinguished his tailoring appeared to have gone into styling his wavy salt-and-pepper hair. Bordano looked like money, and yet Velázquez sensed he was as streetwise as they come.

Bordano smiled at the Inspector Jefe and pointed with his cigar to the humidor. 'Take a load off and help yourself to one,' he said, in a thick voice that was about as Sevillan as the minaret of the Giralda. Velázquez declined the offer of a cigar and sat on the upright chair. 'So how can I help you today?'

'You'll have heard about what happened to the vet that looked after the bulls at the Gutiérrez ranch and the Maestranza.'

'Yes, it was a tragic business, Inspector.'

'Did you know Gelens at all?'

Bordano shook his head. 'To be honest with you,' he said, 'I don't remember ever talking to the man.' He shrugged. 'My job's to take care of the *toreros* I represent, and negotiate their contracts and so on. I never really have much to do with the vets.'

'But the bulls are of interest to you, I imagine?'

'Insofar as my clients have to fight them, yes, naturally.'

'You'd want to make sure your clients are up against good bulls?'

'Yes, but that's all down to the people who rear them.'

'What about them – the owners, I mean? Do you have cause to deal with them very often?'

'Only if one of my *toreros* has a complaint about a bull. In that event, I'd pass his comments on.'

'What would the breeder do, in that case?'

'What anyone would do in their shoes – try to do a better job next time.' Bordano puffed on his Havana. 'So far as this man Gelens is concerned…well, it's terrible what happened, but I really don't see how I can be of help.'

'He was under the impression some of the bulls it was his job to check up on were being tampered with…that someone was shaving their horns and doping them.'

'It's the first I've heard about any of this.'

'It happens, though, from time to time, right?'

'It certainly shouldn't.' The *apoderado*'s eyes flashed. 'I certainly hope you aren't trying to imply that *I* have been involved with anything *untoward*?'

'I'm talking to everyone who's connected to the bullfighting business as a matter of routine.'

'All I can tell you is that nothing like that has been going on at the *corridas* where any of the bullfighters I represent have appeared.' He shrugged. 'I can't speak for *corridas* where I don't have a bullfighter on the card, of course. Although quite frankly, I don't believe a word of it.' He puffed on his cigar. 'But are you saying it was someone in the Gutiérrez family he accused of doing this?'

'We're not sure whether or not he went so far as to accuse anybody. But we do have reason to believe he'd taken samples from some bulls and sent them to a lab in Seville for testing.'

'And?'

'The samples appear to have gone missing.'

'How unfortunate.'

'Perhaps,' Velázquez allowed. 'Then again, perhaps not…'

'You don't think somebody took them?'

'If they did then they also destroyed any record of their ever existing, too. '

'I wish I could help you more, Inspector. I really do.'

Velázquez handed the man his card. 'Give me a call on this number if anything else occurs to you.'

'Naturally.'

Velázquez said, '*Adios,*' and went out.

Chapter 15

Velázquez parked himself on a stool at the counter in the bar across the street and ordered a glass of brandy. A bullfighter he recognized but couldn't put a name to appeared on the screen of the television up on the wall.

The Inspector Jefe felt frustrated by the way the investigation was going. Or *failing* to go. But it was also about being thorough and professional. Fairness came into it, too. If he made an arrest then he'd need to be confident he had his man. Any fool could throw the wrong guy in jail. That said, Velázquez was well aware that a lot of detectives in this city would already have charged Bloem. A lot of judges would have shown the man short shrift, too. Especially if he had the gall to turn up in court wearing that Ziggy Stardust outfit. Seville wasn't Madrid, after all. And General Franco hadn't been so very long in his grave. Not if you were speaking in historical terms, at any rate. Plenty of people wanted change. There was little doubt about that. But not everyone felt the same way. Case of old attitudes dying hard.

Velázquez had the barman bring him the local newspaper, *Sevilla Hoy*. He found the report on the investigation and began to read it. According to the reporter, there was no doubt that Klaus Bloem had murdered his boyfriend. The motive? The oldest one in the book: sexual jealousy. And it seemed all of this was so blindingly obvious that 'any fool could see it. The exception being the man in charge of the murder investigation, Inspector Jefe Luis Velázquez'.

He tossed the rag down in disgust, then dropped some coins onto the metal counter and went out.

Back behind the wheel of his Alfa Romeo, he started the engine up and glanced in his wing mirror. Who should he see coming along the pavement but the girl Gelens had paid to clean his flat, Monica Pacheco. She was wearing the short denim skirt she'd had on when he interviewed her, stiletto heels, and a red top.

He watched her enter the building where Bordano had his office.

Now *there* was a coincidence.

His curiosity piqued, he decided to stick around and play George Smiley. He waited for some ten minutes, and then saw the girl come back out. And she had Bordano with her. This was interesting.

He watched them climb into Bordano's navy-blue Merc and set off, then tailed them through the narrow streets of the Old Quarter. He drove past shops, cafés and bars on either side. They went on past a big church and came out onto the Avenida de Hercules, a long broad avenue that was home to a thousand varieties of low life. The Merc slowed to a crawl and then pulled over up ahead. Velázquez did likewise, before he killed the engine and watched and waited.

On the next corner, men sat at tables outside a bar. They smoked and drank and kept an eye on the girls that worked for them. Just then, Monica Pacheco climbed out of the Merc and set off across the Alameda. She walked with her head high, as she passed the medley of hookers and their pimps, pushers and addicts.

Velázquez wondered where she was going.

Then got his answer as he watched her enter Ziggy's.

Chapter 16

Minutes passed and there was no sign of the girl. Velázquez felt like he was starting to cook as he sat behind the wheel of his car with no breeze coming in. Sweat was pouring off him.

A woman came over and leaned in through the open window. She kicked off by saying 'Hello sailor'. Velázquez was tempted to tell her he was no mariner. Had an aversion to the sea, in fact. But he let it pass.

The girl said he sure was looking mighty serious. Maybe she could help him relax a little. Lighten his load. Didn't he like her *tetas*? She practically shoved them in through the open window at him. Why, all the men were *loco* about her *tetas*. And so they should be after what they cost to have done. He could have a feel if he liked. There was no need for him to be shy.

He could simply have flashed his ID and told her to beat it, but he was worried that the girl might then tell her fellow prostitutes he was a *poli*. If that happened, Manuel Bordano would surely get wind of the fact that he was being tailed.

The girl wondered if he was more of a leg man. She could bend over and wiggle her booty if that's what did it for him. Or was he one of those that like to get straight down to business? Any way he wanted to play it, she knew a place where they could be a little more *intimate.*

Just then, Monica Pacheco emerged from Ziggy's. She had a man with her. The man was tall, dressed in slim-fit denims, white laceless plimsolls (with no socks), a burgundy-coloured T-shirt and shades. He wore his blond hair swept across, and had some indefinable air that marked him out as 'a classy sort'.

They climbed into Bordano's Merc, with the girl in the front seat and the man in the back, before they pulled away. Velázquez turned the keys in the ignition. 'Where we going, hon?' the prostitute asked him. Maybe they could go sailing on his yacht another time, he told her, and set off.

He followed the Merc to the end of the Alameda and off left. The road was lined with rundown blocks, and the cracked pavements were strewn with garbage. Men peered out from doorways, and a trio of tarts in short skirts loitered on the corner up ahead. One of them called to the occupants of the Merc and waved as it went past. The car took a right and Velázquez followed, the loose rocks and potholes in the road giving the Alfa Romeo's suspension a beating. The Inspector Jefe hadn't got far, after turning the corner, before he found himself driving past Bordano's vehicle. Velázquez looked in his mirror as he slowed to a crawl. The last thing he wanted was for Bordano to notice he was being followed.

The Inspector Jefe pulled over on the far side of a row of parked cars, some eighty metres or so further up. He killed the engine and adjusted his wing mirror in time to see Monica Pacheco emerge from the Merc. He watched her go over to the entrance of a rundown block and ring the buzzer.

Velázquez wondered who Monica Pacheco could be calling on. Maybe she'd come here to buy some *maria.* Or something a little more potent, perhaps. While the Inspector Jefe was pondering these questions, Monica entered the block. She reemerged minutes later, and now she had a bottle blonde for company. The bottlehead also wore the tarts' uniform of short skirt with stiletto heels. Velázquez watched Monica climb into the passenger seat, while the other girl sat in the back. Then the car started up, and came sailing past the Inspector Jefe. He counted to five before he pulled out and set off on their tail once more.

He followed as the Merc zigzagged through the Old Quarter, with its narrow streets, and made its way down to the river. They crossed the Guadalquivir and joined the motorway, heading south. It wasn't long before Velázquez found himself passing fields full of olive trees on either side, and he could see the mountains, like huge jagged molars away in the distance. He allowed two cars to get between him and Bordano's vehicle, which cruised at a steady 120 kph in the middle lane. Velázquez played follow-my-leader. It was a straight road all the way down to the coast and they kept going like that for maybe a couple of hours, until the Inspector Jefe saw signs for Málaga and Cádiz.

Velázquez knew he'd better stay on the ball now, because Bordano would have to turn off any time. Sure enough, the Merc took the next exit and joined the Algeciras road. The Inspector Jefe continued to tail Bordano's car in this way for another half hour or so, as they bypassed the city of Málaga and resorts like Benalmadena and Bardino. When they came to the exit for Puerto Banus, Bordano turned off and headed down towards the port.

Velázquez tailed him at a discreet distance, until he saw the man's car pull over. Bordano, Monica Pacheco and the other two they'd picked up climbed out of the vehicle and set off on foot. Velázquez parked any old how, then climbed out of his Alfa Romeo and followed them.

The road narrowed as they approached the quay, where the yachts were moored. Smart restaurants, bars, cafés and boutiques lined the other side of the street. Expensive cars were parked in a line by the harbour wall – Ferraris and Bugattis and Lamborghinis, Bentleys and Rolls Royces. Many of the men and women that passed were elegantly dressed and looked as though they had money and weren't afraid to flaunt it. Or perhaps it would be truer to say they had money and they were here precisely *to* flaunt it.

Velázquez followed Bordano and his three companions off the path and over to the harbour wall, where he lost sight of them for a brief moment when a couple of tall Nordic types blocked his path. Then when he caught sight of the foursome again, they were making their way along the boardwalk attached to one of the yachts. Velázquez held back and watched as an Arabic-looking man welcomed the foursome aboard, and they went through a doorway into the covered area.

The Inspector Jefe found a table outside a café across the street, and kept watch on the yacht. A waiter came over and Velázquez told him he wanted a cup of coffee. He paid the bill as soon as the waiter served him, in case he had to leave in a hurry.

Nearly an hour passed before Bordano finally came back out on deck. He was accompanied by the Arab, the blond man, and Monica Pacheco. There was no sign of the other girl. The trio said goodbye to the Arab, before they came off the yacht.

Velázquez got up and followed them. Seeing the trio get into the Mercedes up ahead, he hurried back to his car. By the time he had climbed in behind the wheel, he'd lost sight of them.

He set off and drove around for a while, trying to catch sight of the Merc. But it was no good. He figured they must be well gone by now. He told himself this was the mother of all fuckups. The *great puta* of all fuckups, in fact. He shat in the milk. Not that his cursing did any good.

Then, just when he'd given up all hope of ever seeing the Merc again, he spotted it up ahead in the distance. Bordano must have taken some kind of detour. Or perhaps he'd stopped to call on someone again. If so, Velázquez had missed it. Anyway, he was back on the man's tail, and he followed the Mercedes out of the *pueblo* and back onto the motorway. He made sure he kept at least one car between him and Bordano's vehicle all the way back to Seville.

When they reached the city, the Inspector Jefe continued to follow at a discreet distance as Bordano zigzagged through the narrow streets of the Old Quarter. Finally, the *apoderado* pulled up outside of the Hotel Madrid, where the trio climbed out. A large affair with an impressive façade and elegant lobby, the Madrid was known to be a favorite among bullfighters that came to the city for the *corridas*.

Now Bordano was talking to the bellboy. He handed him the keys to the Merc, before he and his two companions went in through the revolving door.

Velázquez parked with two wheels on the narrow pavement, a little way down the street, and wondered what to do. If he went into the hotel and they were still in the lobby then Bardino would be sure to recognise him. And if that happened then the *apoderado* would almost certainly cotton to the fact that Velázquez had been following him.

On balance, the Inspector Jefe decided it would be wise to wait outside for a bit. So he stayed put and kept watch on the entrance from behind the wheel of his car. He waited in this way for some ten minutes, then he went into the hotel.

Finding there was no sign of the trio in the lobby, Velázquez figured they must have gone up to one of the rooms. He showed the man on reception his ID. 'A group of three came in here a few minutes ago,' the Inspector Jefe said. 'Two men and a girl.' He took a one-thousand-peseta note from his pocket and placed it on the counter, under his hand. 'I need to know which room they went up to.'

The man said, 'Two-four-two.' Velázquez lifted his hand, and the man made the banknote disappear.

Velázquez took the lift up and found the room. Now he was here, he wondered how he should play this.

Then he had an idea.

Chapter 17

Velázquez knocked on the door to the neighbouring room, once, twice. Nobody came. That suited his purposes nicely. He took out his lock picks and went to work. In next to no time he had the door open.

Once inside, he figured it would be an idea to make sure there was nobody sleeping in the bed or lying in the bathtub. So he took a quick look round. Having ascertained that he had the place to himself, he held the hospitality glass against the wall and pressed his ear against it. He could hear voices in there all right, but they were so muffled he couldn't make sense of anything that was being said.

He went out through the French doors, checked the coast was clear, then climbed over onto the neighbouring balcony. He fell awkwardly from the rail and clattered into a plastic chair as he landed. The next thing he knew, the French doors opened. The occupant of the room had clearly come out to see what caused the noise. It was dark by now, but there was enough light from the moon and stars for Velázquez to be able to see that it was Manuel Bordano. Fortunately, the *apoderado* failed to see him as he crouched under the plastic table in the corner.

Bordano turned and went back inside, without bothering to close the French doors. The Inspector Jefe heard him say, 'It must've been somebody on one of the other balconies.'

'So let's have the stuff, then,' said a man whose voice Velázquez didn't recognize.

Bordano said, 'Get out the baggie for the man, Jaime.'

The voices went quiet for a moment, and Velázquez tried to make himself a little more comfortable without banging into the plastic table he was hiding under. He heard a voice that must belong to the young blond man. Heard him say, 'This is the best stuff on the market…it's come all the way from Colombia. It's your genuine marching powder.'

'How did you get your hands on it, then?' asked the first man.

'You don't want to know, trust me.'

Bordano said, 'Stick to fighting bulls is my advice.'

So the man they were selling the baggie of cocaine to was a bullfighter. It wasn't Alfonso de la Torre, because Velázquez would have recognized his voice. But in all probability it was one of the other *toreros* currently on the card at the Maestranza.

'Here you are,' Bordano said. 'Take a snort and see what this does for you.'

The voices went quiet for a short while, and then the *apoderado* said he'd brought the girl along in case the bullfighter happened to feel like company. 'Monica, meet Jorge,' Bordano said. 'Jorge, Monica.'

'Hello, Monica, nice to meet you,' the bullfighter said. 'Yes, a little company of the right sort would be just what the doctor ordered. Just so long as there are no strings attached.'

'The only strings you need to worry about, honey,' the girl said, 'are the ones that keep my knickers up.'

So the *torero*'s first name was *Jorge*. Velázquez remembered looking at the card for the current week at the Maestranza. He tried to remember…then it came to him. The man in there with them had to be Jorge Belgrano.

The bullfighter said, 'The vet knew about the business with the bulls, didn't he?'

'That's none of your concern, Jorge.'

'Who killed him?'

'How should I know?'

'*You* didn't kill him, did you, Manolo?'

'Of course not. Do I look like a murderer?'

'I don't know. What do murderers look like?'

'Stop fucking with me, Jorge.'

'If it comes out that you've been doping the bulls, we'll both be finished.'

'The samples the vet sent to the lab have gone missing. They ain't got nothing.'

'I sure hope you're right.'

'I *am* right. Ain't I always?'

'The great bullfighters of the past wouldn't of gone in for any of this bullshit. It's dirty, Manolo. And you know it.'

'I didn't hear you complain when I told you how much extra

the Arab was going to pay you. Nor when they carried you out of the bullring on their shoulders in Ronda. Nor when you got two ears in Málaga.'

'Christ, Manolo, a man's been *murdered*.'

'You need to pull yourself together, Jorge. I've got to go now. So stop your whining and enjoy yourself with Monica. You'll find she can be damn good company if you let her. Tell me if I'm not talking sense.'

'Okay.'

'That's better. And by the way, there's no need to thank me for taking such good care of you,' Bordano said. 'It's all going on your bill.'

Velázquez climbed out from under the table and went in through the French doors. Jorge Belgrano got up from his chair, his hands balled into fists ready to fight. 'Who the fuck are you?'

Velázquez held up his ID and introduced himself.

'But how the fuck did you get in here?'

'That's my business.'

'You've got no right to snoop around in people's bedrooms, mister.'

'I've got every right,' Velázquez said. 'I'm investigating a murder.'

Bordano made to leave with the young blond man, and the Inspector Jefe told them to stay put. The *apoderado* said that he was a busy professional. He had commitments, appointments to keep. Velázquez said he knew all about his commitments. 'I listened in on the little conversation you were having.'

'What conversation?' Bordano looked at the bullfighter. 'Did we have a conversation, Jorge?'

Belgrano shrugged. 'Can't say I remember it.'

The Inspector Jefe took out his gun and said, 'Nobody's going anywhere.'

Chapter 18

Velázquez told the three of them to sit down, and they made themselves look uncomfortable on the comfortable chairs. He looked at Bordano. 'Nice little business you've got going,' he said. 'Pimping and providing drugs for rich Arabs and your bullfighters.'

'I do no such thing.' The *apoderado* had switched to his professional voice. 'And quite frankly, I resent the implications of what you just said.'

Belgrano threw the baggie full of cocaine. It went sailing past Velázquez's ear, on out through the open French doors and over the balcony. 'This is a drug-free zone, Inspector.'

'Very funny.'

'I don't see anyone laughing.'

Bordano said he really had to leave. Velázquez told him he wasn't going anywhere, unless he wanted to take a drive down to the Jefatura. 'I can always book you into a cell for the night.'

'You ain't got nothing on me.'

Velázquez smiled. 'So you were tampering with the bulls,' he said. 'Gelens found out about it and challenged you. And you either killed him yourself or had someone else do your dirty work for you. Which was it?'

'You're full of shit.'

'Okay, come on, Manolo.' The Inspector Jefe pointed his gun at Bordano. 'Let's go for a drive.'

'There's no need for that.'

Velázquez said, 'I'm trying to think of a reason why I shouldn't charge you with the murder of Arjan Gelens.'

'What is this nonsense you're talking?'

'You've got a motive and you had the opportunity.'

'It was obviously that boyfriend of his – Ziggy what's-his-face. Don't you read the newspapers, Inspector?'

'You're trying my patience, Manolo,' Velázquez said. 'Let's get one or two things straight here. You either play ball with me or you're screwed, big-time. If you don't go down for murder

70

then the least that's going to happen is, you'll be charged with tampering with the bulls. Your career will be finished, and Jorge here won't exactly come out of it smelling of roses, either.'

'For fuck's sake, Manolo, you heard the man,' Belgrano said. 'Tell him what you know.'

Bordano tented his fingers and looked at the floor.

'I might be persuaded to turn a deaf ear to some of what I've heard this evening,' Velázquez said. 'But only if you come up with something that makes sense.'

'I'd love to be able to make a deal with you, Inspector, if I knew something about what happened to Gelens. But the God's honest truth is, I don't.' Bordano shrugged. 'I ain't no murderer, and I don't pay people to do no stuff like that. And you wouldn't want me to make up a load of lies, would you?'

'Who's the Arab?'

'What *Arab*?'

'The one you went to visit on his yacht in Puerto Banus earlier this evening.'

'You mean you tailed us?'

'You supplied him with a girl and cocaine, and he's financing the bullfights.'

'If I did half the stuff you say, Inspector, I'd been living quite a life.'

'Just tell me the Arab's name.'

'The Arab don't know nothing about the vet,' Bordano said. 'He never even met the man.'

'His name.'

'Okay, sure…it's Mohammed Haddad.'

'Where's he from?'

'He's an Egyptian.'

Velázquez picked up the phone and called Gajardo's number at the Jefatura. The Subinspector answered the call, and Velázquez said he had a job for him. 'I need you to call the Jefatura in Puerto Banus,' he said. 'Have them send a couple of officers down to the port to arrest a man by the name of Mohammed Haddad. They'll be able to find him aboard his yacht, which is moored there. It's a big affair – they won't be able to miss it. It's called *Sweet Moments*. They're to stay with him until you get there, then you take him back to the Jefatura in Seville and wait for me.'

'Okay, boss.'

'And there's one more thing. Be sure to tell the officer you speak to in Puerto Banus that you want to be notified the moment Haddad has been detained. You got that? It's important.'

'Sure.'

'Then you are to call me on this number. I'll be waiting here for your call. I'm in room two-four-two at the Hotel Madrid. It's in the Old Quarter. But first I want you to have a squad car sent over here. You got all that?'

'I got it.'

'Good, so get on it and I'll catch you later.' He hung up.

Belgrano said, 'What's the squad car for?'

'You'll find out.' Velázquez lifted the phone from the bedside table and called reception. He recognized the voice of the person who picked up. It was the man he'd spoken to earlier. The Inspector Jefe identified himself and said a squad car would soon be arriving. When it did, the man was to send the officers straight up to room two-four-two. The man said he would do as the Inspector wished. Velázquez hung up.

Bordano started to grumble. He said he was telling the truth when he said he didn't know anything about Gelens's murder. Velázquez told him he'd better shut his mouth if he knew what was good for him.

The *apoderado* shrugged and bit his tongue.

Velázquez sat with the foursome. He rather liked the idea of watching Bordano and Belgrano sweat. Nor that the girl or the blond kid seemed so worried. They both just looked bored more than anything.

The hands on the clock dragged. Bordano tried to look calm and relaxed, but didn't make much of a job of it. As for Belgrano, he didn't even try to pretend he wasn't worried.

Then there was a knock at the door. Velázquez went and peered out through the peephole. It was two officers in uniform. He opened the door and let the men in. 'These two are suspects in a murder investigation,' he said, pointing first at Bordano and then at Belgrano. 'So I need you men to take them to the Jefatura. I'll take my car and meet you there.'

'What about us?' the girl said.

The Inspector Jefe looked at her and the young man like he'd forgotten they were even there. 'You two are free to go,' he said.

Monica Pacheco went out with the blond lad, and the two uniforms cuffed Bardino and Belgrano.

Velázquez called the Jefatura and booked a couple of incident rooms.

Velázquez found his car and was about to climb into it when he saw that there was a sheet of paper on his windscreen. On closer inspection, he saw that it had been stuck to the glass with adhesive tape.

He peeled off the tape and saw that something had been written on the paper in block capitals.

BACK OFF VELÁZQUEZ OR YOU'LL FORCE ME TO DO SOMETHING WE'LL BOTH REGRET. IT WOULD BE SUCH A PITY IF YOU AND YOUR LOVELY WIFE ENDED UP LIKE THE VET.

And below these words was a rather infantile drawing of a… – was it a bull's horn?

Velázquez looked around, but there was nobody in the street.

Rage fizzed up within him. If the killer thought he could frighten him off with his pathetic artwork then he was grossly mistaken.

Chapter 19

When Velázquez arrived at the Jefatura, Bardino and Belgrano were already in Incident Rooms 1 and 3, making their statements. The Inspector Jefe figured he'd leave them to write their works of fiction and entered Interview 2, where Subinspector Gajardo was sitting with Mohammed Haddad. The Arab was of slight build, and dressed in a newish pair of Levi's, and a plum-coloured Fred Perry. The smell of his expensive *eau de cologne* filled the room.

Velázquez introduced himself and showed the man his ID. 'I expect my number two, Subinspector Gajardo, will already have identified himself to you?'

'But what's all this about?'

'Did you know Arjan Gelens?'

'*Who*?'

'He was viciously murdered after he discovered bulls sent to the Maestranza for the fights were being drugged and having their horns shaved.'

'That's news to me.'

'Where were you on Sunday night and Monday morning?'

Haddad took a moment to think. Or perhaps just to give the impression of doing so. 'On board my yacht, *Sweet Moments*.'

'Have you got anyone who can corroborate that?'

'My crew who were also on board.'

'Are they there now?'

The Arab nodded. 'But you can't possibly think *I* killed this man Gelens?'

'Did you?'

'No…and quite frankly I resent your asking me that.'

'Just doing my job, Señor Haddad.'

'I'd like to call my lawyer.'

'No need for that just yet.'

'I don't agree.'

'Unless you've got something to hide?'

'No, I've nothing to hide, but that's not the point.'

A glance at the clock on the wall told Velázquez it was just coming up to one a.m. He turned to Gajardo. 'Some coffee wouldn't go amiss, José.'

The Subinspector got up and went out. Velázquez rubbed his eyelids before he turned his hawk-like gaze back on Mohammed Haddad. 'You can't charge me,' the Arab said. 'I haven't done anything.'

'Sounds to me like you've been doing plenty.'

'Like what?'

The door opened and the fingerprint man came in. Velázquez asked him if he had taken the prints of Bordano and Belgrano. The man nodded, before he took Haddad's prints and went on his way.

'This just isn't on, Inspector.' Haddad glanced at his Rolex. 'You're holding me under false pretenses.'

'I'm investigating a murder,' Velázquez said. 'And the less you cooperate, the more likely I am to believe that you've got something to hide.'

'But you've had me brought here for no good reason at all.'

Velázquez looked right through the man. 'Let's get one or two things straight here,' he said. 'Earlier this evening, you were seen buying cocaine and paying for the services of a young woman.'

'*Que*?'

'The girl certainly didn't go onto your boat to clean up, I know that much.'

'I'd say you don't know dick,' the Arab said. 'And I never touch drugs. It's against my religion.'

'In that case, perhaps you'd like to do a drug test. I'd be willing to bet the results should prove interesting.'

'Why don't you stop wasting my time? Shouldn't you be out trying to catch whoever it was that killed the vet?'

'That's exactly what I am doing. And you'd better stop wasting *my* time if you want to sleep in your own bed aboard *Sweet Moments* tonight.' Velázquez twirled his pencil. 'What do you know about this business of the bulls being doped and tampered with?'

Haddad shrugged. 'It's the first I've heard of it.'

'You're paying Bordano, right?'

'So?'

'He knows all about it…and since you're bankrolling the man, it leads me to wonder if he's acting under your instructions.'

Haddad threw his arms up in the air. 'This is outrageous,' he said. 'I pay Bordano to do his job and get the best bullfighters for the *corridas*…all of which is perfectly normal and legal.'

Gajardo came in with two mugs of coffee. 'I made it with the kettle, boss,' he said. 'Anything's got to be better than the machine.'

Velázquez nodded and tasted the coffee. It was hot and strong, and it was just what he needed.

'I've cooperated and told you everything I know,' Haddad said. 'Now, either you charge me with something and I call my lawyer, or you let me go. Which is it going to be?'

Even if Velázquez were to try to hold the man, the kind of lawyer Haddad could afford would have him out quicker than you can spit. Velázquez told him he was free to go.

Haddad got up and went out.

Velázquez looked at Gajardo. 'How do you fancy going to see whether the other two have finished writing their statements yet?'

Chapter 20

The Subinspector came back in shortly afterwards with Bordano and Belgrano, along with the two uniforms who had been keeping an eye on them.

'Both done.' Gajardo handed the men's statements to Velázquez.

The Inspector Jefe looked through them quickly, then dropped the papers onto his desk. 'So neither of you know anything, huh?' he said. 'The pair of you are as pure as the proverbial driven snow. If your statements are anything to go by, anyway.' He shook his head in disgust, and told the uniforms to escort Belgrano to one of the other incident rooms and take it in turns to wait with him there.

Gajardo pointed to a chair and the *apoderado* sat on it.

'If you want to waste my time, Manolo, then we can waste yours.' Velázquez shrugged. 'No skin off my nose.'

'You're barking up the wrong tree if you think I've done anything, Inspector.'

Velázquez held up the statement Bordano had written. 'What do you call this?'

'You told me to write a statement.'

'This isn't a statement, it's *bullshit*.' Velázquez dropped the sheet of paper onto his desk.

'I never claimed to be no fucking Cervantes.' Bordano reached into his jacket pocket and pulled out a cigar. 'Mind if I smoke?'

'Go ahead.'

The man lit up. 'Listen, Inspector,' he said. 'I got a reputation to keep up and I don't need any of this shit.'

'You've been drugging and cutting the horns of the bulls,' Velázquez said. 'Either you were doing it yourself or you were getting someone else to do it for you. It adds up to the same thing.'

'That's bollocks.'

'Come on, Manolo. I heard you and Belgrano talking about

it.'

'You must've heard wrong, then.'

'You told Belgrano the Arab wanted him to put on a good show every time for the kind of money he was paying. That's why you were doping the bulls and having their horns shaved down – to make him look better than he really is.'

Bordano shook his head. 'I don't know what you're talking about.'

'And Belgrano practically accused you of killing Gelens,' Velázquez said. 'He reckons you killed the man because he was on to you.'

'Look, Inspector,' Bordano said. 'I didn't even know who this Gelens man was until I read about him in the newspaper. And I never fucking killed him, all right?'

'You're the only one with a motive, Manolo.'

Bordano shook his head. 'We can go on like this all night, but it's not going to change nothing. I didn't kill the man and that's that.'

'I know you were doping the bulls and having their horns shaved.'

Bordano shrugged. 'Even if I did what you're claiming – which I didn't – it'd be no proof that I killed anyone.'

'It's proof that you had a motive. And right now motives are thin on the ground.'

'What about his boyfriend? He had a motive. For Christ's sake, man, the whole fucking city's talking about practically nothing else. The reporter that writes for *Sevilla Hoy* says you're the only person that can't see what's staring you in the face.'

'Klaus Bloem swears he loved Gelens and would never have hurt him.'

'He would say that.'

'He'd no doubt say the same about you.'

Bordano looked at his Rolex. 'It's getting late,' he said. 'Are we going to spend all night like this or what?'

'That depends on you, Manolo.'

'I've already told you everything I know.'

'You've told me a pack of lies.'

'You got me in here to discuss a murder, Inspector, and I keep telling you I didn't do it. That's not a lie.'

'You lied about the business with the bulls. I heard you talking about it at the hotel.'

'Okay,' Bordano said. 'I've said all that I'm gonna say. I came here to try to cooperate, and now you're laying all this shit on me. Either let me go or I'll need to use the phone. And if you're not totally fucking stupid, Inspector, then you must surely realize that my lawyer will have me back out of here faster than you can take a piss.' He brushed something from his trousers. 'Besides, I know people in high places in this city. The Mayor's a friend of mine, and so are a lot of the judges.' He puffed on his cigar. 'It's Judge Bautista that you're up against on this case, isn't it? Miguel's rather a good friend of mine, you know. He's a big bullfight fan. I always save him a ticket for a seat in the front row.'

'Get out of here,' Velázquez said. 'Before I change my mind and charge you with selling class A drugs, pimping and defrauding the public on a grand scale.'

Bordano got up and went out.

He had a sneer as big as a barn door on his face while he was about it.

The guy should've been an actor, Velázquez thought.

The kind that plays bit parts in cheesy third-rate melodramas.

Velázquez told Gajardo to bring Belgrano in, and they went through the same routine with him. The *torero* admitted to having asked Bordano whether he killed Gelens, but said he had no reason to think the *apoderado* did it. 'It was just something that flashed through my mind at the time,' he said. 'But Manolo said he didn't do it and I believe him.' He shrugged. 'He's a streetwise kind of guy, but I can't see him killing anyone.'

'He could have paid someone else to do his dirty work for him.'

'I just can't picture him doing anything like that.'

'So why did you ask him if he was the one that killed Gelens?'

'I don't know...I guess I was just pissed off with him.'

'The man shows up at your hotel room with your night's

entertainment all taken care of, in the shape of a sexy girl and a baggie of cocaine, and you were *angry* with him?'

'I guess I was just nervous about the bullfight tomorrow,' Belgrano said. 'I get like that sometimes the night before a *corrida*.'

'Start accusing your associates of having committed murder, you mean?'

'No, I suffer with my nerves sometimes, and then I say things I shouldn't.'

'Have you ever accused Bordano of murdering anyone else?'

'No.'

'So why did you accuse him of murdering Arjan Gelens?'

'I just told you…my nerves were on edge.'

'That still doesn't really explain it.'

'Look, if you're asking me whether I've got any reason to believe Manolo killed the vet or anyone else, then I already told you the answer is no, I don't. Does that answer your question?'

'What about this business to do with the bulls? You know, doping them and shaving their horns?'

'I didn't know about any of that until it was too late.'

'So you admit that it was happening?'

'I fought a bull one time and it was obvious,' Belgrano said. 'But I didn't know it beforehand. I mean it wasn't until I was in the ring with the bull that I realized.'

'Did you tell anyone about it?'

'Only Manolo.'

'What did he say?'

'You heard us talking at the hotel, didn't you?'

'Why didn't you complain to the proper authorities?'

The bullfighter shrugged. 'I guess I got swayed by the money.'

'The big money Haddad was paying you?'

Belgrano nodded.

'It must've made you feel bad if there's any part of you that's at all serious about what you do for a living?'

'I've been feeling bad about it, sure,' Belgrano said. 'I decided to tell Manolo I wanted out.'

'To stop him tampering with the bulls you had to fight, you

mean?'

'Yes, that's what I was trying to tell him earlier at the hotel – that it's not right. But Manolo's a difficult man to argue with.'

Velázquez had the feeling that Belgrano was basically an honest sort who was being led astray by Bordano. He told him that he was free to leave.

Chapter 21

Velázquez pulled over by a telephone booth on his way home and called his old friend, Teresa Bernales. 'It's me,' he said when she picked up. 'Your favorite cop.'

'Luis, what in the devil are you doing calling me at this hour of the night?'

'How'd you like to hear a bedtime story?'

'Go on, then…just so long as there aren't any ghosts in it.'

'There was this man called Mohammed.'

'Did this Mohammed have a surname?'

'It's Haddad.'

'Can you spell that for me?'

'I can and I will.' And he did. 'He's currently hanging out aboard *Sweet Moments*. That's the name of the big luxury yacht he's got moored down in Puerto Banus.'

'That's nice for him. Now you're going to tell me what's so interesting about this Mohammed Haddad.'

'He finances bullfights,' Velázquez said. 'Nothing illegal about that, of course. Except that a vet who looked after the bulls at the Maestranza and the Gutiérrez ranch was found murdered in his bed on Monday morning.'

'I know. I read the papers as well as write for them. So did our Señor Haddad kill Gelens?'

'You're jumping the gun,' he said. 'I do know he's paying the *apoderado* Manolo Badano, who represents Jorge Belgrano – '

'Where's all this heading?'

'The vet suspected somebody was tampering with the bulls – doping them and shaving their horns.'

'Was he right?'

'He was, and I know who was doing it.'

'That'd be Señor Haddad or Señor Bordano.'

'The latter…although I'm still not sure whether he's been doing it under instructions from Haddad.'

'So are we saying Bordano killed Gelens because Gelens got wind of what he was up to?'

'Maybe.'

'Or maybe this Señor Haddad did?'

'Maybe.'

'That's two *maybes*.'

'You can count. I'd say that's a promising sign in a journalist.'

'Sounds to me like you've got a load of sauce and bones but not much meat, Luis.'

'There's meat on the menu somewhere. We just have to find it.'

'I'm glad to hear it because I couldn't hack life as a vegan.'

'That figures,' he said, 'because I once knew a vegan who couldn't hack life as a hack.'

'Have you been drinking?'

'I also know that Bordano pimps for Haddad and provides cocaine for him via a third party. He does the same for Belgrano and some of his other bullfighters.'

'That's something, too, I guess. But it doesn't add up to evidence to support a murder conviction.'

'Never said it did.'

'So why are you telling me all this?'

'Let's just say I'm getting a little sick of the way the press has set itself up as judge and jury where Klaus Bloem is concerned.'

'You mean you don't think Bloem killed his boyfriend?'

'He might have.'

'Meaning he might *not* have.'

'Exactly.'

'And you're peed off by the way some of my colleagues have it in for Bloem.'

'Did anyone ever tell you that you can be awfully quick on the uptake at times?'

'And let's see…I'd guess you also think homophobia is pretty much the default mindset in contemporary Spain. Am I right?'

'You can think as well as count,' he said. 'I'd say that's a *very* good sign in a reporter.'

'I'll have you know we newspaper people are not all stupid.'

'No, but that fool that's covering the investigation for *Sevilla Hoy* could do with a few lessons from a good teacher.'

'I'd say you're right there. Unfortunately, she's an old-school fascist…the sort that thinks General Franco was a good Catholic. Those types tend to have rather fixed ideas.'

'She's the sort that should be given a different kind of work to do, if you ask me.'

'I agree, Luis…if I were the editor I wouldn't even give her a mop to clean the toilets with.'

'That's an insult to all the decent and intelligent people out there that earn their living by cleaning toilets, Teresa.'

'I guess you're right,' she said. 'So let's see if I've understood correctly. You're giving me this dirt on Manolo Bordano and company, to try to take the spotlight off Bloem and give the guy a break. Is that it?'

'To give myself a break is more like it.'

'Because you're a good cop, and as such you don't want to give in to the lynch mob.'

'You see, I *knew* you'd be able to work out why I called you at this hour.'

She laughed. 'Is there anything else you've got to tell me?'

'Not at the moment, but I hope you enjoyed your bedtime story.'

'It was fun…although I have to say you've left me hungry for more.'

'Isn't that what all the best chefs do?'

'Maybe, but you were a homicide detective the last time we spoke.'

'I've been doing a little moonlighting. Anyway, I've given you a little something to chew on.'

'You've done that all right,' she said. 'But I'll need to be awfully careful about what I say, because Bordano is well in with people in high places.'

'Maybe so, but that doesn't prevent him from being a lowlife.'

'I never said it did,' she said. 'But it might give my editor pause when it comes to printing any stuff about the man that can't be backed up with hard evidence.'

'I'm not asking you to do that necessarily.'

'What do you suggest, then?'

'I just thought maybe you could find a way of muddying the waters a little,' he said. 'Your crime reporter's stirring up the lynch mob, and somebody needs to call her to account. She's been telling her readers it's an open-and-shut case from day one, and that I'm the only person in Seville that fails to realize it.'

'But how am I going to argue she's wrong when I'm unable to print most of what you've just told me?'

'You'll think of a way.'

'Will I?'

'I've every confidence in you,' he said. 'You're a great journalistic talent. And you're also a person of intelligence, wit and charm.'

'Since you put it like that, I guess I'd better see what I can do, Luis.'

'I can't wait to read tomorrow's edition of your newspaper.'

'I just hope my editor doesn't spike what I write.'

'Appeal to the man's better nature.'

'I already tried that and it didn't work.'

'So maybe you should try appealing to his lower nature.'

'You're starting to sound like the sort of man my mother always warned me about, Luis'

'I'd better be going.'

'And I'd better get to my desk and write my article.'

'In that case, all that remains for me to do is to bid you happy writing and sweet dreams.'

'I haven't had a dream that was *sweet* since I turned sixteen, Luis. But I appreciate the thought,' she said. 'And thanks for the bedtime story.'

'It was my pleasure, Tere. Goodnight.'

'But Luis…?'

'*Que?*'

'Listen, I'll do my best for you on this, but don't be surprised if nothing comes of it, okay? I'm just a reporter on the damned rag, not the owner or editor.'

'Okay, I understand.'

'And there's something else,' she said. 'I've heard through the grapevine that Judge Bautista and the Mayor both reckon the German did it.'

'So does Comisario Alonso,' Velázquez said. 'Although he only ever agrees with what the Mayor and other people in high places say, so I guess his opinion doesn't really count.'

'No, I don't suppose it does really…only he's your boss, right?'

'Look, Tere, just do what you can, okay?'

'Okay, I'll try…Ciao.'

'Ciao.'

They hung up.

Chapter 22

When Velázquez got in, he found Pe fast asleep. He made sure all the windows in the flat were shut. Then he double-locked the door and put the chain across. He couldn't remember having felt the need to do this before, and realized that the killer had begun to get to him.

He was angry with himself for allowing fear to creep into his mind. But even police detectives were human and could have their moments of weakness.

He tried not to disturb Pe's slumbers as he climbed into bed beside her. And this desire of his to allow her to continue to sleep in peace was not entirely unselfish. After all, were he to wake her then she might want to make love.

He was at least reasonable enough to realize that she must be feeling terribly neglected, given his recent run of failures in the sack. When was the last time he'd actually managed to *do it* with her?

His memory was not up to the task of remembering that far back.

Unable to sleep, he got up out of bed. He put on some boxer shorts and slippers, and went into the living room. He found the brandy and poured himself a large one, then sat in one of the easy chairs and tried to make sense of the investigation. He wondered whether there were some all-important detail that he might have missed. If so then he couldn't think what it could be.

He downed his brandy in a single gulp and went back to bed. A glance at the luminous dials on the alarm clock on the bedside table told him it had just turned 3.34 a.m. He needed every minute of sleep he could get if he was going to be at his best in the morning. He knew this to be a fact, but knowing it did nothing to help. He continued to toss and turn until close to 5 a.m.

When he finally dropped off to sleep, he had a crazy dream. Doctor Spock from *Star Trek* was accused of murdering some intergalactic vet, and the media were all out to get him. The main piece of evidence implicating Spock was 'the famous Doctor's being possessed of exceedingly long and rather queer-looking ears'. Then Captain Kirk was called as a witness and Velázquez woke up. Somebody was kissing his ear. Was it Captain Kirk?

Velázquez opened his eyes and realized it was Pe that was doing the kissing. The next thing he knew, she was caressing him further down. For most men, being woken up in this way by a woman as beautiful as Pe would have been the stuff of which dreams were made. But given his recent run of low scores in the sack, he had lost all interest in sex of late. In fact, he had come to *dread* it the way students who haven't bothered to study dread their exams. He just hoped that Pe would notice he wasn't in the mood and realize it was useless.

But instead, she was carrying on as if he were some prize stallion she was intent on riding.

Had he realized just how much she had she suffered as a result of being followed and then attacked and left for dead in a burning building, Velázquez might have understood that what Pe was doing right now was about a lot more than just sex.

She was doing this to try to put her bad experiences behind her and reject the role of victim.

She was also trying to save their marriage, for Christ's sake.

But Velázquez had problems of his own. 'Pe, darling,' he said, 'I'm sorry but I'll be late for work.'

Daggers appeared in Pe's eyes as she slid off him. Velázquez jumped up off the bed and hurried into the bathroom. Feeling terrible about what he'd just done, he stepped into the shower. He wondered how he might explain his behaviour away, as the arrows of water rained down on him.

He ended up deciding the less he said, the better his chances were of avoiding an argument. After all, how could a man seek to excuse the inexcusable?

He felt like he'd just broken some fundamental taboo.

He dried and dressed himself in a hurry, before he gave Pe a kiss goodbye. He said he hoped everything went well on the show later. Given recent events, he was worried about Pe being at risk in her place of work. She knew how he felt, and was irritated by his protective attitude. He knew this and so tried to avoid the subject. But not talking about it didn't stop him worrying. And now there was this *other business* that he didn't want to talk about, as well.

Pe told him that they needed to talk. 'That's if you still care at all about our marriage,' she said. '*Do* you?'

'Of course.'

'In that case, I think you can at least spare me a few minutes of your precious time.'

'But there's a dangerous killer on the loose.'

'*Screw* your killer. Who's more important to you – him or me?'

He took a deep breath and blew out his cheeks, figuring he knew what was coming. 'Look, Pe,' he said, 'I know that I haven't exactly been at my best lately in the bedroom, but – '

'So if you know that,' she cut him off, 'why did you push me away like that earlier?'

How could he tell her when he didn't know the answer to this question himself? 'I've been under a lot of pressure lately,' was the best he could come up with.

'You've never been like this with me before, Luis. Is there another woman?'

'No, there's nobody else…it's nothing like that, Pe. I love you.'

She gazed deep into his eyes. 'Honestly?'

'Honestly,' he said, disentangling himself from her embrace. 'But now I really do have to leave.'

Then as he was going out, he noticed that an envelope had been pushed under the door. He picked it up and opened it. Inside there was a single sheet of paper. He unfolded it and read the words:

IF YOU INSIST ON CONTINUING WITH THE INVESTIGATION THEN YOU KNOW WHAT YOU CAN EXPECT. DON'T SAY I DIDN'T WARN YOU.

Chapter 23

Velázquez dashed out the door and ran down the stairs. In his hurry, he bumped into his neighbour, Señora Tejado. She dropped her shopping bag, and potatoes and other groceries went rolling in all directions.

The Inspector Jefe apologized without looking back as he ran through the lobby, his long loping strides eating up the ground in no time. He went out into the street, hoping to spot somebody who looked suspicious.

He saw the familiar face of Pedro Moreno, who lived on the next floor up from him and Pe. The man raised a hand to acknowledge Velázquez and said '*Buenos dias*,' before he climbed into his car. A couple of men in smart business suits were walking along on the opposite pavement.

To his right, a woman was coming towards him, carrying a shopping bag in either hand. To his left, an old man was making his way along with the aid of a walking stick. A car went past. Velázquez peered in through the passenger window, and saw that a young woman was behind the wheel. She was alone in the car.

He shat in the milk as adrenaline pumped through him. For want of an enemy to chase or fight, he turned and punched the wall.

He had never been in a situation of this sort before. Never had anyone come to his home and leave threatening messages under his door.

The killer was letting him know that he was prepared to attack, or even kill, him and Pe if his warnings went unheeded.

Velázquez needed to come up trumps on this investigation to save his reputation. He realized only too well that all eyes were on him. He needed to show Comisario Alonso and Judge Bautista that he was a competent Head of Homicide. And he needed to get the local media off his case, and win back the confidence of the people of Seville, too. But there was much more at stake than that. If he failed to catch the killer, he feared that he and Pe were going to end up on the man's list of victims.

He turned and went back into the building, where he found Señora Tejado struggling to pick up her potatoes. He apologized for banging into her earlier, and helped her pick up what she had dropped. Then he asked Señora Tejado if she had seen anyone leave the building as she came in from the street. She was afraid that she hadn't. But what was it all about? Instead of replying, Velázquez carried the old lady's groceries up the stairs for her and left her at her door.

He let himself back into his own flat, where Pe was tidying up in the kitchen. She said she thought he had left for work. He told her he reckoned it was now time she went and stayed with her mother.

'But what on earth's this about all of a sudden, Luis?'

'This killer we're after on this one is a dangerous maniac.' He showed her the note that had been pushed under their door, and Pe read it. 'Now do you see what I mean?'

She shrugged. 'It's not exactly pleasant having this sort of thing happen, I agree,' she said. 'But it kind of goes with the territory, doesn't it? Do you really expect me to leave home and go into hiding every time you have a murder to investigate?'

He shook his head. 'This is different,' he said. 'I've never worked on a case where the killer has gone out of his way to make it personal like this before.' He took a deep breath and let it out. 'Look at the two incidents where you work...'

'But aren't you confusing two different stories here, Luis?'

'What if it was Gelens's killer that attacked you and burned the studio down?'

'That's a huge assumption you're making.'

'Is it?'

'You're adding two and two and making five.'

'I don't think so, Pe.'

'No, I'm not going anywhere,' she said. 'This is our home, and I refuse to be pushed out of it by anyone.'

Velázquez sighed. 'The fact is, it's no longer safe for you to stay here.'

'I've made my decision,' Pe said. 'I'm not going anywhere.'

'If you won't go and stay with your mother, then at least you can let me get you a gun to carry for your own protection?'

'Okay, that sounds like a more reasonable idea.'

'In the meantime, make sure you keep the door to the flat double-locked at all times when you're here alone,' he said. 'Park your car close to the building when you go to work.'

'You're talking to me as if I were a child, Luis.'

'Make sure you only go to places where there are lots of people.'

'Okay, Luis, I know the routine...but frankly, I think this is ridiculous.'

'I love you,' he said. 'And I couldn't take it if anything were to happen to you.'

Pe looked at him. It had been a while since he'd told her he loved her. She had needed to hear him say it. 'I love you, too,' she said. 'Take care out there.'

'I always do.'

He made to leave, but she called to him as he opened the door. 'What is it?'

'Make sure you catch this bastard. And when you do, don't take any chances,' she said. 'If you have to kill him then do it.'

When he got to the Jefatura, Velázquez briefed his team on what he'd been up to the day before. Once he'd told them everything he had to say, he got his officers to share any information they managed to turn up.

The net result of their combined efforts was that they still didn't have anything to tie any of the suspects to the crime.

Velázquez spoke of his concerns with regard to the press and their desire to see the case 'solved', regardless of whether or not justice was actually done.

Pérez said, 'That's code-speak for them thinking Bloem's our man, right?'

Velázquez nodded. 'I don't think there's any doubt they have it in for him.'

Serrano looked confused. 'But he's still our main suspect, boss, isn't he?'

'Maybe he is, or then again, maybe he isn't. I can't stress enough the importance of keeping an open mind on this one. A media trial is the last thing we need.'

'What about this *apoderado* fellow, Manuel Bordano?' Merino wanted to know.

'He certainly had a motive. So did Mohammed Haddad, the man that's been paying him and his bullfighters. But we've got nothing on either of them.'

Sara asked if there was any sign of the samples Gelens was supposed to have sent out. Serrano shook his head. 'I've checked with every lab in Seville and nobody seems to know anything about them,' he said. 'So it seems they've either disappeared, or they never really existed in the first place.'

Just then, the Inspector Jefe's telephone rang. '*Hola*?'

'Velázquez, there's been another murder.'

Chapter 24

By the time Velázquez arrived at the crime scene, down in Puerto Banus, they had already hauled Mohammed Haddad's body out of the water.

Seeing that his friend Juan Gómez was in the process of inspecting the body, the Inspector Jefe went and hunkered down next to him on the quayside. 'You got anything you can help me with on this one, Juan?'

'Whatever it might be,' Gómez said, 'would be strictly off the record of course.'

'What's the record?'

'I'd say he'd been in the water a good couple of hours, going by the temperature of the body and the water he was in.'

'Any thoughts on the M.O.?'

'Now you know better than to ask me such questions, Luis,' Gómez said. 'It might however interest you to observe there's a large swelling at the back of the head. Some bleeding, too.'

Velázquez nodded. 'Seems to be consistent with the victim's having been struck there with a heavy, blunt object.'

'If you say so.'

'And then pushed overboard,' Velázquez said. 'Where he would have drowned without regaining consciousness.' The Inspector Jefe grinned. 'All very much off the record, of course. Thanks, Juan.'

Velázquez went and spoke to the people that had worked for Haddad on board his yacht. There was a crew of ten people in total, four women and six men. None of them had seen or heard anything suspicious. Or so they claimed.

The Inspector Jefe wondered whether this fact was suspicious in itself.

He figured it might or might not be.

He had squad cars drive the ten members of Haddad's team to the Jefatura, all the way up in Seville. Upon arrival, they were each put in separate rooms and told to write a statement.

Velázquez read the ten statements. They all said the same thing, more or less.

Seven of them claimed to be in bed, sleeping, around the time the murder was thought to have taken place.

Two of them said they were making love at that hour.

He questioned these two separately. Since they'd been awake, perhaps they heard something?

Oh, they'd heard something all right. Lots of groans and 'I love yous', and some dirty stuff that he would have felt shy about writing in any report.

The other person who'd been awake suffered from insomnia. A Spaniard from Toledo by the name of Miguel, he explained how he'd been listening to rock music through his headphones around the time when the murder was thought to have taken place. Even if there had been a loud noise, there was no way he would have heard it.

The man said that he was a big Fleetwood Mac fan. His idea of paradise was having Stevie Nicks all to himself for a night. He'd get her to run through her greatest hits while they drank a couple of his favorite cocktails to begin with, and then – Velázquez cut the man off with a wave of the hand and said he got the idea.

The rest of the team all said they'd slept right through the entire night.

Velázquez envied them. He wished he could get some proper sleep once in a while. All too often nowadays, what little sleep he got was troubled by violent dreams or nightmares.

His thoughts turned on the killer's M.O. The fact that the Arab's killer hadn't used a bull's horn might mean that Haddad and Gelens were killed by different people.

And yet the Arab's involvement in the world of bullfighting suggested that his death was almost certainly tied to the vet's in some way.

When Velázquez got to the ranch, he found Roberto Rios pottering about. The Inspector Jefe said hello to the man and asked him what he knew about Manuel Bordano. 'Not a lot,' the ranch hand said. 'Apart from the fact that he's one of the top *apoderados* and earns *mucho* money.'

'Have you ever had reason to speak to him?'

'No, but Alfonso de la Torre would – Bordano represents him.'

Velázquez nodded and said he would like to talk to Señor Gutiérrez if he was at home. The ranch hand said if the Inspector Jefe would care to wait, he would go and see. Rios then went into the house and reemerged shortly afterwards. He pointed to the side door, which he had left open. 'He says he can see you now.'

Velázquez went inside, through the bead curtain, and Gutiérrez was there to greet him with a handshake. The man had big hands and a firm grip for someone of his advanced years. He was wearing jeans with a white shirt and a leather waistcoat. 'If you'd like to come with me,' he said, and led Velázquez into the sitting room.

It was a large darkened room with a high ceiling. There was a long mahogany table at the far end, and a huge natural fireplace that wouldn't be used until winter. The walls were covered with oil paintings, some of which were clearly very old. All in all, it really was some place Gutiérrez had here. But finding that he liked the property did nothing to help endear its owner to Velázquez. Not that the Inspector Jefe was by nature a jealous sort, but he had reasons for disliking Gutiérrez.

Not so very long ago, all of Andalusia had been owned by a small number of wealthy landowners and everyone else was dirt poor. Velázquez's own father was a peasant. He fought on the Republican side during the Civil War, and was tortured and then killed by Franco's men shortly after the city fell to the fascists.

This man Gutiérrez had fought for the fascists, as had all of his family. To the Inspector Jefe's way of thinking, Guitierrez would have liked to keep the mass of ordinary Andalusians in a state of something close to slavery if he had his way.

If he were honest with himself, then Velázquez would have to admit that he'd disliked the man before he even met him.

He disliked what he had heard about him – and he'd heard plenty.

He disliked what he had read about him in the local rag.

He disliked everything the man stood for.

He disliked the way that he or people like him had ruled this land for centuries, while ordinary folk had lived in terrible poverty.

He disliked the way Gutiérrez and his clan, along with many others, claimed to have jumped ship now that the dictatorship had fallen.

He disliked their hypocrisy and their lies.

He disliked their easy arrogance.

He even disliked their excellent taste in paintings and furniture, and their fine manners.

He disliked everything about them, even the things that you were supposed to like because they were considered admirable.

But the Inspector Jefe was professional enough to know that he had to try to put his personal feelings aside, so that he could see things with a clear head.

Gutiérrez made himself comfortable in one of the leather chairs and invited Velázquez to take a seat. Would the Inspector Jefe care for something to drink? No, thank you. Gutiérrez ran a hand through his thick white hair. 'Okay, so what can I do for you?'

'I have reason to believe that Arjan Gelens suspected the bulls, either at the Maestranza or here at your ranch, were being tampered with.'

'*Tampered* with?'

'Yes, that their horns were being shaved and they were being doped.'

'That's nonsense.'

'He sent blood samples to a lab, but they appear to have gone missing.'

'I wouldn't know anything about that.'

Velázquez decided to try a different approach. 'Do you know Manuel Bordano, the *apoderado*?'

'I know him to say hello to, yes. But why do you ask?'

'I have reason to believe he was behind this business with the bulls.'

'But what you're suggesting is preposterous.'

'Is it?'

'Yes...that sort of thing would make a mockery of bullfighting. And it would also be a criminal offence.' Gutiérrez's brown eyes flashed. 'What exactly is it that you came here to ask me, Inspector?'

'Do you know a Mohammed Haddad?'

'Yes, he's one of the money men in the bullfighting world.'

'Did you know that he's just been murdered?'

'*Que*?'

'They had to fish him out of the water, down in Puerto Banus.'

'That's news to me, I must say.' Gutiérrez scratched his chin. 'I didn't know the man personally, but what happened to him sure sounds like a nasty business.' He looked at Velázquez. 'But I hope you don't think any of this stuff that you've been talking about has anything to do with me.'

'At this stage, I don't think anything.'

Gutiérrez shrugged. 'I'm sorry I can't be of more help.' He got up and walked to the door. 'I can assure you that you're wasting your time coming here and questioning me like this. I only hope the enquiries you make elsewhere bear more fruit. Good day to you, Inspector.'

Velázquez went out, feeling vaguely dissatisfied with himself and with the world at large.

Just as he was about to climb into his car, a red Lamborghini came rolling into the parking area and pulled up. Velázquez waited to see who was going to get out of it.

And who should it be but the blond lad that had been with Manuel Bordano and Monica Pacheco the day before. This was a turn up.

Was Gutiérrez buying cocaine from the man, too, then?

The Inspector Jefe watched the lad go into the house, then he found the ranch hand again and asked him if he knew who the owner of the flash car was. 'Gutiérrez's son, Jaime,' came the answer.

Velázquez asked Roberto Rios if the lad lived here and learned that he did.

The Inspector Jefe figured he should have known better than to let the lad leave the night before, without at least taking his name and details. That had been a real goof. And it didn't make him feel any better if he told himself that he'd just had the lad figured for a small-time drug pusher who was of no relevance to the murder investigation.

Of course the lad still might not be connected to the case in any significant way. It might just be coincidence that he was old Gutiérrez's son. But even so...

He wondered whether to go and get the lad and take him in for questioning now, but decided against it. He would save that for another day.

Velázquez climbed into his car and set off. All kinds of patterns began to weave their way through his mind, so that he didn't see the mountains or the fields full of olive trees and garlic plants. He drove on automatic pilot all the way back to Seville.

Chapter 25

He left the car in the underground car park at the Jefatura and took the lift up. The officers in his team were all out and about, working on the investigation.

He sat with his feet up on his desk and tried to get the details of the case clear in his mind. But it remained about as clear as one of those days in the mountains when the fog descends and you can't even see your own hand in front of your face.

He worked on his report, hammering at the keys of his Olivetti with two fingers.

Gajardo came in and asked him where this latest murder left them. Velázquez said he had no idea, but he could sure do with a coffee. The Subinspector said he thought it was only the wicked there was no rest for. Velázquez suggested in that case Gajardo might seek to enlighten himself by reading up on a little Spanish history. He could perhaps start with the Inquisition. When he'd finished with that, he might want to check out the Civil War and its long and bloody aftermath.

Gajardo said he had no time to read, unless you counted the crime reports and the sports pages in the only rag.

Velázquez said it was to be lamented that the offensive organ the Subinspector had referred to, namely *Sevilla Hoy*, was edited by the Son of the Great Whore. What's more, that party's mother was currently reporting on the investigation it was incumbent on them to solve. But this fact should not come as any great surprise, given Spain's tortured past.

The Inspector Jefe further informed his number two that they were living in a country whose history was steeped in blood. Yes, indeed, the history of this land was a tale of violence and injustice, of torture and famine. You could throw in murder and revenge and infamy of each and every hue, too – much of it having been carried out in the name of religion.

Gajardo wondered whether the Inspector Jefe would like his coffee to be bought from the café on the corner or the machine downstairs?

Velázquez said that while Spain's history was a disaster story, its future was all set to be a plasticated nightmare if the coffee machine downstairs was anything to go by. He preferred the coffee from the café on the corner. And in a glass.

Gajardo made himself scarce.

Velázquez finished the paragraph he'd been in the middle of writing, before he began to study the inventory of calls made to and from Arjan Gelens's home telephone. The calls made in the days leading up to the murder had already been checked out, so he went a little further back in time to the ones that had yet to be looked at.

There was a number that Gelens had called every week or two. It was a foreign number. Velázquez looked at the list of numbers he had copied from Gelens's personal phone book, and saw that it was one of three he had not crossed off. He had written notes beside the other two numbers, to say they had been discontinued. Next to this number he had written: NOBODY PICKING UP.

Before calling it again now, he ran a check and learned that the first four digits made up the code for calling Holland. Perhaps the number belonged to a sibling or other family member. Or maybe an old friend. He dialed the number and a woman picked up and said something in a language Velázquez didn't know – Dutch, presumably.

'Hello,' he said in English, hoping the woman could speak that language. 'I'm calling from Seville.'

Gajardo came in at that moment with the Inspector Jefe's coffee in a glass. The Subinspector placed it down on Velázquez's desk. The Inspector Jefe heard the woman on the other end of the line say, 'From *Seville* did you say?'

'Yes…I've tried calling you several times lately.'

'I've been away in Italy. I just got back last night,' she said in fluent English. 'Is it about my brother?'

'It's about Arjan Gelens,' Velázquez said. 'Is he your brother?'

'Yes,' she replied. 'What's happened?'

'You mean you haven't heard?

'Heard *what*…?'

Chapter 26

'I think you'd better sit down.' Velázquez swallowed hard. Over the years he had told lots of people that their loved ones were dead, but somehow it never got any easier.

'Can you please just tell me?'

There was no easy or gentle way to break the news, so he figured the thing to do was get it over with as quickly as possible. 'I'm very sorry but your brother has been killed.'

'No...there must be some mistake.'

'I'm afraid not.'

'But Arjan is a *veterinarian*.' She spoke as if the notion that a vet – *any* vet – could be murdered were ridiculous.

'I'm very sorry.'

'But who would want to kill a *vet*?'

'That's what I need to find out.'

The woman let out a terrible animal sound that was followed by a succession of sobs, each one longer than the last. 'I'm sorry,' Velázquez said. 'Perhaps I should call you again later?'

'No, please don't hang up,' she said. 'How did it happen?'

Velázquez told the woman that her brother was found dead in his own bed. 'He was murdered.' The Inspector Jefe figured it would be better to spare her the gory details of the killer's M.O. At least for the time being, anyway.

He coughed to clear his throat. 'The girl he had in to clean the flat found the body.'

More sobbing. He waited for the woman to get herself back under control. Then he said, 'I'd really like to talk to you in person.'

'When's the funeral?'

'The body's still with the pathologist, but he should be finished with it soon. Then it's really up to you, as his next of kin.'

'Yes, of course. I'll book myself onto the next flight to Seville.'

He offered to pick her up from the airport, and she said she would appreciate that. If he gave her his number then she would call him just as soon as she had bought her flight ticket and knew her arrival time.

He gave her his number, then expressed his condolences. He said he was sorry, too, that he'd had to tell her the bad news over the telephone.

Not at all, she said. It was hardly the Inspector Jefe's fault.

Velázquez said *ciao* and they hung up.

He let out a heavy sigh. That was one part of the job he sure didn't enjoy.

He saw Gajardo looking over, one eyebrow raised, so he brought him up to speed. 'I'll talk to her when she gets here,' he said. 'See if she can tell me anything I don't already know about her brother.'

He sipped his coffee. 'How would you like to come to the Maestranza this evening, José?'

Velázquez convened the members of his team for a quick briefing in the office. He told them about the blond lad who dealt drugs and how he turned out to be old Gutiérrez's son.

He told about how Manolo Bordano had driven down to Puerto Banus with the blond lad and Monica Pacheco, to pay a visit on Mohammed Haddad on the Arab's yacht. The same yacht Haddad had been on before he was killed.

He explained how he'd figured the blond kid was just a pusher Bordano was using to get hold of product for him.

At least they knew who he was now, anyway.

He told them that Bordano was pimping Monica Pacheco out to his bullfighters and perhaps also to other people.

He asked if anybody had any questions.

Sara wanted to know whether he reckoned the deaths of Haddad and Gelens were linked. Velázquez said it was very likely they were, although he had no evidence as yet to support his hunch.

And that was what they needed to find: more evidence.

It was a matter of keeping on digging. The missing piece in the puzzle might turn up where they least expected it.

Something had to give, sooner or later.

Chapter 27

Before they took their seats at the Maestranza, Velázquez and Gajardo went to take a look at the bulls. They turned out to be strong and impressive-looking creatures. Certainly there was nothing about them that made either of the two detectives suspect they had been doped.

Next they paid a call on Jorge Belgrano in his dressing room. The *torero* was clearly surprised to see them, but Velázquez was quick to assure him he had not come to make an arrest. They were just there to see the bulls and watch the *corrida*.

Belgrano smiled. 'If you have seen the *toros*, Inspector, then you'll have observed their horns are long and sharp enough. And they hadn't been doped, either…not when I went to look at them, anyway.'

Velázquez said he was glad to hear it. He wished Belgrano the best of luck in the *corrida*. With that, the Inspector Jefe and Gajardo went to pay a call on Alfonso de la Torre in his dressing room.

De la Torre was clearly just as surprised to see them as Jorge Belgrano had been. 'You don't want to question me some more now, Inspector, surely?'

'We're only here to watch the *corrida*,' Velázquez said. 'Have you seen the bulls yet?'

Alfonso nodded. 'You never really know beforehand whether they're going to be any good or not,' he said. 'But they looked fine to me.' The *torero* was tying his hair back in a ponytail. He grinned. 'But if you don't believe me then you are welcome to go and fight them yourself, instead of me, Inspector.'

Velázquez smiled. No, he'd stick to leading murder investigations. 'There's one more thing,' he said. 'I wanted to ask you about Manuel Bordano.'

'What about him?'

'Do you trust him?'

'He's my *apoderado*.'

'So is that a yes?'

'I clearly trust him enough to have him represent me.'

'Do you think he is capable of murder?'

'What's this all about?'

'Just answer the question.'

'How should I know? I'd say any man is, if you put him in a corner.'

'Was Bordano in a corner?'

'Not that I know of.'

'Are you aware that he pimps for his bullfighters and gets drugs for them?'

'Nobody pimps for me,' Alfonso said. 'I am a faithful husband, and I don't use drugs of any kind – unless you count the occasional glass of single malt or French brandy. I need to be fit to kill my bulls.' He frowned. 'Look, if you've got any questions regarding Manolo, then you'd better put them to him. I've got a busy evening coming up.'

'Okay, we'll leave you to get ready. Thanks for your time – and the best of luck.'

'*Gracias.*'

Velázquez and Gajardo went and found their third row seats, in *sombra*. 'We've got a great view from here, boss,' Gajardo said. 'I normally sit in one of the cheap seats somewhere near the back in *sol*. It's all I can afford after the divorce.'

Some of the men and women in the neighbouring seats were done up in traditional Andalusian dress. Looking around, Velázquez recognized various members of Seville's smart set among them. He spotted the Mayor and Judge Bautista, as well as Manolo Bordano and Comisario Alonso.

There was a hum of expectation in the air as everyone waited for the *corrida* to begin. The sun was beating down, and Velázquez was glad he had remembered to wear his black leather trilby for protection. Gajardo took out a flask of Scotch and had a drink then passed it to the Inspector Jefe. The Scotch tasted good and burned pleasantly as it went down.

The band started to play and Jorge Belgrano and the members of his *cuadrilla* entered the ring. The bullfighter cut a handsome and impressive figure as he strutted across the sand-covered ring in his suit of lights. He waved his cape at the bull in an insolent manner, but the animal was slow to attack. Belgrano and his team had to work hard to bring it out.

When the bull did finally start to liven up, Belgrano made a number of passes that left the animal looking tired and bewildered. Then the bullfighter sighted the *toro* along the length of his sword. He stood with one heel raised and called to the bull, before he charged.

He went in close to the animal, then reached in over its horns and went for the kill, skipping to the side as he did so to avoid being gored. The next moment, he realized that he had miscalculated and struck bone, so that his sword went flying into the air.

Belgrano went scurrying after it, and picked it up. Watching from his seat, Velázquez wondered whether the bullfighter was allowing his problems outside of the ring to affect his performance. Either way, Belgrano's work lacked elegance. He needed a couple more tries before he finally landed his sword in the right spot and put the poor bull out of its misery.

In the end, the kill seemed to be more an act of gross butchery than one that involved any sort of artistic prowess. Sections of the crowd offered lukewarm applause, while others jeered. Velázquez did neither.

Alfonso de la Torre was next up, and he was under attack from the bull almost right from the start. Nevertheless, he was able to pull off a series of neat *veronicas* that brought applause from the crowd.

Velázquez admired the economy of de la Torre's work. The bullfighter was establishing his dominance over the bull in a quietly efficient way, and all of his movements were calm and unhurried.

When he had worn the beast out, he stood stock-still and sighted it along the length of his sword. And in contrast to Belgrano, Alfonso de la Torre made a clean kill at the first time of trying. Practically everyone in the crowd began to cheer and applaud.

Chapter 28

Velázquez was hammering away in his customary two-fingered fashion at his long-suffering Olivetti the following morning, writing his report, when Gajardo came in. The Subinspector said, '*Buenos dias*,' then asked Velázquez if he'd turned up anything useful. The Inspector Jefe shook his head and told Gajardo what was on his mind.

His verbal account was intercalated with the kind of invective and foul language he would have liked to include in his written report but couldn't.

Gajardo listened then gave an account of his thoughts that included similar vocabulary to that the Inspector Jefe had used.

Gajardo lit up a Winston and started to smoke it. Velázquez said he thought he'd given up the cigarettes.

Gajardo told him *he* thought he had, too.

Ans Gelens called the Inspector Jefe at just after 10.45 p.m., to say that she had arrived. She was now having a coffee at the airport. Velázquez told her he would go and pick her up. He was leaving now. 'I'll be standing by the exit doors in Arrivals,' she said. 'I'm blonde, forty-five, and on the skinny side. I'm wearing blue jeans and a white top with a black linen jacket.'

Velázquez said that he was sure he would recognize her. And in fact he spotted her as soon as he got there. He went over to her and said, 'You would be Ans Gelens, I presume?'

'I would indeed.' She smiled. 'And you must be Inspector Jefe Velázquez.'

'That's what my ID says.' He held his card out for her to take a look at.

She thanked him for coming to pick her up. He said it was the least he could do. She reached for the handle of her grey Samsonite travelling case, but Velázquez beat her to it. '*Please*,' he said, 'let me help you.' She shrugged and asked where he had parked. He waved an arm in the general direction of where he'd left his car and they set off.

As they drove into the city, Velázquez asked Ans Gelens if she was hungry. She said she hadn't eaten anything since breakfast. They'd offered her some food on the flight, but just looking at it was enough to put her off. Velázquez said he knew a place where they did excellent fish and seafood. Ans Gelens told the Inspector Jefe his description was making her mouth water.

He headed through the *casco antiguo,* in the direction of the restaurant he had in mind. There were no parking places in the immediate vicinity, so he had to drive round the block to look for one. Finally he found a space in a narrow side street, and parked with two wheels on the pavement. They climbed out and set off on foot. The pavements were too narrow for the two of them, so they walked over the cobbles. A breeze blew up, carrying the scent of oranges. Somewhere a forlorn trumpet rang out. Young people passed them, talking and laughing. The restaurant Velázquez had in mind was just behind the bullring. As they entered the place, they found it to be humming with the chatter of contented diners.

The restaurant was small and you had the feeling that the clientele had all been crammed into it. But Velázquez had eaten here many a time before, and knew that they served good food at reasonable prices. A waiter came over and asked him how he was keeping. It had been a while since the Inspector Jefe was last in here. 'Too long, Miguel,' Velázquez said. The waiter led them to a small table over by the natural stone wall. There were bullfight posters up, advertising famous names from the past, and a stuffed bull's head was mounted at the end. Its long and dangerously sharp horns were a sight that might give many a young, would-be bullfighter pause.

The waiter gave them each a menu and went away. Then a different waiter came over to take their order. Velázquez went for the monkfish and Ans Gelens opted for *paella.* They ordered a bowl of mixed salad for two, along with a bottle of chilled white Coto.

Ans Gelens said she was still having difficulty taking in the fact that her brother had been murdered. She felt like she would come to her senses any moment and find that this was all just a bad dream. Velázquez nodded sympathetically.

The waiter came over with their wine and two glasses. He uncorked the bottle and poured a little for Velázquez to try. He suggested that Ans Gelens be the one to try it. She did so and pronounced it rather nice. The waiter poured wine into the two glasses and then went off.

Velázquez was conscious of having only just met the victim's sister. He figured he ought perhaps to engage her in a little small talk before he began to question her about her brother. He asked her where she had learned to speak English. 'Why do you ask, Inspector?'

'You speak the language like it's your mother tongue.'

'I was about to say the same thing to you,' she said.

'My mother was English.' He sipped his wine. 'And I lived in England as a young man for some years.'

'Which part of England did you live in?'

'In Bristol, which is where my mother is from. And I lived in London for a time, as well.'

'Me, too.' Ans Gelens took her knife and fork out of the napkin they had come wrapped in. 'I lived in Putney for five years.'

'In that case, we were practically neighbours.' He smiled. 'I lived in Fulham for a time.'

Having exhausted the theme of conversation, they fell silent. Velázquez felt a little awkward. He wanted to keep the woman talking, but he couldn't think of anything to say to her. Finally, he asked if she'd had a good flight over. But as soon as he'd spoken, he remembered that he'd already asked her this, in the car on their way here from the airport. Making small talk was hardly his strong suit. The waiter reappeared with a bowl of salad, and Velázquez and Ans Gelens began to pick at it.

The Inspector Jefe chewed on a slice of cucumber and swallowed, then took a sip of his wine. He looked at Ans Gelens and asked her if her brother had any enemies. She shook her head. 'So he wasn't the sort to go stirring things up, then?'

'Stirring up *what*, do you mean, exactly?' Worry lines appeared on her forehead. 'What is there for a *vet* to stir up – the animals in his care?'

The waiter came with the main course, and Velázquez applied himself to his monkfish. 'Your brother was gay, I understand?'

'Yes.'

'Did he have any significant others?'

'He had plenty of lovers down through the years.'

'Would you say he had a happy love life?'

'Oh, I don't know about that.'

'Disappointments in love, were there?'

She nodded, sipped her wine. 'Although that was long ago, when he was young and idealistic.' Her lean, sharply defined features creased in a fond smile. 'In the last few years of his life, my brother seemed to get tired of practically everyone he became involved with.'

'Were you close?'

'Yes, very.'

'So did he tell you about his lovers?'

'I got to hear about them, sooner or later,' she said. 'If he stayed with anyone long enough to consider them worth talking about.'

'Did he ever mention a man by the name of Klaus Bloem?'

'Oh yes.'

'The way you said that suggests it might have been serious between the two of them,' Velázquez said. 'Was it?'

'At first I think it was…but like I say, Arjan had a way of growing tired of people.'

'And he grew tired of Klaus?'

'Eventually, yes.'

'After how long are we talking?'

.'They seemed inseparable for the first year or so. I even began to think Arjan might have met Mr. Right at last…that he might settle down once and for all.'

'What made you think that?'

'Just being around them.' She shrugged her narrow shoulders. 'I mean, you get a feeling about a couple when you spend time in their company, don't you?'

'So you came over here to stay with them?'

'A few times, yes,' she said. 'They reminded me of some couple that have been married for half a lifetime…almost as if they lived through an entire marriage in the space of a single year. By the end of it they were finished – or Arjan was.'

'And Klaus?'

'That was the sad thing about it, because the poor man was devoted to Arjan.' There was a thoughtful expression in her bright blue eyes. 'I felt sorry for him in a way.'

'So Arjan dumped him?'

'Not exactly.' She waved her fork. 'Arjan asked him to leave to begin with, but Klaus didn't want to. So Arjan threw a tantrum and they had an almighty row.'

'When would that have been?'

'Oh, six or eight months ago.'

'Arjan told you all this?'

She nodded then sipped her wine.

'Klaus told us he and Arjan were still involved,' Velázquez said. 'So are you saying that's not how it was?'

'No, they were, in a way…I guess it depends how you want to use the word.'

'How would *you* use it?'

'Look, Inspector, I loved my brother and the last thing I want to do is speak badly about him now he's dead.' She popped a prawn into her mouth. 'Besides, Arjan was a good man. He was kind and considerate. He was also a first-rate vet.'

'But?'

'I hate to have to say this, but he did treat poor Klaus abominably. He just seemed to pick him up and put him down whenever he fancied. It was like poor Klaus was some sort of toy, you know?'

'It was an on-off affair, then?'

'They separated in the sense that they stopped living together. But then Arjan would allow Klaus to come over and, from what I gathered, they'd end up in bed more often than not.'

'How often would this happen?'

'Every week or two,' she said. 'Or maybe it was more often than that sometimes. I think it all depended on what Arjan was feeling like. Klaus was always phoning him up. Or else he'd turn up on his doorstep and start pleading with him.'

'And Arjan would weaken, is that it?'

'Sometimes he would, sometimes he wouldn't. Like I say, I think it all depended on the mood he was in. But it was always Klaus who did the chasing and the pleading, and…well, from what I gathered, Arjan didn't exactly treat him well.'

'Did Arjan tell you this?'

Ans Gelens nodded. 'We were in regular contact by phone over the past few years.'

'Sounds like your brother had a fair bit to talk about?'

'He probably needed to get things off his chest.'

'Had Arjan been seeing anyone else during this time?'

Ans Gelens's big blue eyes gazed into Velázquez's. 'Is all this really relevant, Inspector?' she asked. 'I'm starting to feel like I'm on one of these gossip shows. It hardly seems right…my brother's still not been buried.'

'My motive for asking about Arjan isn't simple curiosity, Ans, I can assure you.'

'You don't think all this could have a bearing on the case?'

'I won't know that for sure,' he said, 'until I've heard what you have to tell me, will I? But if one thing's certain, it's that the more I get to learn about Arjan's lifestyle and the people he mixed with, the more likely I am to be able to find out who killed him.'

'That's all very well, Inspector, but there are things that Arjan made me promise never to tell a living soul.'

'I need to know, Ans.'

She shut her eyes and sighed. 'Yes, my brother had been seeing someone else…somebody in the public eye.'

'A man?'

'Of course.'

Velázquez shrugged. 'Arjan might have fancied a change for all I know.'

'Oh, he fancied a *change* all right, Inspector,' she said. 'But not a change of gender.' She shook her head. 'No, Arjan only ever had eyes for men.'

'He didn't live with this man, though?'

'No.'

'Why not?'

'The man was married – and still is.'

'I need to know his name, Ans.'

'He's a bullfighter.'

'That's unusual…a bullfighter being gay, I mean.'

'Not so much as you might think, apparently.' Ans Gelens reached for her glass. 'Not according to Arjan, anyway.'

'The name, Ans?'

'Alfonso...' She waved her fork in the air. 'I can't remember his last name…it was *de la* something or other…'

'De la *Torre*…?'

'That's it,' she said. 'Yes, of course – Alfonso de la Torre.'

Chapter 29

After he had dropped Ans Gelens off at her hotel, Velázquez headed over to Ziggy's. He wanted to see if Klaus Bloem was there.

As it turned out, the man was up on stage, singing and playing guitar with his band when the Inspector Jefe walked in. Velázquez eased his way between rucks of bodies, to get to the counter. Many of the men in the place were dressed in leathers. Others were wearing T-shirts with jeans and trainers. A number appeared to have come here straight from work, and were dressed in formal suits or sports jackets and chinos. Then there were a few who were in drag. The air was heavy with the stink of masculine sweat and patchouli. Velázquez got the attention of the barman and had the man serve him with a bottle of Cruzcampo.

He fixed his attention on Klaus Bloem, who was singing the David Bowie number *Watch That Man.* Not that Velázquez could have put a name to the song, even though it was vaguely familiar to him.

The number came to an end, and Bloem's face froze as he noticed the Inspector Jefe looking at him. It was what Velázquez wanted: to keep up the pressure on his number one suspect. Hopefully Bloem would crack sooner or later and spill the beans on the murder.

If he was the killer.

And if he wasn't, then hopefully it would all come out in the wash.

Contrary to what people like Comisario Alonso and the crime reporter that wrote for *Sevilla Hoy* might think, Velázquez had no intention of giving Bloem an easy ride. No more was that his intention than it would have been to charge the man without sufficient evidence.

He finished his beer and left Ziggy's. As he crossed the Alameda de Hercules, he heard Bloem and the band launch into the next number. He vaguely made out the words 'rock 'n' roll' and 'suicide'.

When Velázquez got home, he found Pe sitting on the sofa. She had her feet up on the coffee table and was reading a magazine. Her denim shorts were cut high, so that he had a good view of her lovely brown legs. Classical music was playing: a pianist, unaccompanied – something he didn't recognize. Velázquez leaned over to kiss Pe on the cheek. 'I thought you'd be in bed by now.'

'I don't feel tired.' Pe smiled. And what a smile it was. It had warmth and joy and love in it. It was just the kind of smile any man would dream of coming home to. The kind of smile that would make a man *want* to come home. It made him feel better than he'd felt all day.

He looked down at the page she was reading. 'This must be a first,' he said. 'You reading the gossip columns.' He knew Pe feared the people that funded her show would want to take the programme down market.

She sipped her wine. 'I was reading about the bullfighter's wife, Yolanda de la Torre,' she said. 'They say she's been taking antidepressants for some time and hitting the booze.'

'Do you believe it?'

She shrugged. 'It doesn't sound like the way a woman who has everything would behave.'

'Have you ever met her?'

'As it happens, I chin-wagged with her for a while at Juan Soria's bash back in the spring. '

'What did you make of her?'

'I never said I really knew the woman.'

'But what was your impression of her, I mean?'

'She seemed like a decent enough sort.'

'Did you get the feeling she was depressed? '

'No, but I do recall that she was hitting the gin rather hard.'

Velázquez was woken up by the alarm the following morning, in the middle of a rather nasty dream. In it, a bull with particularly long and sharp horns was charging at him. He got up out of bed, padded into the bathroom, and took a shower.

Dried and dressed, in black chinos with a plum-coloured polo shirt, he went into the hallway and dialed Gajardo's home number. When the Subinspector picked up, Velázquez brought him up to speed regarding what Ans Gelens had told him. Gajardo expressed his surprise. He found it hard to imagine someone like Alfonso de la Torre being gay. 'I know what you mean,' Velázquez said. 'But I can't think of any reason why the woman should lie about something like this.'

'So where does this leave us?'

'I'm not sure, José…but I need you to contact Sara and Jorge and fill them in on what I've just told you. Tell them to go to the Gutiérrez ranch first thing. If they find Alfonso de la Torre there then they're to talk to him and see what he has to say about what Ans Gelens told me. I'll go to the man's house, so we should run into him between us…although I'm also interested in talking to his wife, if I catch her on her own.'

'Right you are, boss.'

'And I need you to go through the bank accounts of Gelens and Haddad, José. You'll need to get a warrant first. Look for anything that appears unusual – any large amounts going in or out. Check out all the regular payments they were making, too. Get Javi to help you.'

Velázquez hung up then left the flat. He found his car and set off through the narrow streets of the Old Quarter. Minutes later, he crossed the bridge, then picked up the motorway and headed south.

The sun's rays were already hammering down out of a Wedgewood sky, and once he had left the city behind fields given over to cereal crops, garlic plants and olive trees flashed by on either side. He drove for a little under an hour before he pulled up outside of the bullfighter's place.

He pushed the button on the security gantry, and moments later Señora de la Torre's voice asked him to identify himself. When he did so, she said she was sorry but her husband wasn't at home. Velázquez said he would appreciate it nevertheless if she'd let him in. He would like to have a word with her about a few things. She couldn't see how that could possibly be necessary, seeing as she had never even met this *Arjon*

Geddins.

The victim's name was Gel*ens*, he corrected her: Arj*an* Gel*ens*.

Whatever his name was, she was quite certain it didn't alter the fact that she'd never met the man and didn't know anything about him.

Velázquez quite understood but would like to talk to her all the same.

She wondered if it was really necessary.

He assured her that it was.

Chapter 30

Yolanda de la Torre buzzed the gate open, and Velázquez entered the property. He breathed in the pleasant scent of jasmine and mown grass, as he walked up the path that bisected the carefully tended front lawn. The villa's white stucco façade was covered with ivy and purple bougainvillea. Overhead, house martens swooped around the eaves. Somewhere a particularly proud cock was crowing.

The door to the house opened before Velázquez reached it, and Yolanda de la Torre stepped into his line of vision. She was wearing a pair of stonewashed Levi's, and a top that had UCLA blazoned across it. The last time he'd come here, she'd worn a top that advertised BOSTON UNIVERSITY. Velázquez wondered how many *American* universities she had attended. He wondered, too, why her pupils were so dilated. As he was wondering about this, he remembered the tidbit of gossip Pe had passed on to him about the woman.

As he drew up to where she was standing, the Inspector Jefe smiled at Yolanda de la Torre and said *'Buenos dias'*. He promised her he wouldn't take up too much of her time. She mumbled something about having a busy day ahead of her, but stepped aside to let him in. Velázquez caught a whiff of alcohol from her breath. He suspected the gossip columnists had finally got something right for once, as Yolanda de la Torre invited him to make himself at home.

He perched himself on the leather sofa and took out his notebook, then waited for Yolanda de la Torre to come and sit in one of the matching easy chairs. He breathed in the smell of polish and lavender, and looked at her and wondered how to begin. No ideas sprang to mind. He looked at his notebook but that didn't help. He rubbed his nose and said he was sure it couldn't be easy, being married to a bullfighter.

'No, "easy" isn't the word I'd use. But it has its benefits.' She gestured with her hand. 'In between worrying about whether your husband's going to get killed on the job, you get to live in a place like this. We also have luxury flats in the city and overlooking the beach in Marbella.' She shrugged. 'We enjoy the good life. And of course in my case, there's the added bonus of getting to sleep with Alfonso de la Torre every night.'

Despite what she had just said, Yolanda de la Torre didn't look like Velázquez's idea of a happy woman. 'Your lavish properties aside, how's married life been going lately?'

'Excuse me, Inspector, but I really don't see how that could possibly be any of your business.' Her eyes flashed with barely concealed anger. 'And neither do I see what it's got to do with the murder you're supposed to be investigating,' she said. 'Shouldn't you be out there trying to catch whoever did it?'

'I can assure you that's exactly what I'm doing.'

'You could've fooled me.'

'When you build a house, you don't begin with the roof.'

'I hope you haven't come all this way just to quote old Spanish proverbs?'

He flipped through his notebook, before he stopped at a random page and looked at it. 'Apparently the gossip columnists are saying you've been suffering with depression,' he said. 'Is that so?'

'Now it's my turn to quote a proverb – harsh words fall on deaf ears.'

'I'm not here to play games.'

'I really don't see what any of this has got to do with anything, Inspector. Now can you either get to the point, or I'm afraid I'm going to have to be getting along. I've got a busy day ahead of me.'

Velázquez suspected that the only thing he was preventing her from doing was mixing her next cocktail or popping her next pill. 'Okay,' he said, 'I'll cut to the chase. I've been speaking to Arjan Gelens's sister, Ans. She told me that Gelens and your husband were very close. That struck me as odd, seeing as Alfonso's already assured me that he hardly knew the man, beyond having the occasional brief conversation with him about the bulls.'

'A lot of people like to claim to know Alfonso when they don't really,' Yolanda de la Torre said. 'It kind of goes with the

119

territory.'

'What particular territory would that be?'

'Being a famous *torero*, of course.' She shrugged. 'For better or worse, Alfonso's a celebrity and everyone wants a piece of him.'

'Ans Gelens seemed to think there was a little more to it than that.'

Yolanda de la Torre reached for her handbag, one of those smart numbers done in ostrich leather. She took out a cigarette and lit up. Her eyes spat venom at Velázquez through a cloud of smoke.

'In fact,' he said, 'Ans assured me Alfonso and her brother were involved in a sexual relationship.'

'*Que?*'

'I can assure you, Yolanda, that having to talk to you about this gives me no pleasure at all.'

'So why do it, then?'

'I should've thought that was obvious,' he said. 'Arjan Gelens has been murdered. And we know that his ex, Klaus Bloem, was still in love with him. But it appears Gelens left Bloem for your husband.'

'I've never heard such a load of rubbish in all my life.'

'So Alfonso has never spoken to you about any of this?'

She shook her head then took a long drag on her cigarette, before she turned her face away and exhaled. Her shoulders began to shake, and then when she turned her head again, it wasn't to look at Velázquez but to bury her face in her hands.

Her cigarette, barnacled to her forehead as it was so that it poked through her parted fingers, lent her the aspect of some dejected female unicorn. Only appearances could deceive, and if anyone was playing the unicorn then it was her husband. And it was with another man that he'd been using his horn.

Yolanda de la Torre lifted her head, her face now blotched and puffy with tears.

Velázquez said, 'You must realize that this could be of vital relevance to the murder investigation.'

'But you can't possibly think that Alfonso killed him?'

'I don't think anything yet. I'm still in the process of trying to find out as much about what happened as I can.'

'You make it all sound so *reasonable*, Inspector.'

'Did you know about it?'

'It's all nonsense what you've been saying.'

'In that case,' he said, 'why the tears?'

'Just get out of my house,' she hissed.

Velázquez sighed. 'It's all going to come out sooner or later you know, Yolanda. You may as well get it off your chest now.'

'There's nothing to talk about.' The cigarette trembled between her fingers as she brought it to her mouth. She took another drag then exhaled twin columns of smoke down through her nose.

'So why have you been depressed of late?'

'Who says I have?'

'All of the gossip columnists can't be wrong, surely?'

'When have those bastards ever been right about anything?'

'Come on, Yolanda,' he said. 'Give the playacting a rest, huh?'

She dried her eyes. 'We've had our problems, Alfonso and I,' she said. 'But all this about him being bisexual's nonsense.'

'And that's your last word on the subject, is it?'

She looked at Velázquez in a way that told him she would rather fight a tiger in a sack than dish the dirt on her husband. Realizing that he wasn't going to get anything more out of her – not today, anyway – he got to his feet. 'If you change your mind and want to talk about it,' he said, 'give me a call.' He took out his card and set it down on the glass coffee table.

Yolanda de la Torre didn't even turn her head to look at Velázquez or his card as he got to his feet and made for the door.

Velázquez kept turning the details of the case over in his mind, as he headed back to Seville. He was nearing the city when Gajardo came through on the radio. 'What's new, José?'

'I've just finished going through the bank accounts of the two victims, boss,' Gajardo said. 'Nothing much has been going on in either of them. How's your morning gone?'

'I spoke to Yolanda de la Torre,' Velázquez said. 'She burst into tears and completely refused to admit the possibility that her husband could be gay.' He touched the brakes as he came to a bend in the road. 'Have you heard anything from the others?'

'No, but I'm sure they'll be in touch if they turn up anything.'

'Okay. I'll see you when I get to the Jefatura.'

No sooner had Velázquez cleared than Sara Pérez came on, saying she'd just finished interviewing Alfonso de la Torre at the ranch. They'd had to wait for him to finish working out with the bulls first, before he agreed to talk to them. 'And?'

'He's sticking to the story he told you, boss,' Agente Pérez said. 'He claims it's true he didn't know Arjan Gelens all that well. And maintains all what the man's sister's been saying about him and Gelens being lovers is nonsense. Anyway, then he got into his car and had just driven out of the gate, when a woman turned up in a red Seat. The woman was some distance away, so I may be wrong, but I'm pretty sure it was Monica Pacheco. Alfonso and the woman spoke to each other, without getting out of their cars.'

'How could you tell they were talking?'

'She leaned her head out of the window.'

'How long did they talk for?'

'Only half a minute or so, boss. I hurried over to try and talk to the woman, but they both drove off before I got near them.'

'Did you get the impression they knew each other?'

'It seemed like it…although it's hard to say, because I couldn't hear them.'

'If it was Monica Pacheco then I'm wondering what she would've been doing at the ranch in the first place.'

'It got me curious, boss…that's why I made a note of the reg on her car.'

'We need to talk to her and find out what she was up to,' Velázquez said. 'And have you tried giving the bullfighter a call to ask if he knows her?'

'Yes, but he's not picking up.'

'Keep trying him.'

'Oh, and I was going to say, boss, there's one more thing,' Pérez said. 'I ran a check on the car she was driving, just to see who the owner was.'

'And?'

'Funny thing is, the car belongs to a Mohammed Ataoui, who lives in Seville. I got the man's number and gave him a call. And guess what?'

'Don't tell me the car was stolen, Sara?'

'It sure was…so if it was Monica Pacheco I saw behind the wheel, she's a car thief.'

'Among other things,' Velázquez said. 'Give me the reg on the car she was driving.'

Chapter 31

Velázquez drove to the address he had for Monica Pacheco. It was on one of the narrow, cobbled streets that lead off the Alameda. The building was a nondescript affair and looked like it might have started out as a warehouse.

The Inspector Jefe pushed the buzzer to the woman's flat, and when she came on he identified himself. She sounded surprised and said he had already interviewed her once. Velázquez knew that. He told her he had enjoyed it so much he would like to repeat the experience.

She was afraid that she didn't have anything new to tell him. It would be a pleasure just to see her again, even so. Should he come up, or would she like to come down? If he had to come up then she'd have to open the door for him. Otherwise she should know that he'd have to force his way in. She said she'd be right down and hung up.

She came to the door dressed in a short black skirt and tight pink top. Her long black hair was tied back in a pigtail. 'What's up this time, then?' she wanted to know.

'Come and get in the car, Monica.'

'Is this a private party or can anyone go?'

'You're the guest of honour, let's put it that way.'

They drove to the Jefatura in stony silence. When they got there, Velázquez showed her into the incident room he'd reserved earlier. He pointed to the chair and she sat down. 'Know why you're here?'

'I'm figuring you didn't get a good enough look at my legs the first time around.'

'Have another try.'

She shrugged. 'You tell me. Maybe you're an ass man? Or the sort that can't get through a day without looking at a nice pair of titties?'

'Carry on like that and I'll book you for insulting a police officer.'

Gajardo came in and sat in the vacant chair next to the

Inspector Jefe. Velázquez set the tape rolling and spoke into the mic. The usual spiel for the record. He said that he and Subinspector Gajardo were at the Jefatura on Calle Blas Infante in Seville. They were about to interview a Monica Pacheco. He said the time and the date. He opened his notebook, found the woman's address and then read it out.

He said he was pausing the tape because Subinspector Gajardo needed to leave the room for a moment. He looked at Monica Pacheco and said, 'We need to talk to you some more about Arjan Gelens.'

'I thought you just said he was going to leave the room?'

'I did.'

'So why's he still here?'

'That was just for the tape.'

'*Que*?'

Velázquez gave her his plastic smile. 'There's a little matter we wanted to talk to you about off the record. I'm sure you can guess what it is.'

'No…what are you getting at?'

'I think you can guess, Monica.'

'I think so, too,' Gajardo said.

She pulled a face like she wasn't impressed. 'Do you two always think the same about everything?'

'Only when we both know we're right,' Velázquez said.

'What about if one of you likes a woman?' She brushed her hair out of her eyes. 'Does it mean the other one's gotta like her as well?'

'We're not here to joke around, Monica.'

'Who says I was joking?'

'We know about the car.'

'What car?'

'The Seat that you nicked.'

'Who in their right minds would nick a fuckin' Seat?'

'You would, for one…you *would* and you *did*.'

'Seats are for cheapos.'

'How about you stop wasting our time?'

Monica Pacheco pulled a face like she didn't know what they were talking about. 'Look, I ain't nicked no Seat, okay?'

'Nice try, but we've got a witness, Monica. So there's no point in your denying it. It was red, if that helps jog your memory.'

She folded her arms and looked at the wall.

'Popular number with thieves, Seats.'

'Good little car, despite everything Monica's been saying,' Gajardo said. 'Economical, reliable, easy to get spare parts for.'

Velázquez nodded. 'Must explain it.'

'Do you two do this double act for everyone, or's all this just for my benefit?'

'Sold it yet?' Gajardo asked her.

'I don't know what you're talkin' about.'

'Automobile theft's a serious charge,' Velázquez said. 'So is prostitution. And those are just the start of your problems, from what I can see.'

'I'm ain't no *puta*, okay?'

'So what were you doing in Jorge Belgrano's room at the Hotel Madrid when I caught up with you there?'

'That was different.'

'What was different about it?'

She shrugged. 'I got a thing about bullfighters…always have. And I'm a big fan of Jorge Belgrano in particular.'

'It's still prostitution, Monica.'

She went back to rummaging in her handbag. 'Fuck it, I'm out of cigarettes,' she said. 'Have you got one?'

'Not until you start to play ball.'

'Never was one for ball games.'

'No…you're more into bullfighting, we know. Or perhaps I mean bullfigh*ters*.' Velázquez set the tape rolling again. He spoke into the mic, saying that he was now starting the interview with Monica Pacheco, Subinspector Gajardo having returned. 'What were you doing at the Gutiérrez ranch earlier today, Monica?'

'Who says I was there?'

'One of our officers saw you there.'

'They couldn't have.'

'She made a note of the reg on the car you were driving,' Velázquez said. 'It was a red Seat.'

Gajardo said, 'Sounds to me like she must nick so many cars

she forgets half of them.'

'That could explain it.'

'Look, I didn't nick no car, all right.'

Velázquez nodded and stopped the tape. 'Listen, Monica, we want to know what you were doing at the Gutiérrez ranch. Tell us that and we might be able to overlook the little question of the stolen Seat. We can always make sure the car's returned to its rightful owner, so he's happy. We could just tell him we found it somewhere – kids'd stolen it and taken it for a joyride then dumped it…happens all the time.'

'Thanks for the warning.' She was scrutinizing her nails. 'I'll make sure I lock the doors of me boyfriend's car the next time I leave it parked somewhere.'

Velázquez said, 'I didn't get you in here so you could entertain us, Monica.'

'How about giving me that cigarette?'

'You can have one when you've told us what you were doing at the ranch.'

'It's a free fuckin' country, ain't it? If I wanna go to a ranch, that's my business.' She shrugged. 'I ain't done nothin' wrong. I come in 'ere after I found the vet's body and told you everything I knew. Tried me best to help you with your enquiries, didn't I? And now you start flinging all this shit at me.'

'We're not flinging shit at you. We're just asking you a few simple questions, that's all,' Velázquez said. 'You give us what we want, you get your cigarette. You keep on wasting our time like this and we really will start flinging shit at you. And you won't like it, believe me.'

'You ain't got nothing on me.'

Gajardo said, 'You're forgetting the car you stole.'

Monica Pacheco looked like she was trying to weigh things up. 'What's the big deal about if I went to the ranch, anyway?'

Velázquez set the tape rolling. He spoke into the mic again, to say he was resuming the interview. Then he asked Monica Pacheco once more what she'd been doing at the Gutiérrez ranch.

She looked at the wall and didn't say anything.

'Went there to see Alfonso de la Torre, did you?' Velázquez said.

'I might've done.'

'So you admit that you went to the ranch to visit Alfonso de la Torre?'

'If you say so.'

'Why did you go to see him?'

'That's my business.'

'Why did you steal a car to go there?'

'You got any idea how much it'd cost to get a friggin' taxi all the way out there?'

'So you admit that you stole the car and drove there in it?'

'No, I never said no such thing.'

Gajardo said, 'Having an affair with Alfonso, are you?'

'Do you think I'd tell you if I was?'

'We need to know, Monica,' Velázquez said.

'I still haven't got that cigarette.'

'There's a rumour going around,' Gajardo said, 'that Alfonso de la Torre was involved with Arjan Gelens.'

'*Involved*?'

'That they were in a gay relationship.'

'Are you pulling me by the hair?' she said, employing the well-worn Spanish idiom.

Velázquez said, 'Ever see Alfonso at Arjan Gelens's place when you were there?'

'No.'

'You're blackmailing Alfonso, aren't you?'

'Of course I'm not.'

'What, then?'

'You do know he's my cousin, right?'

'Who… – Alfonso?'

'Well it ain't the fuckin' Pope we been talkin' about, right?'

Velázquez stopped the tape. 'You'd better not be lying, Monica, because we'll soon find out if you are.'

'Go check it out, Batman. And you can send Robin here to go'n get me those cigarettes while you're about it. I smoke Camels…or if you can't get them then Chesters'll do.'

'It's Subinspector to you,' Gajardo said. 'And I'll go and get you some cigarettes if and when I feel like it. And that means when you've earned them.'

She looked at Velázquez. 'Your boyfriend's a bit sensitive, ain't she?'

'That's enough of the manners, Monica. Unless you want us to keep you here for the next three days,' the Inspector Jefe said.

'You can't fuckin' do that.'

'Say that again and I'll do it, just to show you I can. How does the idea of that grab you?'

She tossed her head in a sulky fashion and looked at the wall.

'Anyway,' Velázquez said, 'even if you and Alfonso are cousins, you still haven't told us what you were doing at the ranch.'

'Like to watch him work out with the bulls, don't I?'

'Only you missed him, I understand?'

She shrugged. 'I got there too late…just as he was leaving?'

'Do you often go to see him?'

'When the whim strikes me.'

'Like the bulls, do you?'

'Is that a crime nowadays?' she said. 'Prob'ly will be soon enough, the way things're going – like everything else that's any fun in this friggin' country.' She crossed her legs. 'Fuck me, anyone could die for want of a smoke in this place.'

Velázquez looked at Gajardo. 'Think you could oblige, Subinspector?'

'I'm not sure she deserves it, boss, the way she's been talking.' Gajardo was still smarting from the insults she'd aimed at him a little earlier. 'She's got a nasty tongue.'

'She's going to be extra good from now on, aren't you, Monica?'

'I guess so.'

Gajardo got up and left the room.

'You shouldn't treat the people that work under you like that, Inspector,' Monica Pacheco said. 'The poor man looked like a dog with his tail between his legs when he went out just then.'

'Carry on talking like that and you won't be smoking another cigarette for the next three days.'

'What would you want to hold me for, if I ain't done nothin'?'

'One reason might be that you're a rude little bitch with a nasty tongue, like the Subinspector just said.'

'Maybe you're right about that.' She chuckled. 'But it's still no reason to hold a person if they ain't broke the law.'

'Apart from stealing a car, you mean?'

'You said yourself the car's small potatoes,' she said. 'Besides, it was only a friggin' Seat. I mean, it's not like it was a Jaguar or a Merc or something.'

'Think of it being like a restaurant, Monica.'

'What?'

'What we really want is one of the big juicy sirloins that the chef's done to perfection. But if they're all gone then we'll just have to settle for the next best thing on the menu.'

'I ain't really hungry at the moment,' Monica Pacheco said. 'I'm dying for a smoke, though.'

'Whoever it was that killed Arjan Gelens is the steak, if you follow my gist. But if we can't get any further with the investigation then we'll just have to settle for the potatoes…and book you for car theft.'

Gajardo reentered the room, holding a couple of cigarettes in his hand. Seeing from the white filter that they were Ducados, Monica Pacheco was quick to protest. 'If you can't get Camels, I'll smoke Chesterfields or Winstons. I'll even smoke Marlboros – or even fuckin' Fortunas at a push,' she said. 'But Du-fuckin-*cados?* Anything's better than that dark shit.'

'Beggars can't be choosers, Monica.'

She snatched the cigarettes from the Subinspector's outstretched hand, then lit up and took a long drag. 'Better than nothing, I s'pose.'

'That's just the way we feel about booking car thieves,' Velázquez said. 'Where's the car now, Monica? And don't try and bullshit me any more if you want to get out of this place before tomorrow.'

'I left it near the flat.'

'In that case,' he said, 'we'll have an officer go with you to get it.'

Chapter 32

Gajardo thanked the person he had been talking to on the telephone and hung up. 'The news is,' he announced to the room, 'Monica Pacheco and Alfonso are in fact cousins.'

'So the woman *is* capable of telling the truth,' Velázquez said.

'When it's in her best interests to do so.'

'What do you make of it, boss?' Pérez asked.

The Inspector Jefe shrugged. 'I really don't know, Sara.' He glanced at his watch: it was just coming up to 8.30 p.m. 'Have yourselves an early night, the three of you, and be here early and ready to put in a hard day's work tomorrow.'

Gajardo asked where Merino was. 'I sent him down to Puerto Banus,' Velázquez said, 'to see if he can turn up anything interesting on Mohammed Haddad.' He stretched his arms then laced his fingers behind his head.

Gajardo, Serrano, and Pérez all finished what they had been doing and then left, leaving the Inspector Jefe in the office alone. He called Pe and told her he would be home some time after ten, so they could go out and eat somewhere if she liked.

He told her he loved her before he hung up.

He tried to think things through. He sketched out a Venn diagram of what he knew about the case so far. He wrote the name ARJAN GELENS in capitals and worked outwards.

Next came Gelens's lover, KLAUS BLOEM. Then there was the ranch owner ADOLFO GUTIÉRREZ, and he wrote the word RANCH and the name ALFONSO DE LA TORRE and that of the ranch owner's son, JAIME.

He drew lines to connect the names of all of the above, with the exception of Klaus Bloem, to the word RANCH.

He wrote the word MAESTRANZA in capitals, and penciled in a big question mark next to it. Next he wrote the name MOHAMMED HADDAD. He factored in MANOLO BORDANO, MONICA PACHECO and the bullfighter JORGE BELGRANO.

He drew a tentative line between BELGRANO and

ALFONSO DE LA TORRE, and wrote the word '*TOREROS*' along it.

He drew more lines to connect ALFONSO DE LA TORRE to the MAESTRANZA and to ARJAN GELENS.

He wrote SEAT and drew a line to connect the car with MONICA PACHECO.

He drew another line, so that SEAT, MONICA PACHECO and ALFONSO DE LA TORRE formed a triangle.

He wrote the name MANOLO BORDANO and drew lines that connected it to the RANCH, to the MAESTRANZA and to ALFONSO DE LA TORRE and JORGE BELGRANO.

He drew a line to connect MONICA PACHECO and ARJAN GELENS.

He drew lines to connect ALFONSO DE LA TORRE with KLAUS BLOOM and ARJAN GELENS and MONICA PACHECO.

He drew a line to connect MONICA PACHECO with BORDANO.

He drew a line to connect MONICA PACHECO with BELGRANO.

He began to wonder whether he had drawn some of the lines twice.

He looked at the diagram. There were lots of names and lines everywhere.

It seemed to him like the case should be about to open up, when he looked at the names he'd written down, all of them linked in different ways.

There was definitely a pattern here of some kind.

He felt like he was on the verge of making some great discovery.

It was all there, and he felt sure he'd find the answer to the mystery if only he kept looking for long enough.

He sat there for close to an hour and pored over the diagram he had sketched out.

But somehow the diagram refused to make anything clearer or offer up any clues. It was like looking at the front of a house and then realizing you didn't have a key to the door. He wondered if there was something he had overlooked.

Something that had been right under his nose all along that he just hadn't seen.

He had that feeling about this case, somehow. Like the answer was there, staring him right in the face, only he'd missed it.

He tore up the sheet of paper and threw it in the bin.

He ran his hands through his thick black hair and puffed out his cheeks. He rubbed his face with his hands. He felt physically and emotionally whacked.

Maybe if he could only stop thinking about the case for a while then he might be able to make better sense of it when he looked at it again.

He left the Jefatura and drove home, willing himself not to think about the investigation. He had decided to take the rest of the night off and start afresh in the morning.

Chapter 33

When he entered the kitchen he found Pe in an apron, labouring over the stove. 'Something smells good,' he said. 'Making *paella*, are we?'

Pe looked over her shoulder at him and smiled. He planted a kiss on her cheek. 'I thought I'd treat us both,' she said. 'There's a bottle of white Rioja open somewhere.'

Velázquez shrugged his jacket off, then went into the living room and draped it over the back of one of the dining chairs. Some sort of piano music was playing: Bach, was it? He found the Rioja and poured himself a glass. It was a little on the dry side but drinkable.

Pe reached for her glass with her free hand and took a sip, stirring the *paella* with the other.

He asked her how her day had gone. 'The usual,' she said. 'I sat on the sofa and chatted and listened. Mostly the latter.' She found the black pepper and sprinkled a little over the pan. 'What about you?'

'I talked to a girl who stole a car and then lied about it.'

'But you're the head of homicide.' She tasted the rice. 'What are you doing worrying about a girl who stole a car?'

'She was the murder victim's cleaning girl, and she's also related to Alfonso de la Torre.'

'The *paella*'s almost ready, if you'd like to lay the table.'

'Sure.'

He realized what a fortunate man he was to have a wife like Pe. Why, he hadn't been able to make love to her in months, and yet here she was treating him to a romantic dinner like everything was just fine between them. He had told her that he loved her and that he didn't have another woman, and that seemed to be enough for her.

He supposed she probably figured so long as they loved each other then they would eventually be able to put whatever problems they had behind them. They had the rest of their lives together to work things out, after all.

First, though, he had to find the killer. He would feel a little better when the gun he had ordered for Pe arrived. He had put in the request and filled in all the forms, and so the weapon should be available to pick up in the morning with any luck.

He would need to teach her how to use it, of course.

He winced at the idea of having to do this, as he finished laying the table.

Pe came in, carrying the *paella* in a big serving dish, and she put it down on the mat in the middle of the table.

They sat down to eat. Velázquez tore the shell off one of the *langostinos* then popped it into his mouth. 'Mm,' he purred. 'This is de-*li*-cious!'

'You're not just saying it to make me feel good?'

'No, of course not.' Velázquez looked at her and shrugged. 'What makes you say that?'

'I often wonder if I make you happy.'

'Of course you do, Pe.' He sensed that they might be going to have one of their 'deep' conversations. 'Has something happened?'

Pe shook her head. 'No, but it's just that I sometimes think I'm not much of a catch. I mean, I don't do the feminine things very well.'

'What "feminine things" would they be?'

'You know, cooking and keeping house.'

'I've never complained.'

'No, but that's exactly it.'

'*Que*?'

'I mean it's like if I cook *paella* then you feel you have to make a song and dance about it.'

Velázquez was taken aback.

Pe said, 'I'd like us to be able to be completely honest with each other.'

'Well we are.' He gave her a searching look. 'Aren't we?'

'Sometimes I wonder.'

'Your dinner will get cold.'

She picked up her knife and fork and tucked in. 'It *is* rather good, actually, even though I say it myself.'

'You're an excellent cook, Pe.'

She gave him her up-from-under look. 'So you'd tell me, then?'

'Huh?'

'If there was something I did that you didn't like, or didn't agree with?'

'I guess so.'

'I mean you wouldn't be too worried about hurting my feelings?'

That was a difficult question. In truth, he'd been brought up to believe that good manners required you to keep your mouth shut on occasion. That was another way of saying 'speaking your mind' was often a synonym for rudeness. 'I suppose it would depend,' he said finally. 'But I really don't see what you're getting at with all this.'

'How about if we play a little game?'

'What sort of game?'

'We both have to say one thing about the way we live our lives together that's true and that we find at least a little troubling,' Pe said. 'And it's got to be something that we wouldn't ordinarily speak about.'

Velazquez shrugged. 'I can't see what all this is in aid of, I must admit.'

'It's about learning to trust each other more, Luis,' Pe said. 'And trying to improve our relationship. It's what we were talking about on the show today. We had a psychologist who specializes in relationships. If we're honest with each other, it should make us stronger...that's the theory, anyway.'

'Okay, then. You go first.'

'I already said mine.'

Velázquez pulled a face like he was confused. 'That was quick. I must've missed it.'

'I just said that I didn't think you'd tell me the *paella* tastes awful if it came out all wrong.'

'But that's not fair, Pe, because it didn't come out all wrong. It's delicious.'

'But if I'd burnt it or something, I mean,' she said. 'And I also said that sometimes I think you'd like me to cook more and show more interest in keeping the flat up together. There, that's

136

two things, when I should really only have said one.'

'But we get a girl in to clean up in the mornings on weekdays.'

'Even so.' She speared a *langostino* and popped it into her mouth. 'Now it's your turn, Luis,' she said. 'You have to fess up to something you've been thinking or worrying about that I've done recently. Or else it can be something that you disagree with me about or disapprove of.'

Velázquez searched his memory for something to say. Then it came to him, what he'd wanted to ask her but hadn't. 'Okay,' he said. 'I saw a home pregnancy test kit in the rubbish bin.' He studied her reaction, to see if she flushed or flinched. She didn't. 'Not the bit you have to pee on. Just the box, you know.' He paused, watching her. 'I was going to ask you what it was all about but then I didn't.'

'Why didn't you?'

'I thought maybe you'd think I was spying on you.' He sipped his wine then set his glass down carefully, as if it were a grenade.

Besides, he might have added, they hadn't made love for ages. So if she turned out to be pregnant then he was more than a little worried that he might not be the father.

'But why didn't you ask me about it the moment you saw it, Luis?'

'I guess I thought I'd wait and give you the chance to get around to telling me in your own sweet time.'

'I forgot to take my pill one time about three months back,' she said. 'I didn't think anything of it at first. But then I had a couple of dizzy spells and so I thought I'd take the test. I didn't say anything because I didn't want to worry you.'

'So?'

'*Que*?'

'*Are* you or *aren't* you?'

'What would you like to hear?'

'The truth, of course.'

'But I mean, would you like me to be pregnant or not?'

That was a tough one to know how to answer. Velázquez knew that Pe didn't think it was the right time to start a family. It was something they had talked about. He had been all for it,

137

but Pe had said she wanted to wait. And knowing this, he didn't want her to be pregnant if it wasn't what she wanted.

'Well?' she prodded him for an answer. 'It's a simple enough question, isn't it?'

The phone began to ring out in the hall. Velázquez sensed it was probably for him. Friends and family wouldn't normally call at this hour. Besides, Murphy's law said it had to be something to do with his job.

His expression, when he looked at her, told Pe he was asking her what he should do. Pe supposed this was one of those rituals that cops and their women find themselves going through. Of course they both knew that he was going to pick up the phone, but he was allowing her to think she had some say in the matter. In a sense Pe figured he was trying to brainwash her. Or maybe the job had brainwashed the pair of them. 'You'd better take it,' she said. 'It might be important.'

He went out into the hall and picked up the phone. '*Hola?*

'Velázquez? It's Comisario Alonso here…there's been another murder.'

Chapter 34

When Velázquez drove in, past the uniform on the gate, he saw light coming from blue halogen lamps away in the distance. He parked and climbed out of his car, then made his way over to where a little crowd had formed. He pushed his way through the rucks of bodies, and saw that the light was coming from the practice ring.

When the Inspector Jefe reached the split-rail fence, a uniform told him to get back. Velázquez identified himself and held up his ID. 'Sorry, boss,' the officer said. 'I didn't recognize you in the dark.'

The Inspector Jefe climbed over the fence, and went and hunkered down next to the body. He took out his torch to get a better view, and was sickened by what he saw. The victim's tracksuit bottoms had been pulled down and a bull's horn had been rammed up into him with such force that the sharp end had come out through his belly.

Velázquez turned the victim's head, to get a proper look at his face. It was Alfonso de la Torre.

The Inspector Jefe heard someone approaching and saw, with the aid of his torch, that it was Juan Gómez. The two men said hello, then the Médico Forense shone his torch on the victim. 'What a mess,' he said. 'I just hope you catch the crazy bastard that did this.'

Velázquez said an estimate as to the time of death wouldn't go amiss. Gómez hunkered down and began to inspect the body. 'He's still warm,' he said. 'Strictly off the record, Luis, I'd say the murder took place within the past couple of hours. Going by the body temperature, at any rate.'

'I don't know if anyone's ever told you this, Juan, but you're a saint.'

Just then, someone climbed over the split-rail fence. Velázquez had to train his torch on the figure before he could see that it was Gajardo.

'*Joder!*' the Subinspector said when he saw the body.

In the light from his torch, Velázquez could see tracks in the dust. He looked more closely, and saw a trail that led over to the fence.

He got the attention of one of the uniforms and told him to move everyone away. 'And be sharp about it,' he said. 'This is a crime scene, for Christ's sake, and you're allowing these people to contaminate it.'

The uniform started to shoo people along. Once the area had been cleared, Velázquez was able to follow the trail of blood. It led him as far as the parking area.

So it looked like the murderer had killed Alfonso de la Torre elsewhere and brought the body here. There was a terrible theatricality about it. Merely murdering his victim had clearly not been enough to satisfy the killer's deranged lust for violence. He had needed to go the extra mile and perpetrate the crime in the most horrendous fashion imaginable.

With the aid of his torch, Velázquez found Roberto Rios and asked him if he'd heard or seen anything. Rios nodded and said, 'I think I mentioned to you once before that we had a heifer at the ranch that was about to calve?'

'Yes, go on.'

'So I knew to expect someone. Only I didn't know what the man would look like, seeing as Gelens was always our regular vet,' Rios said. 'So when this guy shows up in his car at the security gate and says he's the new vet come to take care of the heifer, I assumed he was who he said he was and let him in.'

'But are you saying you let this man in through the gate and he turned out not actually to be a vet?'

'That's what I'm saying.'

'So how did he know to tell you about the heifer to get in?'

Rios shrugged. 'Search me.'

'Okay, so then what happened?'

'Once he'd got out of his car, I said I would take him to where we had the heifer.'

'And?'

'Next thing I know, he hits me with something hard on the back of the head. When I came round, I was lying gagged and bound over by those bushes.'

'Who found you?'

'Señor Gutiérrez,' Rios said. 'He'd come out to introduce himself to the new vet and see how things were going with the heifer...only by then the guy had scarpered. So Señor Gutiérrez untied me, and then we took a look around to see if any of the bulls or heifers had been taken. That was when we spotted poor Alfonso and saw what'd happened to him.'

'When would this have been?'

'Getting on for an hour ago.'

'Would you recognize the man that hit you if you saw him again?'

Rios shook his head. 'It was dark, and I didn't really manage to get a good look at him. I just said hello and then set off walking in front of him.'

'And that's when he hit you?'

'That's right.'

'Did you notice what kind of car it was?'

'One of them Seats, I think.'

'Colour?'

'Like I said, it was dark, but I seem to recall seeing that it was red in the light by the security gantry.'

'What about the licence plate?'

'No idea. I didn't feel there was any need to check the man out like that. I already told you I assumed he was the vet we were expecting.'

Velázquez pocketed his notebook. 'Where's Señor Gutiérrez?'

'He's standing just over there.' Roberto Rios pointed to Adolfo Gutiérrez, and shone his torch so that the Inspector Jefe could see the man.

'One more thing,' Velázquez said. 'Am I right in understanding that Señor Gutiérrez told you to expect a vet to come?'

'Yes.'

'Did he say what time you were to expect him?'

'No...he just said he shouldn't be too late.'

'So it was your responsibility to let the vet in through the gate when he arrived?'

'That's right.'

Having finished with Rios for the time being, Velázquez went over to the ranch owner and asked him if he knew anything about what had happened. 'No, I'm afraid not, Inspector,' Gutiérrez said. 'But you can rest assured that you'll be the first person I'll tell if I do get to hear anything. I was fond of Alfonso de la Torre.' The man shook his head. 'He was a decent young man and a damned fine *torero*, and some evil bastard's killed him in the most despicable fashion imaginable. What's more, they did it on *my land*. Now I take that kind of personal.'

'Have you any idea who might've wanted Alfonso dead?'

'None at all…it sure beats me.'

'Were you expecting a vet?'

'Yes, one of the heifers is about to calf.'

'Has the vet arrived yet?'

'No…he called a short while ago to say he should be here within the hour.'

'So who was the man that arrived claiming to be the vet?'

'I've no idea.'

'Did you get a look at him?'

'No, I was inside the house.'

Velázquez looked Gutiérrez in the eye. 'So you were fond of Alfonso, you say?'

'He was practically like a son to me.'

'That's strange.'

'What do you mean?'

'There's a rumour going around that Alfonso reckoned the bulls coming out of your ranch were doped and had their horns shaved.'

'That's a damned lie,' Gutiérrez said. 'I'd like to know who told you that.'

'Why? So that you could have them beaten up?'

Velázquez could practically see the man choking back a quantity of bile and rage. 'We'll probably have to talk to you down at the Jefatura at some point, Señor Gutiérrez,' he said. 'So if you've got any plans to go on holiday you're going to have to put them on ice.'

'I'm not planning on going anywhere, Inspector. And I don't

have anything to hide from the likes of you.'

'If that's true then we'll get along just fine.'

'I sincerely doubt that – and I resent your impertinence, if I might say so.'

'Sure you can say so.' Velázquez said. 'It's a free country, so they tell me.' With that he turned, and left the man before he could come back with a reply.

The Inspector Jefe hadn't got far before he heard another car pull up, its wheels biting on the loose gravel in the parking area. The door of the vehicle opened, and Velázquez saw in the light from his torch that it was Agente Pérez who climbed out. He held up a hand, and she made her way over.

'I came hurrying here as soon as I heard, boss,' she said.

'It's a nasty one, Sara.' He nodded in the direction of the body. 'The victim's taken a horn right through him. It's the same MO as was used on Gelens.'

'So it's probably the same killer.'

'I think it's safe to assume so,' he said. 'I need you to go with Subinspector Gajardo and find Klaus Bloem then take him to the Jefatura. I'll be going back as soon as I've finished here.'

The two officers headed off, and Velázquez stayed at the ranch to wait for the vet to arrive. And when he did, he asked the man if he had told anyone else he was coming here.

'That's an odd question.' The man's long, lean face creased in a frown. 'Obviously the people here at the ranch were expecting me.'

'Apart from them, I mean?'

'No…only my wife.'

'You're quite sure about that?'

'Yes, totally.'

Velázquez explained that he was asking this because another man had shown up here earlier, claiming to be a vet. 'Have you any idea how that might have happened?'

The vet shook his head. 'No, I'm afraid not,' he said. 'None at all.'

Velázquez took down the man's details, and went with him to see the heifer that was about to calve, just to check that part of the story was true. And having satisfied himself that it was, and that the man who claimed to be a vet actually was what he said he was, Velázquez headed off back to the Jefatura. And all the way he kept wondering how it was that Alfonso de la Torre's killer could have known a heifer on the ranch was about to calve.

Or had he just figured he would try to bluff his way in and got lucky?

Chapter 35

It was coming up to 2.30 a.m. when Velázquez pulled over outside the Jefatura on Blas Infante. There was nothing useful he could do until Gajardo and Pérez showed with Klaus Bloem, so he figured a little shut-eye was in order. He reclined the seat all the way back and lay there with his eyes closed, and it wasn't long before he fell asleep.

A voice coming out of the radio woke him up just over an hour later. It was Gajardo. 'Had any luck tracking Bloem down yet?' Velázquez asked him.

'We have as a matter of fact, boss.'

'So bring him in.'

'We can't very well do that right now,' Gajardo said. 'He's in the hospital…somebody gave him a real beating.'

'Who?'

'He says he isn't sure. Whoever it was, he says they were wearing a balaclava. The door to his flat had been forced when we got there, and we found him lying on the carpet.'

'What sort of shape's he in?'

'Looks as though his arm might be broken,' Gajardo said. 'And he's got a black eye and a few other cuts and bruises.'

'Which hospital is he in?'

'The Virgen del Rocio. We're in Emergencies, getting him checked out just to make sure he's not suffered any serious internal damage.'

'Stay where you are and don't let him out of your sight, José,' Velázquez said. 'I'm on my way.'

Klaus Bloem had his arm put in a sling, and he was given some painkillers and allowed to leave the hospital at just after 4.25 a.m. Velázquez drove him over to the Jefatura, with the man whining all the way. Bloem said he had no idea who'd beaten him up, so what was the point of interviewing him now? 'I'm in pain and I'm exhausted. I just want to go to bed.'

'Do you think you're the only one?' Velázquez said. 'My wife made a wonderful *paella* earlier, with *langostinos* as big as your middle finger. The Bach's coming out over the sound system, and I've uncorked a decent white wine…then the phone rings…'

'So you answered it?' Bloem shook his head. 'You should've unplugged the phone before you sat down to eat.'

'You'd have liked that, wouldn't you, Klaus?'

'I'm thinking of your wife and all the trouble she must've gone to, to make that *paella*.'

'And I had to leave it.'

'That was your first big mistake of the night, Inspector,' Bloem said. 'And you know the way these things tend to go.'

'No, you tell me.'

'It's like a domino effect…once you make one bad decision it's like it sets up a chain reaction.'

Velázquez flashed him a quick sideways glance. 'Is that the way you feel about having killed Arjan?'

'No.'

'You mean you don't feel bad about doing it?' the Inspector Jefe said. 'Or do you mean you don't feel as if by murdering him you set up a chain reaction of negative events?'

Bloem let out a loud and rather theatrical sigh. 'I mean I didn't kill him,' he said.

Velázquez turned onto the bridge and they crossed the river in silence, then headed on up towards the Jefatura. The Inspector always loved the city at this time of night. It was so wonderfully quiet.

Minutes later, they were in Incident Room 1 and the tape was rolling.

Velázquez said, 'So perhaps you'd like to tell us what happened?'

'I told you that on the way here.'

'So tell me again for the record.'

'Somebody broke into my apartment.'

'Who was it?'

'I already told you, it was a tall guy wearing a balaclava,' Bloem said. 'I didn't get to see his face.'

'You must have some idea who it was, though, right?'

'How'd you arrive at that idea?'

Velázquez sensed that the man was holding out on him. 'Your story doesn't add up,' he said. 'Do you really expect us to believe that this guy just turns up in your apartment and beats you up, and you have no idea who he was?'

The German shrugged. 'Having spent far too much time in your company recently, Inspector, I've learned not to expect you to believe anything I say. But I'm telling you the truth.'

The door opened and Gajardo came in. He acknowledged the Inspector Jefe with a nod of the head, then came and sat in the vacant chair next to him. Velázquez turned back to look at the suspect. 'What time did all this happen?'

'Around three-ish, I think. I'm not totally sure.'

'What were you doing at the time?'

'Sleeping.'

'Alone? Or with someone?'

'Alone.'

Velázquez tamped his pen on the metal desk. 'It's been a difficult time for you lately, I should imagine?'

'I guess so.'

'Must all be rather hard on the nerves, too?'

'If you mean has what happened to Arjan upset me, then yes, you're too damned right it has.'

'What's the first thing you remember seeing after you woke up?'

'The guy attacking me.'

'Wearing a mask, was he?' Gajardo asked.

'How many times do I have to say it?'

'Correct me if I'm wrong,' Velázquez said, 'but I thought you said he was wearing a *balaclava*?'

'Same thing, isn't it?'

'Not in my book.'

'It was dark.'

'But not too dark for you to be able to see he was wearing a mask?'

'That's right.'

'What is?'

'It was dark, but not too dark for me to be able to see his face was covered, just like you just said.'

Velázquez said, 'With a mask and not a balaclava?'

'A balaclava, then.'

'Which was it, a mask or a balaclava?'

'I told you, a balaclava.'

'What did he attack you with?'

'A baseball bat…that's how he broke my arm.'

'And you didn't hear him enter the flat?'

'No.'

'I see.' Velázquez nodded like he didn't really *see* at all. 'He got in through the front door, you said?'

'That's right.'

'So he must've forced the lock?'

'I guess so.'

Gajardo said, 'The lock had been bust open, boss.'

'In that case the intruder must've made a fair bit of noise doing it, I should imagine?'

'If you say so.'

'Wouldn't *you* say so?'

'I really don't know.'

'You *don't know*?' Velázquez's eyebrows were arched like scorpions' tails. 'A racket like that would've woken anyone up, I should've thought.'

The German shrugged. 'You tell me, Inspector.'

Velázquez exchanged glances with Gajardo. 'We'll need a photographer and fingerprint expert to go over there.'

'I've already taken care of it, boss.'

Velázquez turned back to Bloem. 'You went to meet Alfonso de la Torre at the ranch earlier, didn't you, Klaus?'

'No.'

'You're lying.'

Bloem shook his head. 'Either let me go now or I want to speak to a lawyer.'

'It'll be a lot better for you if you tell us everything, Klaus.'

'I already have.'

'We might be able to work out a deal.'

'Listening's obviously not your strong suit, is it, Inspector?'

'Prison can be pretty tough on guys like you, Klaus.' Velázquez looked Bloem in the eye. 'I doubt whether you'd make it.'

'I'm not saying another word until I've got a lawyer here.'

'I think we'll take a break.'

Chapter 36

'I can see where you're coming from, boss,' Gajardo said, once they'd left the room. 'You're thinking how is it he didn't hear the guy breaking in if his assailant had to bust the lock...must've made a fairly loud noise.'

'You'd think so, wouldn't you?' Velázquez puffed out his cheeks.

'The man's story doesn't add up.' Gajardo shook his head. 'But what's he trying to hide?'

'Maybe he doesn't want us to know how he got his arm broken.'

'He could've got it broken fighting with Alfonso de la Torre, before he killed him,' Gajardo said. 'What do you think?'

'I think I need a coffee, José.'

When Velázquez and Gajardo returned to the incident room, some twenty minutes later, the Inspector Jefe asked Klaus Bloem if he had a lawyer he wanted to call. Bloem said he'd never had anything to do with lawyers. 'I thought they were supposed to hang round police stations, ready to represent people who're accused of doing things?'

'If you want, we can take a look?'

The German nodded.

Velázquez gestured to Gajardo, and the Subinspector left the room.

'You might as well just confess, Klaus,' the Inspector Jefe said. 'You'd save us all a lot of time and bother.'

'You'd like that, wouldn't you?'

'You'll feel a whole lot better afterwards, trust me.'

'What makes you so sure I'm your man?'

'I've got a nose for these things.'

'Look into people's eyes and read their thoughts, can you?'

'Enough to know you did it, Klaus.' In reality Velázquez knew no such thing – although he did have a strong sense that the man was lying to him about something.

'That's just where you're wrong.'

Velázquez stifled a yawn and figured it was turning out to be one of those nights. Or mornings. Bloem said, 'What's the matter, Inspector – not tired are we, surely?'

'We could both get some sleep if you'd only confess to what you did, Klaus.'

'I bet your wife's wondering where you are.'

It occurred to Velázquez that if Bloem were the killer then it must be him that had left the threatening notes on his windscreen and under his door.

A part of the Inspector Jefe wanted to take hold of the man and beat the holy crap out of him. And when he'd finished with the holy stuff he'd start on the less than sanctified material.

It was what a lot of cops in his shoes would have done, given the pressure he was under.

But if he were to go down that road then he would be no better than the likes of Comisario Alonso. The times had changed and Velázquez liked to think he had changed with them. He told himself that lynch mobs and cops beating up suspects were things of the past. The Inspector Jefe wanted to be part of the new, democratic Spain. He believed in a Spain in which men like himself could be fair and just but also decent.

Besides, he couldn't be totally sure that Bloem was the killer.

So he resisted the temptation to give vent to his primal urges and simply said, 'My private life is none of your business.'

'Maybe not,' Klaus Bloem sneered. 'But neither's *my* private life any of *your* business, only that hasn't stopped you sticking your big fat nose into it.'

'You lost the right to a private life, Klaus, when you killed Arjan Gelens.'

'I loved Arjan.'

'I believe you, Klaus. I think that you did love Arjan. I also believe that you miss him.'

'So do you mean that I'm free to go?'

'I'm afraid not,' Velázquez said. 'You see, I think you miss him because you loved him. But I also happen to think you *killed* him for the same reason.'

Bloem's upper lip curled in a sneer. 'That's just stupid.'

151

The door opened and Gajardo came back in, followed by a tall man dressed in an elegant light-blue suit. The man was of slim build and his deep tan suggested he spent more time lying on beaches than was good for him. In contrast, the dark bags under his eyes told a story of long hours spent burning the midnight oil. Velázquez had crossed swords with the man in the past. His name was Fernando Belloso, and he was a wily customer. Belloso acknowledged Velázquez with a nod of the head, before he set his briefcase down on the gunmetal-grey desk.

He said he would like to have some time alone with his client before they proceeded.

'I thought you were going to say that.' Velázquez turned to the suspect and said, 'You see, Klaus, I can read people's minds.'

Up in the office, Velázquez went over to the window and gazed out over the sleeping city. What he saw resembled a lot of gleaming jewels on a dark satin background. It was strange the way everything appeared different from the way it did in the daytime. And of course there was so much that you just couldn't see at all.

He thought of all those people out there sleeping in their beds, each with their own lives, their own hopes and worries, their own pleasures and problems. Pe was one of them, presuming that she was in fact sleeping – which he very much hoped.

Velázquez reminded himself that *he* was the one who often suffered with insomnia, not Pe.

His thoughts turned on the *paella* Pe had made earlier, and the truncated conversation they'd had.

He wondered whether she was pregnant…

Back in Incident Room 1, Velázquez set the tape rolling again. He said the time and date, before he explained that they were about to resume the interview with Klaus Bloem. He said that Bloem now had his lawyer, Fernando Belloso, with him.

'So, Klaus, let me think,' he said. 'Where were we?' He leaned on the desk and looked at the suspect. 'I believe we'd established that your assailant must've made quite a racket when he smashed his way in.' Velázquez made a tripod with his hands. 'So we were wanting you to explain to us how it could be that you didn't hear him?'

Fernando Belloso said, 'Don't answer that, Klaus.' Then, to Velázquez: 'It's my understanding that my client has already told you what happened. He assures me the version of events he's given you is correct and accurate, so I really see no reason why he should be subjected to any further questioning of this sort at this stage.'

Velázquez took a deep breath and let it out. 'Klaus, it's my belief that you know who beat you up. If you tell us who it was, we can find the man and maybe put him in prison where he belongs.'

Fernando Belloso said, 'My client has already told you that he doesn't have any idea as to the identity of his assailant, Inspector Jefe.'

Velázquez knew only too well the way the law worked, and so he knew that the suspect's lawyer was within his rights in advising Bloem in this way. Yet try as he might, the Inspector Jefe failed to understand the mentality of people like Fernando Belloso. So far as he could see, the role of such individuals was to seek out ways of obstructing the path of justice. How could such people live with themselves? Didn't they realize they were little or no better than the criminals they represented?

Velázquez chewed on his lower lip. 'You knew that Arjan was having an affair with Alfonso de la Torre, didn't you, Klaus?' he said. 'But of course you did…that's what pushed you over the edge, isn't it?'

Bloem's eyes flashed with anger. 'Whoever told you that's a fucking liar.'

'It was Arjan's sister, Ans.' Velázquez smiled. 'It seems they were close, the pair of them. They shared all their secrets…told each other about their lovers – intimate stuff, you know…'

Fernando Belloso said, 'I fail to see what any of this tittle-tattle has to do with my client.'

Velázquez would have liked to see the lawyer spend a year or two living in the world of the people he defended. Maybe a short stretch in the prison out at Alhaurin de la Torre might show him

153

the error of his ways. 'It has everything to do with your client and the investigation.'

'With the greatest respect, Inspector,' Fernando Belloso said, 'it's up to you to prove a link between these deaths and my client. And that's something you have clearly and demonstrably failed to do.'

'He was Arjan Gelens's lover – what's that if it isn't a *link*?'

'Mere coincidence is what it is, Inspector Jefe, and you know it.'

Velázquez sighed as he exchanged glances with his number two. Gajardo shrugged and straightened the collar of his silk shirt. The Inspector Jefe turned back to the suspect. 'Okay, Klaus, we'll need you to put your side of what happened in a statement,' he said. 'When you've written it, you can leave.'

In his statement, Bloem trotted out the story he had already told Velázquez.

When he read it, the Inspector Jefe considered charging the man with the murder of Arjan Gelens. But then he wondered whether that would be such a good idea. He was tired and angry, and figured that it would be wiser to sleep on it.

Chapter 37

Velázquez entered the flat like a cat burglar for fear of making any noise. He opened the door to the bedroom gently. In the light sweeping in through the window, he could see that Pe was fast asleep. He pulled the door to, padded along the hallway and entered the spare bedroom. No sooner had he lain out on the bed than he fell asleep.

He was in the middle of a strange dream when Pe woke him up the following morning. Velázquez looked at his watch, and saw that it was coming up to ten. '*Joder*,' he cursed under his breath.

'What time did you get in last night?'

'Late.' He swung his legs over the side of the bed and stretched. 'I didn't want to wake you.'

'*Gracias*.' Pe set a mug down on the night table. 'I thought you might like some coffee.'

He picked up the mug and took a sip: it was just what the doctor ordered. 'I really don't deserve you, do you know that?'

Pe smiled at him, and he saw from the look in her eyes that she'd forgotten about the night before. Or at least she had managed to forgive him. She said, 'I hope whatever you had to go dashing off like that for was worth it?'

'It was the bullfighter, Alfonso de la Torre.'

'What about him?'

'He was murdered…and in the most horrific fashion, too.'

'Oh no.' Pe's brown eyes flashed. 'How did it happen?'

Velázquez described the shape he had found the victim in when he arrived at the ranch. Pe's lips parted but no words came out at first. Finally, she said, 'But what kind of person would do something like that?'

'That's what I need to find out.'

Velázquez got up off the bed then padded off to the bathroom and took a shower. He enjoyed the feel of the hot arrows of water raining down on his skin, washing the sweat from his body. Dried and dressed in clean denims, sky-blue polo shirt and brown leather loafers, he went into the kitchen. Pe was sitting at the pinewood table, eating a mixture she'd made up of fruit, nuts and natural white yoghurt.

Velázquez popped a couple of slices of Bimbo into the toaster and fixed himself another mug of coffee. When the toast was ready, he dripped olive oil onto it then joined Pe at the table. He bit into his toast and said, 'We need to talk at some point.'

'What about?'

'You know, what we were talking about last night before I had to leave.' He gave her a tentative, questioning look. 'You're *not*…are you?'

'Not, *what*?'

'Pregnant?'

'The test was inconclusive, so I made an appointment to see my doctor,' Pe said. 'I'll let you know as soon as I get the result.'

There was a group of reporters by the front gate when Velázquez pulled up outside the de la Torres' place. They all turned to point their cameras in his face as he climbed out of his car. 'Can you give us a statement, Inspector Jefe?'

'Still early days, I'm afraid.' He was pushing his way through the ruck of bodies. 'But I can assure you we're doing all we can. Hopefully I should have something to tell you before too long.' He went for his best PR smile, but sensed it came out more like an angry snarl. Turning, he pushed the buzzer on the security gantry.

Nobody answered.

But that wasn't so surprising. The grieving widow would hardly want to come out and face all these vultures, would she? For all Velázquez knew, she might not even be in there.

But then the door to the house opened and Yolanda de la Torre emerged, dressed in jeans and T-shirt. She looked over and saw Velázquez, then went back into the house and buzzed him in. The newshounds tried to follow him inside, and he had to push a couple back.

'Listen, everyone,' the Inspector Jefe said. 'Señora de la Torre has given me, and me alone, permission to enter the premises.

Anyone else who tries to get in will be guilty of trespassing and duly arrested.'

He shut the self-locking gate behind him, before he hurried up the garden path. He stepped inside the house, and the widow shut the door behind him.

'Thanks for letting me in,' he said. 'I'm so sorry about what's happened.'

Yolanda de la Torre appeared to lurch towards him for a moment, before she regained her balance, and Velázquez caught a whiff of alcohol on her breath. The widow allowed him to lead her over to the sofa and they sat down next to each other. She brushed some stray strands of hair out of her face, and Velázquez noticed the dark bags that underscored her bloodshot eyes. She buried her face in her hands and began to sob.

When she finally lifted her head, her eyes were wet and her cheeks puffy. She began to dry her eyes with her hand. Velázquez took out a handkerchief. 'Use this,' he said. 'It's clean.'

The widow dabbed at her eyes with it, then sat very still and looked at the wall. 'How did it happen?' she asked finally.

'We still aren't totally sure – but it's my job to try and find out.'

She took a deep breath and let it out slowly. 'Now everyone wants to come and dig up the dirt.' Her forced smile was as terrible as it was false. 'How perfectly sweet and charming it's all going to be.'

'I'll do my best to keep the press off your back, Yolanda.'

Looking out through the window, Velázquez could see the garden and then the gate, with the newshounds on the other side of it. A number of cameras were pointing this way. Yolanda de la Torre sighed and said, 'They're like bloody sharks.'

'It will die down eventually, once they've written their story.'

'That's easy for you to say.'

Velázquez got up, then went and closed the curtains. And finding it was now a little dark in the room, he turned on one of the table lamps before he returned to the sofa.

Yolanda de la Torre said, 'Have you any idea who killed my husband?'

'There are various possible suspects.'

'But no clear favorite as yet, is that it?'

'That's a fair description of the way things stand,' he said. 'What about you? Have you got any idea who killed Alfonso?'

The widow shook her head.

'Do you know of any enemies he might have had?'

'No.'

'Was Alfonso cheating on you, Yolanda?'

'You tell me, Inspector.' The widow shrugged. 'You're the one with all the ideas and the ear for nasty gossip. The last time you came here, you suggested Alfonso was gay and that he was *involved* with that vet.'

'Was he?'

When she looked at him, the anger had gone out of her eyes so that they looked flat and empty. 'As I told you during your previous visit, if Alfonso was bisexual then he certainly never let me in on it.'

'He never did anything that gave you reason to suspect he might be attracted to men?'

'Beyond the fact that he used to have to squeeze himself into pink tights before a *corrida*, you mean?' She snorted at her own joke then wiped away a tear. 'On the contrary, he was always so macho – too much so for my liking at times.'

'Meaning what, exactly?'

'The marriage had been on the rocks for some time.'

'Did you love him?'

'Yes, but love can sometimes be a hard ride,' she said. 'We didn't always see eye to eye or understand each other.'

'Did he ever hit you?'

'No, but I once threw a solid glass ashtray at his head,' she said. 'It would've smashed his skull to a pulp if it'd hit the mark. And it only just missed by a whisker.'

The widow's face creased in a taut smile that was full of sadness and bitterness. 'One thing about Alfonso, he had lightning-fast reactions. I suppose you need to have if you fight bulls for a living.' She shrugged. 'There. Does *that* give you your motive, Inspector? It was in front of a lot of people at a party, too, so there were plenty of witnesses,' she said. 'I have something of a temper, as you've probably guessed from what I've just told you.'

'Were there other women?'

'You've already asked me that...' She sighed and shook her head. 'Not that I know of.'

'Did you kill Alfonso, or have him killed?'

The widow's surprise was clear to see when she looked at him. 'You can't be serious?'

'Where were you yesterday evening and night?'

'I was at home.'

'Alone?'

She nodded.

'Doing what?'

'Reading and watching TV.'

'What was on?'

'*The Manchurian Candidate,* with Frank Sinatra and Laurence Harvey. Perhaps you know the film?'

Velázquez wrote in his notepad.

Yolanda de la Torre turned her face away. 'I've told you everything I know,' she said. 'Are you going to arrest me?'

'No...not unless I need to.'

'In that case,' she said, 'please leave.'

Chapter 38

Velázquez drove back to the Jefatura, where he briefed his officers. Then he and Gajardo went to pay a call on Monica Pacheco and her boyfriend. The girl answered the intercom when Gajardo pressed the buzzer to their flat. 'We need to talk to you,' the Subinspector told her. 'You'd better hurry up, unless you want us to break the door down.'

'Wait a minute.'

She came down wearing a black T-shirt and frayed denim cutoffs. 'Where's the Seat, Monica?' Velázquez asked her. 'Apparently the officer that was sent round to collect it didn't get any joy.'

'Juan was driving it, but I think he said it was nicked.'

'Let's get this straight,' he said. 'You steal a car and let your boyfriend drive it *and it gets stolen by someone else*?'

'*Si.*'

'And you expect us to *believe* that?'

She shrugged. 'You know what this area's like.'

'Where's your boyfriend?'

'He's upstairs.'

'Get him down here now.'

She pushed the buzzer to her flat on the intercom. Moments later, her boyfriend answered, and she put him in the picture and told him to come down.

Velázquez said, 'What does your boyfriend do to make ends meet?'

'What's that got to do with anything?'

'I'll do the questions.'

'He does a bit of this and that,' she said. 'But what's it to you?'

'Don't tell me,' the Inspector Jefe said. '*This* is selling drugs, right? And *that* would be the prison time he does when he gets caught?'

'He's done a bit of time in the past, yeah. But he's going straight now.'

'What's he into, Monica?' Gajardo asked her.

'Juan ain't done nothin'.'

Velázquez said, 'We need you both to come down to the Jefatura.'

'What for?'

Gajardo said, 'It's not to sample the coffee, that's for sure.'

'Your boyfriend's taking his time, isn't he?'

'He'll be down in a minute,' Monica Pacheco said. 'He was in the shower when you first called.'

Moments later, the door to the building opened, and a tallish man of lean build dressed in jeans and a green T-shirt stepped out. He blinked as his eyes adjusted to the light of the street, then ran a hand through his mop of greasy black hair. 'Did you wanna talk to me?'

Velázquez held his ID out as he introduced himself, then he said, 'And you are?'

'Juan Muñoz.' His surname sounded like Munn-yoth.

'Where's the Seat, Juan?'

'What?'

'Better stop wasting my time, unless you want me to arrest you here and now.'

'I ain't done nothin'.'

'Where's the car?'

'Which car are you talking about?'

'The Seat that Monica stole.'

'It got nicked...honest it did...I told the officer that came round to pick it up.'

Once they arrived at the Jefatura, Velázquez had Monica Pacheco and Juan Muñoz shown into different interview rooms. He told the uniforms keeping watch on the pair that statements were to be taken from each of them, and they were to be held until he'd returned. Then he went up to the office, to follow up on what had happened to the stolen Seat. He sat at his desk and made some telephone calls.

Minutes later an officer called him back, to say the stolen vehicle had been found. Velázquez arranged for the vehicle to be brought over to the Jefatura and left in the underground car park.

Once he'd got off the phone, the Inspector Jefe got hold of Gajardo. He told him to find out if Alfonso de la Torre had a life insurance policy. And if so then how much his widow stood to receive.

Sara Pérez came hurrying in. 'This was in the post for you, boss.'

Velázquez opened the envelope, then took out the single sheet that was inside. The killer had left him another typed note.

INSPECTOR VELÁZQUEZ, IT'S TIME TO STOP THIS INVESTIGATION OR I WILL HAVE TO STOP YOU – FOR GOOD. THIS IS MY FINAL WARNING FOR YOU AND YOUR LOVELY WIFE.

Velázquez folded the letter and put it in his jacket pocket, then he sent Pérez and Merino out to find Klaus Bloem and bring him in for further questioning.

Minutes later, the Inspector Jefe's telephone rang. He picked up the receiver. '*Hola*?' It was the police psychologist, Ana Pelayo. She told him she was calling, to remind him that he had a session with her on the hour.

He told her he wouldn't miss it for the world.

Chapter 39

Ana Pelayo kicked off by asking him how things were going. Velázquez wondered what she meant by 'things'.

She shrugged. 'Whatever you care to talk about…your home life, the investigation – any of it.'

'Okay, I guess.'

'You *guess*?'

Velázquez nodded. He wasn't going to tell her about the death threats. Why should he?

'Don't you *know* whether things are going okay or not?'

'Insofar as the investigation is concerned,' he said, 'we put in the hours. We talk to the suspects and so on, and collate the information we turn up. But then it's a question of seeing what we've got and hopefully getting a break or two.'

'You make it sound like a question of luck,' Anna Pelayo said. 'Is that the way you feel?'

'Some of the time.' He shrugged. 'It depends on the direction any given investigation takes.'

'And what about this particular case you're investigating now?'

'We have suspects I'll be wanting to talk to, once we finish here.'

'Meaning you consider these sessions to be merely a nuisance and a waste of time, is that it?'

'You said it, not me.'

'But it's the way you feel – like you can't wait to get this over with. Am I right?'

'You tell me.' He cracked a plastic smile. 'You're the shrink.'

Ana Pelayo sighed. 'The more evasive you are, Luis, the longer all this is likely to go on.'

'I'm not sure I follow you.'

'Once I'm satisfied you're in a fit state to work,' she said, 'I can tell the Comisario and you won't have to come to any more of these sessions.'

'So what's stopping you?'

163

'It's all really in your hands.' Ana Pelayo made a note in her pad.

Velázquez took the plastic top off his coffee and had a sip.

'It can't be easy for you and Pe to keep your private lives to yourselves, what with her working on television?' The psychologist tamped her pencil on her desk. 'How would you describe your relationship?'

'We get along great.'

'But Pe must be a pretty formidable sort of woman to have as a partner, I should imagine?' Ana Pelayo said. 'What with her being a television personality, I mean? A lot of men would feel intimidated by someone like her, I'm sure.'

'Not me.'

'Okay...so perhaps you can talk a little more about the investigation you're currently working on?'

He sipped his coffee. 'Another victim's turned up.'

'I read about it in the newspaper,' she said. 'Have you got any leads?'

'We've got lots of them.' Velázquez felt more comfortable, now they'd shifted the topic of conversation away from his personal life. 'The problem is knowing which ones to follow.'

'Such as?'

'You already know about Klaus Bloem.'

'So tell me about the other suspects.'

'There's Adolfo Gutiérrez, the owner of the ranch where the vet was on a retainer,' Velázquez said. 'Then there's his son, Jaime, who sells cocaine to contacts he's introduced to by the *apoderado,* Manuel Bordano. Bordano, incidentally, represented Alfonso de la Torre, and he also represents Jorge Belgrano. He pimps for the latter, too, as well as for the second victim, Mohammed Haddad. All the people I've just mentioned, with the possible exception of Haddad, had access to the ranch and the Maestranza.'

'So?'

'Any one of them could have tampered with the bulls.'

'But what's that got to do with the murders?'

'Whoever doped the bulls would've had a motive to want Arjan Gelens out of the way,' Velázquez said. 'Presuming the vet was on to them and they found out.' He smiled. 'Shall I go on?'

'Sure, this is interesting.'

'Then there's Monica Pacheco. It turns out she's one of Bordano's girls that he pimps to his bullfighters and other clients. She stole a car to drive to see Alfonso at the ranch the day he was killed. As it happens, she and Alfonso were cousins.

'And there's Alfonso's widow, who's been suffering from depression. She told me herself she's got a bad temper. On one occasion she threw a solid ashtray at her husband's head – and this was in public. And we have it on good authority that Alfonso was having a gay affair with the first victim.'

'A gay bullfighter, huh?'

'That's according to the vet's sister, anyway, and I can't see any reason why she should lie to me,' he said. 'Then there's the second victim I referred to a moment ago, Mohammed Haddad. He financed bullfights and had professional associations with Bordano and Alfonso de la Torre, before he was found drowned after falling from his yacht. For "falling" we can read "pushed". And then there's the gruesome nature of the way in which Alfonso and Gelens were both killed that needs to be taken into account.'

'Yes, I read about that. It must be a first, I should think – having people murdered by a bull's horn in that way, right?'

'Let's just hope it's not the start of a new trend.'

'It's uncanny,' she said. 'I was only talking about that recently.'

'You were?'

'Not Alfonso de la Torre being murdered, I don't mean, but...' Ana Pelayo made a quick sweeping gesture with her hand. 'You know, the whole subject of bullfighters and their sexuality. It's a fascinating field, I think.'

'Is it?'

'Have you never stopped to consider the erotics of it?' She sat forward in her chair. 'The bullfighter gets himself up in pink tights and tight trousers of the sort a young woman who wants to show off her butt might wear. Then he struts his stuff in front of this enormous beast, an animal that's a mass of solid muscle and with this *huge horn*. And of course, the bull's probably wondering what it's doing there, so the *torero* has to wind it up to begin with. You know, he has to act the *coquette* a little, and give the poor beast the come-on.'

'You make it sound like a porn movie.'

'This isn't just my idea but the actual theory of the art of bullfighting I'm talking about now,' the psychologist said. 'According to the experts, the bullfighter has to feign femininity in order to make the bull charge…then when it does, the *torero* quickly flips from female to male, from passive coquette to macho man. It's all got to do with the essential androgynousness of the artist, apparently.'

Velázquez glanced at his watch. 'Listen,' he said, 'as much as I'd love to sit here and talk with you like this all day, it looks like our time's up. And I've got suspects to interview…'

Chapter 40

Velázquez went down to his office and called Ans Gelens. When she picked up he said, 'Ans? Inspector Jefe Velázquez here.'

'Hello, Inspector. Have there been any new developments in the case?'

Clearly she hadn't seen the news. But of course, if she didn't have any Spanish, then it was unlikely that she would even bother to turn the television on while she was over here. 'Yes, I wondered if I could talk to you again later?'

'Sure…or I can talk now, if you'd prefer?'

'No, not over the phone,' he said. 'Perhaps I could invite you to dinner again this evening?'

'But it's my turn to invite you, Inspector.'

'Nonsense…it all comes out of my expense account, anyway.'

'Okay, then, as you wish.'

'Does eight o'clock suit you?'

'Yes, all right,' she said. 'Can you pick me up at my hotel?'

'Of course.'

'Eight it is, then. *Ciao*.'

They hung up. Then Velázquez called Pe and told her he might not be back until late again, so she shouldn't bother to cook anything for him.

'So no *paella* this evening, then?'

He was temporarily lost for words, and Pe broke the silence with a chuckle. 'I'm just joking,' she said. 'Thanks for letting me know.'

'*Te quiero*.'

'I love you, too.'

They hung up.

Minutes later, Gajardo came hurrying into the office with the news that Yolanda de la Torre stood to receive five million US dollars from her late husband's life insurance policy. The bullfighter, Gajardo explained, had the lion's share of his

167

money tied up in the USA, and took out a policy with a company based in New York. Then there were the three properties the couple owned, as well as the cars.

With this new information percolating through his mind, Velázquez called in on Monica Pacheco's boyfriend, Juan Muñoz, in Interview Room 2. He cast Oficial Merino, who had been keeping watch on the man, a questioning glance. 'He's made his statement all right,' Javier said. 'Only problem is, what he's put in it's a sack of shit. He claims he doesn't know *nada* about any of it, boss.'

Velázquez turned to look at the suspect. 'Make it easy on yourself, Juan,' he said. 'We know you're in this up to your neck. Play ball with us, and we might be able to go light on you.'

'You must think I'm stupid,' Muñoz said. 'You're trying to lay this on me because you've got nobody else to pin it on.'

'That's not what Monica's saying.'

'*Que*?'

'She tells me the pair of you were blackmailing Alfonso de la Torre,' Velázquez said. 'She says she saw Alfonso and Arjan Gelens in bed together one day and when she came home and told you about it, you got to thinking. She said it was all your idea, and that she didn't want to go along with it. She says you forced her to steal the car, but didn't tell her what you needed it for.

'Now she's had a little time to think and developed one or two theories of her own. She seems to think you killed Gelens because he refused to cough up the blackmail money and threatened to go to the police. So then you had to get rid of Alfonso, too, because you couldn't be sure if he knew about it. She reckons you got her to steal the Seat because you wanted a car that couldn't be traced to you to drive to the ranch to kill Alfonso.'

'That's a pile of shit.'

'You mean she was in it from the start, as much as you were?'

Muñoz looked like he was about to say something, but then he appeared to think better of it.

'Monica says she didn't want to do it, but you threatened to kill her if she didn't,' Velázquez said. 'She says you held a knife to her throat on more than one occasion.' He shrugged. 'Why would she lie about something like that?'

'I've told you everything I know.' Muñoz crossed his arms. 'I'm not saying another word without I got a lawyer here.'

His gambit having failed, Velázquez turned and made for the door. Merino followed him out into the corridor. 'Was all that true what you said in there, boss?'

'It might be.'

'You mean you think they might've been blackmailing him, but the girl didn't tell you they were?'

Velázquez smiled. 'I'll go and see her now, and find out what she has to say for herself.'

It was the same story with the girl, in Room 3. Sara Pérez, the officer in the room with her, summed the situation up for Velázquez. 'She's made a statement,' the Agente said, 'saying she doesn't know anything about it, boss.'

The Inspector Jefe threw a plastic smile at Monica Pacheco. 'That isn't the version your boyfriend Juan's giving us in the other room,' he said. 'According to him, you were blackmailing Alfonso de la Torre. He says you saw him in bed with Arjan Gelens at the house one day and managed to take a photo of them *in flagrante*.'

A nice little imaginative touch, Velázquez thought. 'Juan says you had the idea of using the photo to blackmail Alfonso, Monica, but that you wanted him to back you up. He says you wanted some muscle behind you and he was it.'

'That's a lie.'

'Juan swears it's the whole truth and nothing but the truth. He looks like a fairly honest sort to me – and he says he's willing to swear to it under oath in a court of law.'

'I ain't never blackmailed nobody.'

'Not what your record says,' Pérez said.

This was news to Velázquez.

'I did a little research earlier, Monica,' Sara said. 'It seems you were charged with stealing from a lady you worked for as a cleaner in the past...a Señora Fuentes.'

'That was a fuckin' lie. I never took nothing from that lying

169

old bitch. She had to retract it in the end.'

'Yes, you settled out of court.'

'She retracted.'

'The way I heard it,' Pérez said, 'you had to pay back every penny you'd stolen from her first. But you tried to force her to let you keep the money by threatening to make public a lesbian affair she'd been having behind her husband's back.'

Monica Pacheco turned her head away and looked at the wall.

'Have to sell your car after that, did you?'

No answer.

Velázquez said, 'Did you kill Arjan Gelens and Alfonso de la Torre, Monica?'

'Don't be stupid.'

The business with the car was niggling at the Inspector Jefe. And it was also true that as Gelens's cleaning lady, Monica Pacheco was ideally placed to carry out the first murder. Then there was her association with the third victim's *apoderado*, Manuel Bordano, to take into account. And she knew Jaime Gutiérrez, as well.

Velázquez's mind was buzzing as he tried to weigh up all the angles. His thoughts turned on the woman's boyfriend. He figured Monica Pachecho would have needed the help of a man if she were involved in the murders. He couldn't see her being strong enough to do what the killer had done to Arjan Gelens and Alfonso de la Torre if she'd been operating alone. 'How's Juan making ends meet – on the dole, is he?'

'Sometimes.'

'At the moment, I mean?'

'It ran out.'

'So he's got no income whatsoever, then?'

'Only what he gets from doing odd jobs he can pick up here and there.'

Velázquez nodded. 'What odd jobs would they be?'

'Whatever he can find.'

'Find a little *maría* to sell every now and then, does he, your Juan?'

'That's not what I said.'

'Or maybe it's cocaine or heroin he deals in more?'

'Stop putting words in my mouth.'

'He must get his money from somewhere, Monica.' Velázquez shrugged. 'The last I heard the stuff wasn't growing on trees.'

She shrugged and looked at the wall.

'Did Arjan Gelens pay you much?' Pérez asked.

'Just amounted to pocket money, really.'

'How do you manage to get by, then? You've got your rent and bills to pay, right?'

'Tell me about it.' Monica Pacheco rolled her eyes. 'You guys should try makin' ends meet on what I have to sometime.'

'I'd prefer to work for a living, thanks.'

Monica Pacheco looked at Velázquez. 'You wanna watch her, Inspector,' she said. 'She's a right bitch, that one.'

'I'd watch your mouth, if I were you, Monica,' Pérez warned her. 'Any more of that and I'll do you for insulting a police officer.'

'Just 'cause you got a job for life workin' for the government, you think you can lord it over people like me.'

'Agente Pérez's got a point. Your outgoings are several times more than your income,' Velázquez said. 'How do you explain that?'

Monica Pacheco tossed her head and looked at the wall.

'Of course you do a little moonlighting for Manolo Bordano, don't you?'

'I only do that when I'm really hard up.'

'It sounds to me like you must be short of money practically all the time.'

'Did you two just get me in here to take the piss out of me for being poor, or what?'

Chapter 41

Velázquez nodded hello to the Subinspector upon entering Room 1, then he looked at the suspect. 'It's good to see you again, Klaus,' he said.

'Such a pity the feeling's not mutual, Inspector.'

Velázquez turned to Gajardo. 'How have we been doing here?'

'He's made his statement, boss.'

'And?'

'He's still saying he's got no idea who broke into his flat and beat him up.'

Velázquez looked at Klaus Bloem. 'Why won't you help us try to find the person who killed Arjan and Alfonso de la Torre?'

'My client has already told you everything he knows,' said Fernando Belloso. 'He's made a statement and cooperated in every way that can be expected of him.'

Velázquez ignored the lawyer and kept looking at Bloem. 'What have you got to hide, Klaus?'

'Nothing.'

'How could you possibly not have heard your assailant breaking in at your place, if you were in bed like you say?'

'I have no idea.'

'You have no idea because it's a lie, isn't it?'

'No.'

'The man had to bust the lock to get in,' Velázquez said. 'That means he must've made a hell of a lot of noise.'

'I'm a deep sleeper.'

'Unless there was no intruder, of course.'

'What?'

'Perhaps you broke the lock yourself, Klaus?'

Bloem looked confused. 'Why would I do that?'

The lawyer said, 'Suggesting my client broke the lock to his own apartment is mere supposition.'

'You did it, Klaus,' Velázquez said, 'to make it look like there'd been an intruder...this phantom guy that's supposed to

172

have attacked you with a baseball bat, but whom you didn't hear bursting his way in or get a good look at.'

'I already told you he was wearing a balaclava.'

'Yes, you did already tell us that, I know, Klaus.' Velázquez nodded. 'But we didn't believe your story the first time you told it, either.'

Fernando Belloso said, 'Inspector Jefe, either get to the point and charge my client or we are going to have to bring this interview to an end.'

'But it's your client's lover that was murdered.'

'I am well aware of that.'

'In which case you'll understand why Klaus should want to help us with our enquiries,' Velázquez said. 'Assuming of course that he's actually innocent.'

'That's all very well,' the lawyer said. 'Just so long as you don't intersperse your questions with insinuations and accusations based on false supposition, as you have been doing, Inspector.'

'I'm merely trying to get at the truth.'

Fernando Belloso turned to look at his client. 'You're within your rights to end this interview now, Klaus,' he said.

Bloem appeared to be paying little attention to his lawyer. 'The man I loved has been murdered, and you've decided to persecute me because I'm the soft option, Inspector,' he said. 'You're too lazy and incompetent to go out and find the killer, so it has to be the victim's gay boyfriend, doesn't it? It's a lot easier and a lot less work that way. And besides, I'm sure you think gay people like me should all be locked up anyway, simply because of our sexual orientation.'

'I resent what you're saying, Klaus.'

'In that case you know how I feel…except you don't, of course, because you're the copper and I'm the suspect.' Bloem shook his head in disgust. 'You cops are all the same,' he said. 'You're all homophobes and *Franquistas*.'

'That's both untrue and unfair. It's my job to lead the investigation into Arjan's murder, no more and no less.' Velázquez flipped through the pages of his notebook. 'I realize this must all be very hard for you, Klaus,' he said. 'Just as it must be hard to have a lover reject you for somebody who's younger…somebody who really *is* famous and not just a wannabe.'

The lawyer said, 'You don't need to respond to comments of that sort, Klaus.'

'What?' Bloem said. 'Who told you Arjan rejected me?'

'His sister Ans told me he was tired of you, but you kept running after him like a puppy dog.' Velázquez sat back in his seat and crossed his arms. 'It seems Arjan was involved with the bullfighter, Alfonso de la Torre.'

'That's nonsense.'

'Not according to Ans Gelens it isn't,' the Inspector Jefe said. 'It can't have been easy, finding yourself being replaced by a younger man. And I'm sure you would have felt it in other ways, too. Because Arjan paid for everything when you were together, didn't he? So when he dumped you, there'd have been no more money for the nice things in life. No nice holidays or meals in good restaurants, huh?'

'This is mere supposition,' the lawyer said. 'You don't need to respond to any comments of this sort, Klaus.'

'No, it's okay, I want to set the record straight. I've had this homophobic claptrap up to here.' Bloem held his palm sideways and lifted it to his throat. His eyes were spitting fury at the Inspector Jefe. 'I know my rights and I haven't killed anyone.'

'No, so you keep saying,' Velázquez said. 'But if that's the case then why are you still hiding things from us?'

'Why don't you talk to the widow? If you ask me, it must've been her that sent someone over to beat me up.'

'And just why would she want to do that, do you think?'

'Obvious, isn't it?'

'No, I can't say it is.'

'Jealousy…what d'you think?'

'Are you saying you were involved with her husband in a romantic affair?'

'I'm not quite sure that's the term for it, Inspector.'

'Perhaps you'd like to use your own words, then?'

'We had a few threesomes.'

'Who did?'

174

'Me and Arjan, and Alfonso de la Torre.'

'How many's "a few"?'

'It happened five or six times.'

'Over what sort of time period are we talking?'

'The past six months.'

Fernando Belloso said, 'This is neither here nor there. You shouldn't be telling him all this, Klaus.'

'And the widow knew about it, you're saying?' Velázquez said.

'I really have no idea.' Bloem shrugged. 'But if Alfonso told her or she found out about it somehow, then it would certainly explain a few things, wouldn't it?'

'Such as?'

'What's happened to me and Arjan – as well as Alfonso, of course.'

Velázquez exchanged glances with Gajardo, then he turned back to the suspect. 'What proof have you got that Alfonso took part in these threesomes?'

'It's not exactly the sort of thing a person can very easily prove unless there are witnesses, is it?'

'Exactly…and seeing as they're both dead, we can hardly ask them.'

'No, of course not. But why would I lie about something like that?'

'To muddy the waters, perhaps.'

'What?' Bloem pulled a face. 'Give me a break, will you?'

Velázquez eyed the suspect coldly. 'For someone who wants to see the man who killed his boyfriend – or boyfriend*s* – caught, Klaus, you don't half whine a lot.'

'Right, I really think we have to stop there,' Fernando Belloso said. 'You started off by harassing my client, Inspector, and now you've resorted to insulting him. The fact is, you've yet to produce a single shred of evidence to suggest my client has done anything illegal, or is in any way involved in the murder case you're investigating. In fact, the only thing that you have been able to ascertain with any certainty is that my client is the victim of a violent attack, and yet you continue to bully and insult him. My client has helped you all he can with your enquiries. Now you can either charge him with something, or I really must insist that the interview be brought to a close.'

Chapter 42

Velázquez was sitting across the table from Ans Gelens, in the same restaurant that he'd brought her to the previous time they dined together. Looking at the large bull's head over on the wall, the Inspector Jefe couldn't help but think of Alfonso de la Torre's tragic and violent demise, as if he needed to be reminded of it.

'So how's the investigation going, Inspector?' Ans Gelens sipped her wine. 'Have there been any more developments?'

'It's all been in the news.'

'You forget that I don't speak Spanish, so I can't read the newspapers. And I haven't seen any TV at all. Not that I would understand anything if I did.'

'Yes…there's been another murder.' He wiped his lips with his napkin. 'And it's your brother's friend, Alfonso de la Torre, that was killed.'

Ans Gelens's eyes flashed and she set her fork down. 'Where did it happen?'

'His body was found at the ranch.'

'You said that as though you think he might not have been killed there, Inspector?'

'We're looking into it.'

Ans Gelens put a hand to her cheek. 'Do you think it's the same person that killed them both?'

'I think we can say that's a pretty safe bet at this stage.'

'Arjan told me the bullfighter wanted to leave his wife.'

'Did he tell you whether Alfonso had told her of his plans?'

'No, he didn't say.'

Velázquez said, 'I was wondering if there's anything else you can think of, Ans?'

'Like what?'

'I don't know.' The Inspector Jefe shrugged. 'It could be anything, that's just it.'

'There is one thing.' Ans Gelens sighed. 'Perhaps I should have told you when we met before, Inspector, but I didn't see

177

the need for it. It didn't seem to have any connection with what had happened. Or at least, I couldn't imagine how it could.'

'And now you are not so sure?'

'That's it, exactly, yes,' she said. 'It's something I have always been a little ashamed of. Perhaps I should say that I always loved Arjan, but I did not always approve of everything he did. He was the black sheep of the family in many ways.'

'Being gay, you mean?'

'Oh no, that was the very least of it.'

'What, then?'

'Arjan had Nazi sympathies.'

Well, this was a turn-up for the books. 'Did he keep in contact with other Nazis he knew from the past?'

She nodded.

'In that case, I need the names of the fellow Nazi sympathizers he hung out with.'

'It really wasn't my intention to come here and dig all this up.'

'I realize that, Ans, but it could be important.'

She frowned and looked down at her plate. 'Arjan knew some people down on the coast.' Her voice was barely more than a whisper. 'He would go down there to meet with them now and then.'

'How often is "now and then"?'

'They would meet up every few weeks, so far as I could gather.'

'The coastline stretches for hundreds of kilometres, Ans.'

'The place was called *Bad*-something.' She closed her eyes as she tried to remember. '*Badno,* was it? Or *Bordno*?' She sighed. 'No, it ended 'with *ino*…yes, something – *ino.*'

'*Bardino,* do you mean?'

'Yes, that's it.'

'The *pueblo* is a refuge for gangsters and their minions,' Velázquez said. 'That's to say the people who live off the industries those people generate. But it's the first I've heard of there being a group of Nazis in that part of the world.'

'But they are all harmless, Inspector.' She gripped the stem of her wineglass. 'I mean they're all old men living in a lost dream of the past – *Deutschland uber alles* and all that. Everyone

178

knows that's all over and done with, but they refuse to give up on their fantasy.'

'Whereabouts in Bardino did Arjan meet up with these people?'

'All I know is that they rented some place. Apparently they'd put swastikas on the walls and get themselves up in uniform.'

'And carry on like the Second World War never ended, is that it?'

'More or less, I think, from the way Arjan described those meetings.' She laced her fingers, and Velázquez saw that her hands were trembling. 'Of course, they all idolized Hitler.'

'I need some names, Ans.'

'Kurt Prall was one of them.'

He made a note in his pad and had Ans Gelens check the way he'd spelt it. Then he asked her to tell him what she knew about this Kurt Prall. 'He lives in the south of Spain somewhere, I think,' Ans Gelens said. 'And Arjan was on friendly terms with him.' She massaged the stem of her wineglass. 'He's in his sixties but is still strong and robust, by all accounts.

Velázquez caught the attention of the waiter and waved his plate away.

Ans Gelens told the waiter he could take her plate, too.

'But you've hardly touched your sea bass, Ans,' Velázquez said.

'No, I'm afraid the subject of conversation has rather taken my appetite away.'

The waiter asked if they would like any dessert. Velázquez translated for Ans Gelens. She shook her head. 'I'm quite full up,' she said. 'But I wouldn't say no to a glass of brandy.'

Velázquez told the waiter to bring them two glasses of Magno, and the man nodded and went off. The Inspector Jefe asked Ans Gelens if she knew how many people were involved in this Nazi group. 'Very few, according to Arjan,' Ans Gelens said. She reached for her handbag and found her cigarettes and lighter. 'It was all very hush-hush, as you can imagine.'

The waiter returned with the two glasses of brandy. Ans Gelens lit her cigarette, and took a drag. 'Did your brother and his friends restrict themselves to meeting up and reminiscing about the past? Or were they involved in any activities that might have been part of an overt political campaign?'

'Arjan never liked to talk about it much, so I really can't say.'

'Did he ever mention whether he had any enemies – anyone who might want him out of the way?'

'Beyond the part of the world's population who are either Jewish or left of being right-wing extremists, do you mean?'

'I'm talking about individuals who knew what he was up to and were *actively* out to get him?'

'He did mention a group that call themselves ACCIÓN DIRECTO.' Ans Gelens sipped her brandy. 'They were made up of communists and anarchists, mostly, I think…although I do remember Arjan telling me that two of their number were survivors from the concentration camps.'

'There's still too much I don't know about your brother's lifestyle,' Velázquez said. 'I need to know exactly what it was he'd got himself mixed up in.' A thought occurred to him. 'And what about Alfonso de la Torre and Klaus Bloem – were they Nazi sympathizers, too?'

'Arjan told me Alfonso was really into the fascist cause.' Ans Gelens exhaled smoke out of the side of her mouth. 'Although he wasn't allowed to attend the Nazi revivalist meetings.'

'Because he wasn't German, you mean?'

She nodded. 'I imagine his swarthy looks and Spanish origin would probably have gone down like a lead balloon.'

'Yet Alfonso shared Arjan's political ideas?'

'Apparently he was most enthusiastic.'

'And what about Klaus Bloem?'

'No…Arjan thought it was important to keep him in the dark about it all.'

'Why?'

'I think he thought Klaus wouldn't understand what it was all about,' she said. 'Or maybe he didn't think he'd be in sympathy with the cause.'

Chapter 43

As Velázquez walked to his car early the following morning, a motorbike came roaring up the narrow street. He paid no attention to it at first, but then the vehicle slowed to a crawl as it drew level with him. Velázquez glanced to his side in time to see the rider reach inside his jacket and bring out a gun. The Inspector Jefe threw himself on the pavement and scrambled behind a parked car.

The motorcyclist rode past the parked car then came up onto the narrow pavement. Velázquez poked his head out and to try to get a quick look at the man. His assailant was wearing a helmet with a visor, and had a scarf wrapped round the lower part of his face, so that it was impossible to tell what he looked like. Seeing the man raise his arm to fire, Velázquez moved his head back then heard the bullet ricocheting off one or more of the cars parked behind him.

The Inspector Jefe had his gun out by now, and he fired back at the man, blind – and missed. He fired a second shot but missed again, then heard the sound of the motorcyclist's engine revving up.

He got to his feet and gave chase, as the motorcyclist drove off at speed then took a left and disappeared out of sight.

Velázquez cursed, shitting on his assailant's ancestors, then doubled over as he caught his breath.

He returned to the flat. Finding that Pe was asleep, he woke her up and told her what had just happened. Things were getting serious, he said.

He asked her again if she would please, please, please go and stay with her mother.

No, she wouldn't – and he knew very well why not.

He gave her the police issue Glock he'd had to put in a special request for, and showed her how to use it.

Then he dialed Gajardo's home number. When the Subinspector picked up, Velázquez told him to see what he could find out about any anti-Nazi groups in the area. 'In particular, see what you can turn up on a group that call themselves ACCIÓN DIRECTO,' the Inspector Jefe said. 'Get Javi and Jorge to help you…and get on to Sara. I need her to find out if there are any survivors from the Nazi concentration camps living in the region. And get back to me when you've got something.'

'Right you are, boss.'

'Now I'm going to drive down to Bardino,' Velázquez said. 'See what I can find out about the murder of an old Nazi by the name of Kurt Prall.'

'Why do I feel like I've missed something?'

'No time to explain now, José,' the Inspector Jefe said. 'Just do what I said and I'll bring you up to speed later.'

Situated on the south coast, Bardino had a history of piracy and violence that dated back to pre-Roman times, and its forbears would no doubt have been pleased to learn that this ancient tradition of lawlessness continued unchecked to the current day.

The proximity of Morocco meant that the *pueblo* had become a magnet for drug traffickers, and ensured that Bardino attracted the wrong sort of people. They came in the shape of hookers and pimps and hustlers, as well as drug pushers. Wars broke out between rival gangs and the name of the town became a byword for violence and bloodshed. The local police found they had so much work on their hands they were unable to cope, and this helped to explain why a number of private detectives had been drawn to the area and come to thrive in its shady environs.

Velázquez had little time for these private operators, but there were the odd few for whom he held a grudging respect. And PI Arthur – Art to his friends – Blakey was such an individual. This explained why the Inspector Jefe decided to call in on the private op no sooner than he had arrived in the town.

The man's office was situated at the top of a flight of stairs accessed via a narrow doorway on Calle Mijas, a busy street in the *pueblo*. Finding the door locked, Velázquez pushed the buzzer. A female voice said, '*Hola*?' and the Inspector Jefe explained that he had come to speak to Mr. Blakey. The door buzzed open and he entered into a perfumed antechamber.

A young woman was sitting behind a walnut desk, oozing youthful feminine charm and well-dressed respectability. Either Velázquez had entered through the wrong door or Art Blakey had come up in the world, because the last time the Inspector Jefe called in on this particular private dick the man had a fleapit for an office. Now the freshly painted walls gleamed under the mounted light fixtures, and the wooden boards had been polished to a perfect sheen. The furniture was new, too. So was the secretary. She was *particularly* new. 'Señor Blakey is free now if you'd like to go in and see him,' the girl said. 'It's just through that door.'

Velázquez found the man he'd come to see sitting at a large rosewood desk topped with green leather. There were a couple of notepads and a telephone on the desk, but otherwise it was bare. 'Long time no see, Arthur,' Velázquez said.

'That it is, Luis.' The private op waved a hand in the general direction of the chair across the desk from where he was sitting. 'Do make yourself at home.'

Velázquez parked himself on the upright chair. 'How's the world treating you, Arthur?'

The dick smiled, revealing two rows of white teeth. He was a handsome devil, and the robin's-egg-blue linen jacket he had on went well with his canary-yellow Fred Perry polo shirt. 'Can't complain, Luis,' he said. 'One thing about this town, there's always enough work to keep a body busy.' That was certainly true so long as you were involved with the law in one capacity or another, whether enforcing or breaking it. 'Something to drink?'

Velázquez declined and fixed the dick with an expectant smile. Art Blakey leaned back in his chair. 'So what can I do for you, Luis?'

'Does the name Kurt Prall mean anything to you?'

'It's funny you should ask that.'

'You must forgive me, Arthur, but I fail to see the humour.'

'As in coincidental, I mean.' The dick's eyes narrowed. 'You got here fast, I must say. How did you hear about it?'

'Here about *what*?'

'The murder of course?'

'What *murder*?'

'Are you and I talking the same language here?'

'You tell me, Arthur. I've been speaking Spanish.'

'Me, too.'

Velázquez nodded. 'Accent's a little fucked-up but I guess you could call it that.'

'So?'

'Perhaps you can begin by telling me who it is that's got dead, Arthur?'

'Your man.'

'You wouldn't be meaning Kurt Prall?'

'The very same.'

'When did it happen?'

'Some time during the night.'

'And we're definitely talking murder and not death by some other means?'

'It was murder most foul, no question.'

'What is it you know that I don't, Arthur?'

'In order to answer that, Luis, I'd first have to know what you know.'

'Let's say I don't know much.'

Blakey nodded. 'A client came in here a couple of days ago and asked me to follow Kurt Prall.'

'Who's this client?'

'I'm afraid I can't tell you that.'

'*Won't* you mean.'

Blakey gave the Inspector Jefe the benefit of his broadest smile. 'Wouldn't want to put me out of business, now would you, Luis?'

'That would depend.'

'I thought we were *amigos*?'

'I thought so, too, Arthur. But I've driven all the way down here from Seville, to investigate a certain individual,' Velázquez said. 'It turns out said individual's just been murdered and you're holding out on me.'

'"Holding out" isn't the term I'd use, Luis.'

'What term would you use, Arthur?'

184

'I was about to tell you everything I know.'

'Except for who your client is.'

'That's right – everything except for that. Where would I be in this racket if I failed to respect client confidentiality, do you think, huh? I'll tell you where I'd be, Luis – out of this racket altogether, is where…out of it *on my ass*. I'd be without a client list – which is another way of saying I'd be a private op who's no longer operational.'

Velázquez waved away the man's complaints. 'You're starting to give me a headache,' he said. 'Why don't you just tell me what you know?'

'As I was saying, my client asked me to tail Prall.'

'Did she say why?'

'Nope.' Blakey grinned. 'And I don't recall saying my client is a *she,* either.'

Velázquez got to his feet. 'I've had enough of this bullshit,' he said. 'Let's go.'

'Where are we going?'

'Where do you think?' the Inspector Jefe said. 'You can drive.'

Chapter 44

They passed out of the *pueblo* and headed for the hills. After they had been driving for some twenty minutes, they turned onto a dusty track then went through an open gate that led into a graveled forecourt. The property was situated in the foothills and you could see the stony peaks of the medium-sized mountains in the distance. At their back the land sloped at a gentle gradient down to Bardino, and the *pueblo* was bordered by the giant blue bib that was the Med.

Turning to look at the house, Velázquez saw that there were two casement windows to the left of the entrance and one to the right, both upstairs and downstairs. He climbed out of the dick's Porsche and breathed in the scent of lilac and roses. The air was alive with birdsong that seemed to disclaim the close proximity of death and wrongdoing.

But what did birds or flowers know about murder?

Velázquez looked at the other vehicles parked there. The Land Rover probably belonged to the deceased, but the three squad cars sure as hell didn't. A female police officer was sitting in one of the squad cars with another woman – probably Prall's widow.

The Inspector Jefe and the private op headed over to the front door to the house, where a uniform stood on guard. Velázquez showed the man his ID. 'He's with me,' he said, referring to Art Blakey. The officer stood aside to allow them to enter. It was hot and stuffy inside, without the boon of the cooling breeze.

They passed a man who was busy scouring the hallway on the lookout for prints, then went through the paneled oak door at the end. There were six men in the room, one of them a plainclothes detective that Velázquez knew.

The victim was lying faceup on the bed and had fallen so that he was positioned sideways, parallel with the wooden headboard. His feet were splayed and a leather slipper had fallen from his right foot, and lay looking rather pointless and forlorn on the bedside rug. From the position of the body, Velázquez would have said the victim had either been sitting on the side of the bed or standing there when he'd been shot.

A big man, his broad shoulders and belly filled out the top of the striped pajamas he had on. There was a large red stain around the region of the heart, where the bullet went in. The sheets and coverlet were also stained with blood. Velázquez noticed that blood had even sprayed over the photograph that was hanging on the whitewashed wall above the headboard.

Velázquez studied the photograph. The victim would have been in his thirties at the time it was taken. He was standing proudly with his young bride on their wedding day. Prall had clearly been a strong and handsome young man back then. His blond hair (which had since turned white) and bright blue eyes might have served as an advertisement for Hitler's eugenic ideal.

The bride was holding a bouquet of flowers and smiling. She was slim yet shapely and rather pretty. Velázquez didn't doubt that the Fuhrer would have considered her a suitable prize for one of his Teutonic heroes.

Shafts of sunlight came in through the window, creating stripes of shadow and lozenges of amber that played over the night table, wardrobe and dressing table, as well as the whitewashed walls. A fingerprint expert was going over the headboard with a small brush, while a colleague of his applied himself in similar fashion to the night table.

The doctor, who had just finished his inspection of the body, was putting the instruments of his profession back into his case. Velázquez wanted to talk to the man before he left. But just then he noticed that the detective at the scene was coming towards him. The man was of stocky build, and was dressed in grey slacks with an orange shirt that he wore open at the collar. 'Long time no see, Luis,' he said.

'Sure is, Miguel.' Velázquez smiled. 'What have you got on this one?'

'Before I answer that, perhaps you'd like to tell me what your interest is in this investigation? This is my jurisdiction, in case you'd forgotten.'

'I have reason to believe this murder could be connected to a case I'm currently investigating in Seville.'

'Perhaps you'd care to tell me about it?'

'We talking *quid pro quo* here, Miguel, I assume?'

'I can stretch to that, Luis, so long as you can,' Inspector Jefe Miguel Rojo said. 'And just so long as an exchange of info is all you want here. I mean, it's strictly hands-off where you're concerned. This one's mine, you do understand that?'

'I understand, Miguel.'

Rojo tucked his thumbs inside his belt. 'The honest truth is,' he said, 'we don't have much yet. The victim was clearly killed by a gunshot wound, but there's no sign of the murder weapon as yet.' He shrugged. 'What's this link with your investigation up in Seville?'

'It seems this man Kurt Prall was a friend of the victim in the case I'm working on.'

'What victim would this be?'

'Name's Arjan Gelens. He was a vet.'

'Yes, I heard about that,' Rojo said. 'It's been in the news.' The man ran a finger over his black moustache. '*Gelens*,' he said. 'That sounds Kraut.'

'Dutch.'

'Prall was German.'

The doctor, a pale man of slight build in a grey summer suit, placed a hand on Rojo's arm. 'I've finished here,' he said. 'It's all yours.'

Rojo said, 'I meant to ask for your thoughts on the time of death, Raul?'

The Médico Forense shrugged his narrow shoulders. 'You know I can't possibly give you an accurate time, Miguel.'

'Strictly off the record, I'm talking. And don't worry about these two' – he meant Velázquez and Art Blakey – 'they're both deaf.'

'Going by the body temperature and ambient conditions, I'd say somewhere between three and four a.m…four-thirty at the latest.'

'*Gracias*, Raul.'

'I'll be performing the autopsy at half-nine tomorrow morning.' With that, the doctor went out.

Rojo looked first at Velázquez then at Blakey. 'You two gents didn't hear any of that.'

'Hear what?' Velázquez said. 'We can't hear anything – we're both stone deaf. You just said as much yourself.'

'Sure you are.' Rojo grinned. 'This vet of yours,' he said. 'Did he have any previous?'

Velázquez shook his head. 'Clean as a veritable whistle.'

'Is that so?' Rojo didn't look convinced. 'You got any suspects or a motive?'

'We've got one possible.'

'Who is?'

'The man's boyfriend was the jealous type.'

'Can you place him at the murder scene?'

'Nope.'

'Managed to turn up the murder weapon?'

'Yes, it was a bull's horn.'

'That's a new one.'

Velázquez nodded. 'We're just hoping it's not the start of a new trend in this part of the world.'

'I'll second that.'

'There are no prints on it and so far there's nothing to connect it to anyone.'

'Sounds like you've got plenty of *nada*.'

'That's about right.'

'But your vet was friends with Prall, huh?'

'It seems so.'

'Who told you this?'

'Gelens's sister.'

'She tell you anything else about Prall?'

Velázquez was conscious of the fact that this was supposed to be a *quid pro quo* arrangement he had with Inspector Jefe Rojo, but as yet the other man had come up with precious little in the way of *pro*. So he said, 'Nope.'

'That all you got?'

Velázquez nodded. 'It doesn't add up to much, I know.'

Rojo looked at Art Blakey then back at Velázquez. 'How come you brought your friend along?'

'Oh sorry, I forgot to introduce you – Inspector Jefe Miguel

Rojo, Art Blakey.'

'It's okay,' Rojo said. 'We've already met.'

'He's here in his capacity as driver.'

'That would explain it.' Rojo scratched his bulbous nose. 'Except that it doesn't really explain jack,' he said. 'Why do I get the feeling there's something you're not telling me?'

'You're just the suspicious type, Miguel,' Velázquez said. 'You always were.'

'Perhaps you'd care to lay my suspicions to rest for me, Luis?'

'There's no mystery to it,' Velázquez said. 'Arthur here makes it his business to find out what's going on in this part of the world, so I figured I'd call in on him to ask if he knew one Kurt Prall and if so then where the man lives. Arthur was able to supply me with the information I asked for, and was even kind enough to offer to drive me here to the man's house.'

Rojo looked at the private op. 'What's the matter, Arthur, can't you make ends meet nowadays working as a dick? You got to double up as a cab driver?'

The private op didn't say anything. Insults just bounced off the guy. It was one of the things Velázquez admired about him.

Rojo looked at Velázquez. 'So what are you hoping to get out of coming here, Luis?'

'A word with the widow, if that's all right with you?'

'What do you want to talk to her for?'

'I'd like to ask her what she knows about her husband's association with Arjan Gelens.'

Rojo thrust his hands deep into the pockets of his trousers, as he took a moment to consider. 'Okay,' he said finally. 'Just so long as you stick to your end of it, and keep me updated on what you and your team turn up concerning any links between Prall's death and that of your man Gelens.'

'Sure.' Velázquez would feed the man such tidbits as he reckoned might keep him quiet.

Rojo looked about the room and shrugged. 'I've finished here,' he said. 'It's just a question of seeing if the print guys or Ballistics can come up with anything. And of course there's the autopsy in the morning.'

The three men left the house, and Rojo went over to the squad car with the widow in the back. He opened the door and looked over the roof at Velázquez. 'See you at the Jefatura, then.' With that, he climbed in behind the wheel and set off, raising a cloud of dust in his wake.

Chapter 45

When they arrived at the Jefatura in Bardino, Inspector Jefe Rojo showed Velázquez and Blakey into the incident room, where Prall's widow was being held. A slim, blonde woman in her late fifties or early sixties, she looked elegant in her beige trouser suit.

Rojo introduced himself to the widow, before he asked her if she'd seen the man who killed her husband. She shook her head. 'It was too dark. All I could see was that he was wearing some kind of mask or scarf to cover his face.' She shrugged. 'And it happened so fast. He was gone out of the room before I could react.'

'Can you think of any enemies your husband might have had?'

'No…we lived a simple life.'

'So your husband wasn't involved in anything he shouldn't have been?' Rojo said. 'He wasn't having an affair with anyone's wife? Or else involved in drug trafficking or arms dealing or something of that order?'

'No.' Her blue eyes flashed as she looked at him. 'I'm surprised that you can even ask such a thing.'

'I don't mean to be insensitive, Señora Prall, because I know this is a tough time for you. But these are routine questions that I need to ask.'

'My husband and I retired some years ago, Inspector,' she said. 'Kurt had a good pension, so we had no need to work or worry about money.'

'But whoever killed your husband must have had a motive.' Rojo exchanged glances with Velázquez. 'My colleague here is investigating the murder of a Dutchman up in Seville…an Arjon Gelens.'

'Arjan Gelens,' Velázquez corrected him. Then he said to the widow, 'He appears to have been an associate of your husband's.'

Señora Prall took a moment to think, then shook her head. 'The name doesn't ring any bells. What did this man do?'

'He was a vet.'

'I'm afraid I've never heard of him…and we never had any pets.'

Rojo said, 'Your husband was in the war, is that right?'

'Yes, he was a brave servant of his country.'

'Of the Fatherland.'

'Yes, of course. He was German, as am I.'

'So you were proud of him, then?'

'Yes.'

'We have a file on him. Did you know that?'

Hearing this, Velázquez wondered how his colleague could possibly have known about Prall's past, seeing that he had changed his name upon coming to Spain. Perhaps Rojo was bluffing to try to unnerve the widow. If he was then his plan seemed to be working, judging by the look on Frau Prall's face.

'He was made welcome here in the times of the dictatorship,' Rojo said. 'That's hardly surprising, seeing as General Franco was a big admirer of Hitler. But it may not have escaped your attention that things have changed a little here recently.'

'I really don't see what this has to do with what happened to my husband.'

'He served as a guard at Mauthausen concentration camp in World War Two, didn't he?'

'Yes.'

Rojo took a deep breath and let it out slowly. 'They specialized in dealing with political prisoners at Mauthausen, I understand?'

'I really wouldn't know. Kurt never liked to talk about it.'

A look of disgust and contempt appeared on Rojo's face. 'Of course it's all in the history books now, isn't it?' he said. 'How they used to treat the prisoners, I mean.'

'Whatever they did, it was in time of war,' Señora Prall said. 'Awful things happened on both sides. But that's only to be expected. War is a terrible thing.'

Rojo nodded. 'They made them play leapfrog and do other pointless activities until they were worn out,' he said. 'And then they forced them to continue past the point of exhaustion. Many died that way. It was a deliberate ploy, to kill off the ones who

193

couldn't take it.'

The widow's eyes flashed. 'Where did you get all this nonsense?'

'I did a little reading up on it. It's all in your husband's file. All the concentration camps were tough and cruel, but Mauthausen was perhaps the worst. It was meant to be, because the prisoners were mostly politicals and as such were considered enemies of the State.'

'I'm afraid I really don't see where you're heading with all this. And nor do I see what possible relevance it might have to Kurt's murder,' she said. 'It all happened such a long time ago. Besides, none of the rules that govern civilized society apply at such times. My husband didn't start the war. He was merely a brave and faithful servant of his country.'

'The judges at Nuremberg would surely have taken a different view.'

'This really is too much, Inspector. I came here thinking I was going to be asked to help you with your investigation into my husband's death. But here you are talking about... ' Words failed the widow for a moment. '...About *history*,' she finally said. 'You're talking almost as if you think you're some judge at Nuremberg, instead of a police detective in Bardino investigating a murder. Now either get to the point and stop talking all this nonsense, or I'm going to issue a formal complaint to your superiors.'

'But what I've been talking about may well be of the utmost relevance to this investigation, Señora Prall.'

'I'm afraid I really can't see how.'

'What if the murderer was out to take revenge for what happened at Mauthausen?'

'What nonsense.'

'What makes you so sure of that?'

'Why would anyone have waited all these years until now?'

'I quite agree with the Inspector,' Velázquez said. 'This smacks of a hit to me.'

'A *hit*?'

'A pre-planned murder carried out in return for a fee.'

'This is all preposterous,' the widow said, and then she broke

194

down in tears.

'I don't think Rojo handled the interview very well,' Art Blakey said. They were driving back to the private op's office.

'I'm not sure it was the kind of interview that could have been handled well. Rojo was up against a brick wall in Señora Prall.' A kind of professional solidarity made Velázquez loath to criticize the best efforts of a colleague in the presence of a private op like Blakey.

'If you say so.'

'Rojo suspects someone from Prall's murky past has come back to bite him. But he's got nothing to go on. And if the widow refuses to help then she's within her rights.'

'Maybe she just doesn't know anything.'

'*Joder*,' Velázquez cursed. 'Rojo's reached a dead-end on this one and so have I. The only person who knows anything about what's going on is you, Arthur. But unfortunately you can't find it in you to give any of us a helping hand.'

Blakey stopped for a traffic light. 'Now wait a minute, Luis,' he said. 'I've told you everything I possibly can.'

'But it's not enough and you know it. I need the name of your client.'

'You know as well as I do, it's the one thing a private eye can never disclose if he wants to stay in business.'

'You've already told me all that, Arthur,' Velázquez said. 'And it's fair enough some of the time. But not on this occasion.' The lights changed and they set off. 'You're withholding vital information, possibly even evidence in a murder investigation. And that amounts to aiding and abetting a murderer. I've a mind to throw you in a cell.'

Blakey pulled up across the street from his office. 'Is this the way you treat me after I tip you off about Prall, and taxi you to the crime scene and back without even asking for a fee?'

'Don't push your luck, Arthur.'

The two men climbed out of the car. 'If I find out anything new about Prall,' Blakey said over the roof of the Porsche, 'I'll let you know.'

'You be sure to do that.'

Chapter 46

Velázquez entered a café and sat at a table by the window. From there he had a clear view of the entrance to the building where Art Blakey had his office. A waiter came over and Velázquez ordered a ham roll *a la catalana* and a bottle of Cruzcampo. The waiter went off and came back with the bottle of beer, a tube glass and a dish full of olives.

Velázquez took a swig of the cold beer straight from the bottle, then ate an olive. Someone entered through the doorway across the street. Velázquez took the stone from his mouth and dropped it into the dish. He could only see her from the back, but he thought it was Blakey's secretary. Presumably she'd returned from lunch or from a brief trip to the shops.

Velázquez wondered how many other people used the same doorway.

The waiter came back with his roll. Velázquez bit into it and chewed, keeping watch on the front of the building across the street.

He finished his beer then ordered another. He took sips from it as he continued his vigil. The propeller fan hummed overhead. Over by the wall, a man was stuffing coins into a fruit machine. Velázquez was somehow aware of all this on one level and yet detached from it. In the same way, he was now chewing on his ham roll without really tasting it.

Then she showed. Velázquez watched her as she came along the pavement, an elegant figure in her slim-fitting linen trouser suit and ballet pumps, her blonde hair tied back in a bun. She was wearing sunglasses, but there was no mistaking her even at this distance.

Velázquez dropped some coins onto the table and went out. The widow had already entered the building by the time he reached the pavement. He allowed her enough time to go up, before he crossed the street and went in after her. He climbed the stairs and pushed the buzzer. The secretary's voice asked who was there. He identified himself, and was buzzed in.

The girl looked up from her desk when Velázquez entered. She asked how she could help him. He told her he was here to see Señor Blakey. The girl said Señor Blakey was busy with a client right now, but if he –

Velázquez crossed the room and went in through the private op's door without knocking.

Blakey and his client turned their heads like they were attached to strings. 'Hello again,' Velázquez said. 'I hope you don't mind my dropping in on you both.'

'You can't just barge in here like this, Luis,' the private op protested.

'Can't I?' Velázquez shrugged. 'That's funny, I thought I just did.'

'I'm with a client.'

'I can see that.'

'We were having a private conversation.'

The Inspector Jefe perched himself on the edge of Blakey's desk. 'In that case, don't let me disturb you.'

The widow scowled at Velázquez. 'What is the meaning of this?'

'That's what I'm trying to get to the bottom of.' Velázquez made a show of examining his nails. 'Arthur here tells me a client of his who can't be named – *you,* Señora Prall – hired him to keep an eye on your husband. And then your husband promptly gets dead.'

'Yes, Inspector, that is right.'

Velázquez shrugged. 'Sounds to me, Señora Prall, like you knew something was about to happen to your husband. Maybe you even killed him, or had him killed.'

Blakey said, 'You need a warrant to come busting in here like this.'

'Either you shut up,' Velázquez told him, 'or I'm going to arrest you.'

'But Luis –'

'I mean it,' the Inspector Jefe said.

He turned to the widow. 'I think you owe me an explanation.'

'I owe you nothing, Inspector. But even so I will tell you as much as I can. Because, believe it or not, I loved my husband

197

and want to help you catch the man who killed him.' The widow spread her palms on her lap, and took a deep breath then let it out. 'I hired Señor Blakey to keep an eye on Kurt,' she said. 'I sensed that something was wrong and I didn't know what it was.'

'You didn't think to ask your husband if he had a problem of some sort?'

'Kurt liked to keep things to himself. I think it was partly because of his past.' She dropped her head. 'My husband was a Nazi, you're probably thinking, and the Nazis were all monsters. But what you fail to understand is that men like Kurt had no choice. If he had refused to follow orders he would have been killed himself, and nothing would have been achieved.'

Art Blakey said, 'There's no need to rerun the Nuremberg trials here, Señora Prall.'

Velázquez told the private op to button it. 'It's all right, Señor Blakey,' the widow said. 'I appreciate your concern. You're probably feeling you've let me down in allowing the Inspector to come into your office and interview me like this. But it's not your fault.'

'I didn't tell him you were my client.' Blakey opened the top drawer in his desk and brought out a roll of banknotes. He counted off one hundred thousand *pesetas*, tamped the notes into a neat pile and held them out. 'Here,' he said. 'I feel like I owe you a refund.'

The widow seemed confused. 'But why?'

'I've hardly earned it.'

'Please keep it.'

Blakey shrugged and dropped the banknotes onto the desk.

Velázquez reckoned the man sure did have a funny way of doing business. He'd never heard of any of his colleagues wanting to give back their salary, that was for sure.

Señora Prall looked at Velázquez. 'Kurt was a tortured man,' she said. 'He rarely slept before two in the morning – and only then with the aid of alcohol and sleeping tablets.'

'That's all very well, but it doesn't help me much.'

'I'm telling you the truth.'

'And I'm listening. But you can skip the bit about your

husband's bad conscience. I'm sure he earned it.'

'If that's supposed to be funny, Inspector, then you'll have to excuse me if I say I don't share your sense of humour.'

'I don't joke about such matters, Señora Prall. The idea of the Nazis murdering several million Jews and then burning the bodies to destroy the evidence doesn't strike me as the least bit funny.'

The widow turned her head with a jerk as if she'd been slapped.

Velázquez said, 'Now how about if we get to the point?'

'As I was saying, my husband was acting strangely.'

'In what way?'

'I had the feeling he was afraid for his life. And I was also worried that someone might have been blackmailing him.'

'Have you any idea who?'

'No, that's why I hired Mr. Blakey,' she said. 'I was hoping he might be able to find out whether my suspicions were correct.'

'And you didn't have any ideas yourself as to who it might have been?'

She shrugged. 'I didn't even know for sure that it was happening. It was just a hunch of mine.'

'Based purely on his behaviour?'

'Yes…he seemed very nervous all of a sudden. I tried to talk to him about it, but it was useless.' Señora Prall shook her head. 'You have to understand that my husband was a very proud man, Inspector. He wasn't in the habit of talking to me about his problems.' She brushed away a tear. 'And there's another thing,' she said. 'Kurt Prall isn't the name my husband was born with. His name by birth was Hans Graf. He was made welcome in Franco's Spain as a Nazi, but felt it might be wise to change his name anyway. After the fall of the regime, he probably feared an ex-Nazi might find himself at risk should someone find out about his past.'

'And who might have found out about it, do you think?'

'If I could tell you then I would.' The widow held Velázquez's glance, and he had the feeling she was being straight with him.

'Was your husband friendly with the politician, Pedro

Villalonga?'

'I really can't say, I'm afraid,' she said. 'But I know the man you mean. I saw your wife interviewing him on television.'

'Do you think whoever killed your husband was after revenge?'

'What else can it have been?'

'Are you sure the name Arjan Gelens means nothing to you?'

'I think I've already told you that I've never heard of anyone by that name.' She got to her feet. 'And now I've told you everything I know. So if you've finished with your questions, Inspector, I'll be on my way.'

'Okay,' he said. 'But don't leave town because I may have to talk to you again.'

Velázquez watched the widow go out. Then he turned to the private op. 'You know, Arthur,' he said, 'contrary to what you may think, I rather like you.'

'Sure you do. You just have a funny way of showing it, that's all.'

'I think we've got off on the wrong foot on this investigation, is our problem. Perhaps it's partly my fault. There are a few things that you need to know. Maybe I should have pointed them out to you when we first ran across each other. You see, I'm an officer of the law. That means I can throw your ass in jail any time I want to. Now, it doesn't have to be like that. In fact, as I just said, I like you. So there really is no reason it should be. But in order for things to run smoothly where you and I are concerned, one or two things need to change. You need to cut out all this talk about stuff you know being 'private information'. In other words, I need you to cooperate with me and then I can cooperate with you.'

'I haven't seen much sign of any cooperation on your part, Luis,' Blakey said. 'You've just cost me a client and now you're talking about throwing me in jail.'

'You held out on me with the widow, Arthur. You shouldn't have done that.'

Blakey gave his Parker fountain pen a thoughtful twirl. 'Okay,' he said finally, 'I'm just wondering what I'll get out of this if I agree to play ball more?'

'You'll get an easy ride.'

'As in your protection from all the other cops out there who try and make life difficult for me?'

'Up to a point, yes.'

'You know who my client is now and you've even had the opportunity to question her,' Blakey said. 'What more do you want?'

'What I want right now, Arthur, is for you to tell me if you know where these Nazi goofballs meet up.'

'I do,' Blakey said. 'And after what happened to Prall there has to be a big chance they'll convene sometime soon – like this evening, perhaps.'

'To talk about what happened and what they're going to do about it, you mean?'

'I shouldn't be at all surprised.'

'That makes sense.'

'Okay, so if you like I'll take you over there. We can see if anything's going on,' the private op said. 'Now it's your turn to tell me something.'

'All right, it's a deal.' Velázquez paused to think. He didn't want to tell Blakey too much. But on the other hand, he wanted to give the man an incentive to play straight. 'Ever heard of Manuel Bordano?'

'The *apoderado*, you mean?'

Velázquez nodded. 'He pimps for his bullfighters, to keep them happy when they're in town.'

'That's interesting – which bullfighters are these?'

'Jorge Belgrano is the only one I know about for sure, so far.'

'Most of the *toreros* normally use the Hotel Madrid when they go to Seville,' Blakey said. 'I suppose he takes the girls over there to the guy's room – is that how it works?'

'You got it in one.'

'Be a little difficult to prove, I should think, what with the pull someone like Bordano has – as well as the bullfighters he represents, for that matter. You'd risk being laughed out of court if you were to try to make a case against any of them.'

'I'm not going after them. Not for that, anyway.'

'You don't think Bordano's involved in these murders?'

201

'I can't say for sure.'

'So he's a suspect?'

'I've got a list of suspects that's as long as your arm.' Velázquez pushed himself off the desk and stretched. 'Let's go and see this place.'

Blakey glanced at his watch. 'It's still a little early,' he said. 'If the information I've received is correct, they never meet up before sevenish.'

'Okay, so let's go and eat someplace first.' Velázquez made for the door, and Blakey got up out of his chair and followed him. 'Know any good seafood restaurants that don't overcharge too much in this part of the world, Arthur?'

'I know just the place.'

'Good,' the Inspector Jefe said. 'I could murder a *paella*.' He winked at the secretary as they passed her desk.

Chapter 47

At just after seven that evening, Arthur Blakey pulled up on the outskirts of the village of Bardino, near to the rectangular-shaped redbrick building the Nazis used for their get-togethers. It was the kind of place you might have expected to be used for boy scouts' meetings or Sunday school classes if they had been in England. The building fronted onto a dusty parking lot, which extended to the road on which Art Blakey's Porsche was now parked. The other side of the road, to Velázquez's right, was taken up with a block of flats that had seen better days. The paint was flaking from the walls of the block, and the residents' washing hung from the balconies. This was clearly the poor end of town. In areas like this practically anything could – and often *did* – happen without causing too much of a stir. People who lived in rundown blocks like the one Velázquez was now looking at learned early in life that it wasn't just the cat that could get into trouble for showing too much curiosity.

He turned his head, to look at the redbrick building that was situated to his left. To the other side of it, there was a stretch of wasteland. He could see the motorway, and beyond that the hills stretching into the distance.

Velázquez could see why a bunch of neo-Nazis might have chosen such a spot to hold their meetings. It was just about far enough from anywhere of importance for them to be able to make all the noise they wanted without attracting the attention of the locals.

The Inspector Jefe counted the cars that had been left parked in the dusty lot. There were six of them. And there was no sign of any of their owners – or of anyone else for that matter. He suggested they go and take a closer look. So the two men climbed out of the Porsche and made their way over to the redbrick building.

It was impossible to see inside because the windows were blacked up.

Velázquez tried the doors at the front. They were locked.

He placed his ear against one of the windows. All he could hear was the purr of the traffic speeding along the motorway at his back. If there were any people inside the building, then they were behaving more like a bunch of Trappist monks than a group of neo-Nazis intent on celebrating and reviving the Hitlerian spirit.

The two men went and climbed back into the car and waited. Time dragged and Velázquez wondered if the dick had brought him down here on a wild goose chase. Then a couple of blond men showed up carrying briefcases. One of them brought out a key and opened the door to the redbrick building, and the pair disappeared inside.

Velázquez asked his companion if he recognized either of the men. Blakey told him the tall blond one was Albert Klein. He didn't know about the other man. The Inspector Jefe wondered what they had in the briefcases they were carrying. 'Most probably their uniforms,' the private op said. 'Rumour has it they change into them once they get inside. Do you want to go in and talk to them?'

'Let's wait a little first and see if anyone else comes.'

Sure enough, more men began to arrive in dribs and drabs over the next twenty minutes or so. Velázquez counted them and got up to fifteen before he decided it was time to go and investigate further. They climbed out of the car and went over to the building.

Velázquez tried the door and it opened, but there was a tall blond man standing on guard just inside. 'I'm sorry,' the man said, 'but you must have come to the wrong place.'

Velázquez smiled. 'I don't think so.'

'This is a private members club.'

'I know all about that.' The Inspector Jefe showed the man his ID. 'I want to talk to Albert Klein.'

'I can go and get him for you, if you'd like to wait here. But I'm afraid you won't be able to come in, Inspector.'

'I don't think you quite understand,' Velázquez said. 'I'm going in whether you like it or not.'

'I'm afraid you'll need to show me a warrant before I'll be able to let you enter.'

Velázquez reached under his jacket, took his Glock from its holster and pointed it at the man. 'Is this good enough for you?'

The blond man's blue eyes lit up. 'But this is quite out of order and totally unnecessary.'

'I'll be the judge of that.' The man moved aside, and Velázquez and Blakey brushed past him. They went through another door and found themselves in a large hall. Swastikas were hanging from the walls, and men were busy changing into their Nazi uniforms. The tall man who had tried to bar their entry came rushing in after them. He shouted something in German, and the men in the room all turned to look at the two intruders.

'Good afternoon, gentlemen,' Velázquez said in English. 'Please allow me to pass on my condolences after what happened to Kurt Prall.'

One of the men – it was Albert Klein – approached them. Velázquez exchanged glances with his companion, and saw that Art Blakey had already taken his gun out as a precautionary measure. It was obvious to both men that while the war had ended half a lifetime ago, for these Nazi goofballs it was still very much in progress. 'Thank you for the kind words,' Klein said. 'But why the guns? And who are you two exactly?' He spoke good English with a Germanic accent.

'I'm Inspector Jefe Velázquez. I'm leading the investigation into the deaths of Kurt Prall and Arjan Gelens.'

'You can't seriously believe that one of his own people killed him?'

'Not necessarily, but I do need to ask you some questions.'

'Go ahead.'

'We'll start with your name.'

The man confirmed his name was Albert Klein. Then he said, 'But Kurt was one of us.'

'Did he have any enemies that you know of?'

'We all have enemies, Inspector.'

'I need some names.'

'You might start with the Jewish race.' This comment brought a round of laughter from those Germans in the room that understood English.

205

Velázquez said, 'I'm thinking of any specific individuals who might have wanted to get rid of Prall?'

'There are none that I know of.'

'What about your friends here? Might any of them know who could have killed him?'

'I can ask them if you like, just to make sure the men among us who don't have any English understand?'

Velázquez nodded his assent, and Klein barked something out in German.

Some of the men shook their heads as they replied in their mother tongue. Klein turned to look at Velázquez. 'I'm afraid not, Inspector.' The German shrugged. 'If we could help you then we would,' he said. 'Nobody would like to see you catch the man who killed our friend more than us, I can assure you.'

'I'd appreciate it if you'd let me know if you or any of your friends hear anything.' Velázquez handed the man his card.

Klein offered up a chilly smile. 'Of course, Inspector. It would be my pleasure.'

Velázquez turned and went out, with Art Blakey close on his heels.

They hurried back to the car and climbed in. 'Those guys sure give me the willies.' Blakey slipped the car into gear and they set off. 'Tell anyone about a group of aging Nazis that dress up in their old uniforms and it sounds harmless enough.' He checked in his mirror, to make sure they weren't being followed. No, it was all right. 'Like it's a bunch of overgrown Boy Scouts you're talking about, you know? But I don't reckon it's like that with those guys. They're *serious*. You could feel it in the air, as soon as we went in there. It's quite clear that so far as they're concerned, the Third Reich is still very much alive.'

'And kicking,' Velázquez said.

Blakey came to a roundabout and saw a sign for TODAS DIRECCIONES, with an arrow pointing straight on. 'If you ask me,' he said, 'they're just biding their time until the moment is right to make their move back onto the world's political stage.' They came to another roundabout. There was a sign to say the second turning would lead them to the motorway back to Seville. 'I wouldn't have put it past them to try something in there, if we hadn't been armed.'

'Nor me,' Velázquez said. 'And we were seriously outnumbered.'

'I wouldn't have fancied your chances much if you'd gone in there alone, Luis.'

Velázquez turned his head to look at the private op. 'Sounds like you expect me to thank you, is that it?'

'Not exactly,' Blakey said. 'I just figured you might bear it in mind the next time you threaten to throw my arse in jail.'

Velázquez had better things to concern himself with than the Englishman's hind parts. 'One thing I don't get's why all these ex-Nazis should come to a little place like Bardino.'

'Prall settled here first, after coming over from Buenos Aires. He went there after the war. The story is, he first made his way to Rome, where he was given shelter by a priest with close links to the Vatican. They put him on a plane to Buenos Aires and even gave him his ticket and some spending money.'

'How do you know all this, Arturo?' Velázquez asked, unconsciously translating Blakey's Christian name into Spanish.

'Bardino's my patch, Luis. Besides, it's a small town and people talk. There isn't much that goes on in this neck of the woods that I don't get to hear about one way or another. So, once Frau Prall came to ask me to look into what was bothering her husband, I made it my job to investigate the people he hung out with.'

'Okay. Carry on.'

'Prall was working over in B.A. for a while in some car plant. But then when he retired he decided to come back to Europe. He fancied Spain, because he'd been down on the Costa del Sol before on holiday, so he knew this part of the world fairly well and liked it.'

'And then there's the fact that General Franco would have been amenable to men of his political persuasion and past.'

'Yes, there's that, too. So he came over and settled. And once he gave Karlmann the all clear, he decided to come over and join him. It seems neither of them had ever really settled in Buenos Aires. And the other one who lives fairly local is Albert

Klein. He's based somewhere in the Grazalema mountains. But of course they come from all over. A few live in Germany and Austria. One lives in Rome, another in Sicily. Three others are scattered across the Greek islands.'

'And they come all this way just to attend these meetings?'

'From what I can gather, Klein, Karlmann, and Prall were the only regulars to attend all the meetings. Those that live farther afield only come once or twice a year. I suspect so many of them came over for this evening's meeting, to give a show of strength and *esprit de corps* after what happened to Prall. They fly in, meet up in that anonymous-looking little hall, and then fly out again the next day. They're not here long enough to get themselves noticed.'

Chapter 48

When Velázquez got home that night, he found the front door to his flat had been left open. Sensing that something was wrong, he took out his gun as he entered.

The place had been trashed

Where was Pe?

Moving from room to room with his gun up, Velázquez made a quick tour of the flat.

He ran back out, down the stairs and out through the door to the block. His heart pounding in his ears, he looked up and down the street. But there was no sign of anyone other than a woman walking along the pavement with her daughter.

He ran back into the building, and went up and rang the bell to the flat that neighboured his. When Señora Tejado opened up, Velázquez asked her if she'd heard anything. She shrugged and asked him what had happened. He explained that he'd just got home and found the front door to his flat open. More worrying still, there was no sign of Pe.

Señora Tejado shook her head. She had been at home all day but hadn't heard anything out of the ordinary. She hoped Velázquez hadn't been burgled?

The Inspector Jefe went back into the flat, his imagination now having gone into overdrive.

What if the killer had abducted Pe?

He felt like he'd never really known the meaning of anger until now – or of fear.

He called Gajardo and told him what had happened. 'What,' the Subinspector said, 'you don't mean to say the killer's taken Pe?'

'I don't know anything for certain.'

'But what are we going to do, boss?'

'That's what I've been asking myself.'

At that moment, Velázquez heard footsteps out in the hallway. He set the phone down, then held his gun up and crept over to the door – and Pe walked in. 'Luis,' she said. 'What's the gun

209

for?'

'But where have you been?'

'I went to the gym and then I stopped off in the Corte Ingles on the way home, to buy some things. I got some beef, chickpeas and vegetables.' She held up her shopping bag. 'I thought I'd make a *cocido*.'

Velázquez hugged her like love was about to go out of fashion. Pe said she knew she made a great *cocido*, but even so wasn't he overreacting just a little? Velázquez told her he'd been worried that something might have happened to her. Pe wanted to know what could possibly happen to her in the local supermarket? 'The killer's been here,' he said.

Pe brushed past him, and he said, 'I wouldn't go in there if I were you.' But she ignored his advice.

Velázquez figured he couldn't very well have kept Pe from seeing what a mess the place was in anyway.

He picked up the telephone. Gajardo was still there, on the other end of the line. The Inspector Jefe told him that it was a false alarm. 'Pe's just come back.'

'Thank God for that.'

'Yeah, I was getting worried there for a moment,' Velázquez said. 'And not without good reason. The door had been left open and the flat's been trashed.'

Gajardo shat in the milk. 'Who'd do a thing like that, boss?'

'If I knew that, José, then I'd know the identity of the killer.'

'But you don't really think - '

'It was *him* all right,' Velázquez said. 'No question.'

Gajardo shat on the killer's ancestors.

'Anyway, I'll catch you later.' The Inspector Jefe hung up then went into the dining room. Pe was standing with her mouth open, looking at the mess the flat was in. 'I did warn you not to come in here,' he said.

'What kind of son of a bitch would do this?'

'It was the killer,' Velázquez said. 'He's letting us know he can get at us whenever he wants to.'

He set about tidying up the front room, and Pe went to see what kind of state the rest of the flat was in. Then he heard Pe scream from the master bedroom. He rushed to her, and immediately saw the cause of her alarm. There on the bed lay a long bull's horn.

On the floor at Pe's feet was the cardboard box and wrapping paper it had been in.

Velázquez hadn't noticed there had been a parcel left on the bed when he'd looked in the bedroom minutes earlier. He was too taken up at the time with making sure the killer wasn't in the flat.

It didn't take a genius to work out what was going on here. The killer was letting Velázquez and Pe know that he intended to kill them the same way that he had Arjan Gelens and Alfonso de la Torre, unless the Inspector Jefe dropped the investigation.

Velázquez took Pe in his arms and did his best to console her. Part of him realized he wasn't making much of a job of it.

How could he possibly hope to allay his wife's fears when he was spooked out of his wits himself?

Gazing over Pe's head, through the bedroom window, the terrible and horrifying thought took root in Velázquez's mind that the killer was out there somewhere. And this man was no ordinary killer, either. He was clearly a vicious and sadistic lunatic, a monster of the worst and most dangerous sort.

What made things far worse, the man knew where to find him and Pe, while Velázquez was still practically at square one in so far as the investigation was concerned.

The Inspector Jefe felt like he was taking part in a contest that was as unfair as it was unnerving. The killer was holding all of the cards.

It was only by a stroke of great fortune that Pe hadn't been at home when the man came here.

Or had the killer known that nobody was home?

Perhaps he knew Pe's routine and had chosen to come here when she was out, so as to leave the bull's horn and put the fear of God into them.

If that was the case, then the man had certainly achieved his goal.

And what was to prevent him from returning whenever he chose to do so?

Pe said, 'What I don't understand is how he could've got in

here without a key?'

Velázquez shrugged. 'Expert criminals have their ways,' he said. 'He could have used lock picks. Or else there's stuff some burglars use. They pour it into the lock. It quickly solidifies into the shape of a key, which they then use to open the door.'

He looked Pe in the eye. 'You must know by now that you really can't stay here any longer,' he said. 'It's just too dangerous. The killer has made this personal. It's between him and me. We're both together in this crazy sort of endgame. And there's only going to be one winner.'

This time Pe saw the sense in what Velázquez was saying. He helped her pack and then drove her out to her mother's cottage in the village of Modrigones.

Señora Sanchez was delighted to see them. But then when Pe explained that she would be staying for a few days, her mother began to worry. She hoped that Pe and Luis weren't 'having problems'. Velázquez hastened to reassure her that it was 'nothing like that'.

Pe made coffee and they were in the small kitchen, drinking it, when the telephone rang. Velázquez took the call. A man with a foreign accent said he wanted to speak to Inspector Jefe. 'Speaking,' Velázquez said.

'I saw you at the reunion in Bardino yesterday.' The man sounded nervous. 'I believe you're investigating Kurt Prall's murder?'

'That's correct.'

'Kurt and I were close friends.'

'Is there anything you can tell me about how he was killed?'

'I don't know anything for certain, but let's say that I have a hunch.'

'Go on.'

'Kurt had been having weekly sessions with a psychologist in Bardino. You see, he was haunted by some of the things our superior officer, Albert Klein – the man you spoke to in Bardino yesterday – made us do when we were guards at Mauthausen. Then one day not so long ago, Kurt saw Klein and the psychiatrist together. They were holding hands coming out of a restaurant in Bardino.'

'So Kurt began to worry that the psychiatrist might have told Klein all about what he had confided in her about the man during their time at Mauthausen, is that it?'

'Exactly.'

'Do you think Klein decided to kill Kurt because of that?'

'I don't know anything for certain, Inspector,' the man said. 'But Klein is a particularly nasty piece of work, even judging by the standards of the Nazis. He is not a man to be crossed.'

'This is all very interesting, Herr um…sorry, what did you say your name was again?'

'If I tell you then I will be placing myself at great risk.'

'What if I promise to keep all this between you and me?'

'Listen, Inspector, if anything happens to me – if I end up like Kurt, I mean – then you will know who is behind it.'

'But if something happens to you and I don't know your name, then I won't be able to link it to Klein, will I?'

'No, that's true, I suppose. Okay, my name is Ben Karlmann.' He spelt his surname so that Velázquez could make a note of it.

'And your address?'

'Is that necessary?'

'I can find it out anyway easily enough.'

The man told him. 'I hope you realize that I am placing my life in your hands, Inspector?'

'Yes, I appreciate that Herr Karlmann and you have nothing to fear,' Velázquez said. 'There is something else I must ask you. Does the name Arjan Gelens mean anything to you?'

'That would be the vet who was murdered. I read about it in the newspaper.'

'Was he part of your group?'

'Yes, he attended meetings. And he was a guard at Mauthausen, too, the same as us.'

'Did you and your Nazi friends in the group know that Gelens was homosexual?'

'No…that is I, for one, had no idea.'

'What does Albert Klein think of gay people?'

'He hates them.'

Velázquez wondered whether the vet's being gay might have been reason enough to drive a psychopath like Klein to murder him. 'Do you know anything about Klaus Bloem?'

'I don't know anyone by that name.'

Velázquez thanked Herr Karlmann for his help and hung up. Then he called the Jefatura and found Gajardo at his desk. The Inspector Jefe brought him up to speed regarding the break-in at his flat, before he told him to send Serrano and Merino out to Señora Sanchez's place in Modrigones. 'Tell them to come armed,' he said. 'They should also know that they're going to have to spend the night here, guarding my wife and her mother.'

Chapter 49

Ana Pelayo kicked off the session by reflecting on the fact that the local newspapers were saying the investigation should have been an open-and-shut case. 'And yet it seems you see it all very differently, Luis?'

'They're out to get Ziggy Stardust, that's for sure,' Velázquez said.

'But you still have your doubts as to whether he's your killer?'

'I'm not the kind of detective who charges a man with murder merely on hearsay,' he said. 'I happen to believe in a more modern concept of justice.'

The psychologist made a note in her pad. 'How have you been feeling about your work lately?'

'I love my job.'

'There are aspects of it that can be a pain, though, right?'

Now we're getting to it, Velázquez thought. He looked at her and didn't say anything.

'I get the impression,' she said, 'that everything isn't sweetness and light between you and Comisario Alonso. Would that be fair?'

Velázquez didn't say anything.

'How could things between you be improved, would you say?'

'Wait a minute,' the Inspector Jefe said. 'Comisario Alonso has directed you to ask me this, right? So you can trot back upstairs and tell him what a rotten employee and terrible team player I am, is that it?'

'I think you need to realize that I'm independent here.'

'But the Comisario's the one who set these sessions up.'

'That's true. But that doesn't mean he can have any say over their outcome.'

'Didn't you say in one of our previous sessions that the Comisario's threatening to put me on the sick if I don't say the right things here?'

'You still don't get it,' Ana Pelayo said. 'Comisario Alonso can and will put you on the sick, if that's what I say in my final report.'

'So it's all down to you, then?'

'That's about where we're at, yes,' she said. 'The Comisario can still take you off the case for other reasons. But insofar as whether or not you're in a fit mental state to be able to do your work, then it's my call.'

'Doesn't that give you an inordinate amount of power over me and my situation?'

'If you don't agree with my final report then you can always appeal.'

'What would that get me?'

'A second opinion.' Ana Pelayo played with her St. Christopher. 'That would mean having to undergo another course of sessions with a different psychologist, and at the end of it he or she would produce a second report. Then if you disagree with the second opinion, you could always hire a lawyer…although I wouldn't recommend that you go down that road. One officer who tried it ended up losing everything – his home, his car, his wife…and he lost his job at the end of it all, too.'

'Sounds like that would be enough to drive most people crazy.'

'But it doesn't have to be that way where you're concerned.'

'It doesn't?'

Ana Pelayo shook her head. 'I just need you to play ball and convince me you're mentally fit to do your job,' she said. 'Do that and you'll get me off your back.'

At just after five that afternoon, Velázquez's telephone rang. 'Hello?'

A woman's voice asked if it was Inspector Jefe Velázquez she was speaking to. He told her it was. 'Can I help you?'

'I'm calling to tell you about my husband, Ben Karlmann,' the woman said. 'He told me he called you this morning, and that you talked…so I thought you ought to know that he is now in the hospital in Bardino.'

'What happened to him?'

'He was attacked and badly beaten up.'

'I'm very sorry to hear that, Frau Karlmann,' Velázquez said. 'But who was it that did it?'

'I'm sure you don't need me to tell you that, Inspector.'

'Your husband mentioned that he was frightened of some of his fellow Nazis. But I don't see how they could have found out that he talked to me.'

'It seems they did. And since you've got him in this mess, perhaps you'd be kind enough to offer my husband some kind of protection?'

'I can assure you that I'll do everything in my power to make sure your husband is safe.'

'If you ask me,' she said, 'he was a fool to talk to you.' With that, she hung up.

Velázquez and Gajardo went to pay Ben Karlmann a visit in the hospital, and they found him in a bad state, just as the man's wife had said. His head was bandaged up, his arm was in a sling, and his face was a patchwork of cuts and bruises. 'So they got to you, then, Herr Karlmann,' the Inspector Jefe said.

'I'm sorry.' The man squinted at Velázquez. 'I don't think we've ever met?'

Velázquez introduced himself, then took out his ID and held it out so the man could see it. 'We spoke on the telephone this morning. Don't tell me you've forgotten?'

'I'm afraid you're mistaken, Inspector. I didn't speak to any policeman on the telephone – not this morning or at any other time.'

'Oh come on, Herr Karlmann. You told me you were living in fear for your life and it seems you were right.' Velázquez pointed to the man's arm. 'Broken, is it?'

Karlmann nodded. 'But I don't know what you're talking about,' he said. 'You must have me mixed up with someone else.'

'Who was it that beat you up – Albert Klein and his cronies?'

'Nobody beat me up, Inspector. I was hit by a car.'

'Were you really?' Velázquez shook his head in disgust. 'They really have put the fear of God into you, haven't they?'

'Goodbye, Inspector, and I do hope that you find the person you're looking for.'

'I hope you know what you're doing, Herr Karlmann.' Velázquez gestured to Gajardo and they left.

Chapter 50

Velázquez pushed the buzzer for one of the flats on the ground floor, and got them buzzed in. It was an old trick. A way of entering a building without letting the person you were going to visit know you were coming.

There was no lift, so they took the stairs. The stone steps were crumbling in places, and there were random outbursts of graffiti on the walls. It wasn't the kind of graffiti you'd want to keep or try to sell. The person they had come to see lived on the third floor. They heard music and television sets blaring out, as they walked along the hallway. The air was alive with the smells of poverty and misery. They found the door, and the Inspector Jefe rang the bell.

A pale, blonde woman in her late fifties or early sixties came and opened up. She was wearing grey slacks and a blue pullover. Velázquez introduced himself and showed her his ID. 'We've come here,' he said, 'to ask you some questions about your husband, Frau Karlmann.'

She glanced right and left, to make sure the coast was clear, then let them in. They passed through a small hallway and into the living room at the back. There was a three-piece suite done in synthetic leather, and a small television set rested in a pinewood console. On the deal dining table, by the window, was a plate with what was left of the woman's dinner on it. Sauerkraut, if Velázquez wasn't mistaken. 'Don't let us ruin your meal,' the Inspector Jefe said.

'It doesn't matter.' Her shoulders offered up a tired shrug. 'What's happened to my husband has rather taken my appetite away.' She pointed to the sofa. 'Please make yourselves at home.'

The two officers parked themselves, and Frau Karlmann sat in the easy chair. Velázquez looked at the woman. 'Perhaps you'd like to tell us a little about your husband's situation?'

'He's very frightened of that man Albert Klein, Inspector. He seems to feel that Klein's responsible for what happened to Kurt

Prall – although we have no proof of that.'

'Without evidence we won't get very far, I'm afraid.'

'But surely you must be able to do something?'

'We're doing everything within our powers to investigate the murder of Kurt Prall. That's why we are here now.'

'But you've seen what Klein and his cronies did to my husband. What if they decide to finish the job?'

'If they had meant to do that, then I'm sure he'd be in the morgue right now instead of the hospital.'

'They gave him a frightful beating. It's a miracle he's still alive.'

'He's got a broken arm, and a few cuts and bruises here and there, but I can assure you that he's going to be fine. Just give him a little time,' Velázquez said. 'Now, is there anything you can tell us about Albert Klein and his cronies?'

'They fly here from all over.'

'Yes, I know that.'

'Klein himself lives in the Grazalema mountains.'

'I already know that, too.'

Frau Karlmann looked surprised. 'You are surprisingly well informed, Inspector.'

'Do you know where exactly the man's place is?' Velázquez asked. 'The Grazalema mountain range covers a fairly large area.'

'I think Ben said it was three or four kilometres from the village of Grazalema itself. But that's all I know. I've never been there. I don't know if Ben has it written down somewhere.' She got to her feet. 'Wait a moment and I'll take a look.' Frau Karlmann left the room, then returned moments later. She had a little address book in her hand and was looking through it. 'Here it is.' She found pen and paper and copied down the entry her husband had made under Klein's name, then gave it to the Inspector Jefe.

Velázquez looked at what she had written. THE MEADOWS. NEAR GRAZALEMA VILLAGE. He thanked her for her help, then he and Gajardo hurried out to the car.

Velázquez called his mother-in-law's number and Pe picked

up. 'It's me,' he said. 'How's everything going?'

'All quiet on the western front,' Pe said. 'Mum's making herself busy in the kitchen. She's been feeding Serrano and Merino with the cakes she's made.'

'That's what I like to hear.'

'It's all right for you, but I'm going to die of boredom at this rate.'

'Hopefully it won't be for long.'

'Are you any closer to finding the killer?'

'We've had a break on the case, yes. But I'll tell you about it when I see you later.'

'I love you.'

'*Te quiero también.*'

'One thing, Luis,' she said. 'You do know I'll have to go on the show tomorrow morning.'

'But you can't, Pe.'

'I can't just not turn up. I have my viewers to think of.'

'I'm sure they've all got your best interests at heart.'

'They want to see the show, Luis.'

'The studio will have to get somebody to stand in for you.'

'But the killer's hardly going to try and kill me while I'm on national television.'

'You never know with this guy.'

'I recognize the need to show caution here, Luis. But aren't you just being a little paranoid?'

'Have you forgotten what he left on our bed?'

Pe didn't say anything.

'Sorry,' Velázquez said, 'I didn't want to remind you of it.'

'No, it's okay. I suppose you've got a point.'

'With any luck, we should be able to catch the guy before too long.'

'What about if Jorge was to go to the studio with me? And Javier could stay and keep an eye on *Mama*, in case the killer were to come here after we've left?'

Velázquez gave it some thought. 'Okay,' he said finally, 'if you must go. But Serrano is to be with you at all times. And you're to go straight back to your mother's place with him, just as soon as the show's finished and stay there.'

'Okay, I will. I promise.'

Velázquez told Pe he wanted to speak to Serrano, and she put the phone down and went to call him.

When the Agente came on, Velázquez explained the revised plan for the following morning. 'And don't leave her out of your sight for a second, do you understand, Jorge?'

'Of course, boss.'

'This guy has already broken into our home and left a bull's horn on our bed,' Velázquez said. 'And you hardly need me to tell you what he did to Gelens and Juanito de la Torre.'

'I hear what you're saying.'

'Just don't relax your guard, the pair of you.'

'It'll be okay, boss. Don't worry.'

Velázquez crossed his fingers as he told Serrano he wanted to speak to Pe again. And when she came back on the line, he told her that he'd call again the next day, after she'd returned from the studio. 'Have a good night.'

'You, too.'

They hung up.

Chapter 51

First thing the following morning, Velázquez and Gajardo made enquiries in the village of Grazalema regarding the whereabouts of Albert Klein's property, and the Inspector Jefe finally found a postman who was able to give them directions. The man assured them that the German lived only a short drive away.

The two officers climbed back into Velázquez's Alfa Romeo and set off. Just a few minutes later, they saw a property some seventy or eighty metres further up the road. 'That must be it, boss,' Gajardo said.

'I think you're right, José.' Velázquez killed the lights of the car and slowed to a crawl. Then he pulled over, still a little way down the road from the house. He and Gajardo climbed out of the car and set off on foot.

The property was a large, sprawling building with a pitched roof, and a hedge separating the land that surrounded the property from the narrow mountain road. The gate creaked as Gajardo opened it, and Velázquez gestured with his hand to tell his number two to go round the back.

The Inspector Jefe gave Gajardo time to get into position before he went and rang the doorbell. He waited a short while and then rang it again.

Nobody came to open up. But then he heard a noise coming from the back of the house and set off.

When Velázquez got round there, he found his number two lying on the concrete. He shook Gajardo's arm and the Subinspector opened his eyes. 'Where is he, José?'

Gajardo made an inarticulate growling noise.

'Klein?' Velázquez said. 'Where did he go?'

Gajardo blinked and came to his senses. 'Dunno, boss,' he said. 'I didn't see anything…something hit me on the head.'

Velázquez saw a shattered vase on the concrete. And looking up, he could see that the upstairs window was open. Klein had clearly dropped the vase from above.

Just then, it occurred to Velázquez that Klein might have made his exit through the front door, and he set off up the narrow path that ran along the side of the house. No sooner had the Inspector Jefe got to the end of the path than a shot rang out. Then he saw a tall, strong-looking man with blond hair…it was Klein…and he was making for the Range Rover parked in the driveway.

Velázquez raised his gun and fired, then heard the bullet ricochet off the bodywork of the Range Rover. He fired again and missed Klein a second time.

He shat in the milk.

But at least the wayward shots he'd fired served to force Klein to reject the idea of trying to climb in behind the wheel of the Range Rover, and instead he ran out through the gate at the end of the driveway.

Velázquez fired another shot but missed, as Klein disappeared out of sight, and the Inspector Jefe went after him.

Once he was out in the road, the Inspector Jefe had Klein in his sights. The German was running at full pelt. Velázquez fired a couple of shots at him and missed. Klein got as far as where Velázquez's Alfa Romeo was parked and stopped. The Inspector Jefe had a horrible sinking feeling as he realized that in his hurry he'd left the door of the vehicle unlocked. Not only that but he'd left the keys in the ignition.

He fired again on the run, and missed, as Klein climbed into the car.

He fired more shots, but missed each time.

Then he fired again and hit metal.

Realizing that firing on the run wasn't bringing him much success, he stopped and took proper aim. But when he fired nothing happened. *Damn.* His gun was out of ammunition.

He started running again, but could only watch as Klein revved the engine up, then set off with a great screech of rubber on tarmac.

Velázquez could have kicked himself.

Then again, how was he to know that Klein was going to do a runner like that?

Moments later, Gajardo appeared at his side. 'The crafty

bastard,' the Subinspector said. 'How did he manage to give us the slip like that?'

'You just said it, José – the man's a crafty bastard.'

'What I don't get, boss, is why he made a run for it like that.'

'I wasn't expecting that either, José.' Velázquez gave the matter some thought. 'Perhaps it was him that killed Prall, and he figures we must have more on him than we actually do.'

'That's possible, I suppose.'

'It might explain why Ben Karlmann is now lying in a hospital bed.'

Velázquez continued to chew the matter over. 'Who knows, he might even have Jews on his trail, trying to take him to court for crimes he perpetrated back in the war.'

The Inspector Jefe's Alfa Romeo Sport Coupé was found in Bardino later that morning, but there was no sign of Albert Klein.

The German Eagle had flown the coop.

Chapter 52

When he got back to the Jefatura, Velázquez briefed the rest
of his team on what they had missed. He skipped over the bit
where Klein outwitted him and Gajardo, then stole his car and
made his getaway in it.

If he had told his team that then they would have wanted to
know how Klein managed to get into the vehicle and then start
the engine up so quickly, without the keys. In order to answer
that, Velázquez would have had to confess to them that he had
left the car unlocked…and with the keys in the ignition.

But he wasn't going to tell them any of that. Jesus, the officers
in his team would take him for an idiot.

And Amaya Pelayo would no doubt have a field day with
information of that sort. She would probably stick it in her
report, and then it would get back to Comisario Alonso and the
Comisario would reckon he finally had just cause to take him
off the case.

It had been a stupid mistake to make all right, and the
Inspector Jefe could have kicked himself for it. But everyone
was allowed to cock up from time to time. And besides, he'd
been in a hurry.

Not only that, but he'd had no real reason to expect Klein to
do a runner like that.

Even so, it was one of those episodes that he and Gajardo had
agreed to keep to themselves and put down to experience. José
might not be the most imaginative of Subinspectors, but
Velázquez knew that the man always had his back. And that was
what mattered most.

When the Inspector Jefe had finished giving the team his
abbreviated version of what took place earlier that morning,
Merino asked him what exactly he suspected this man Albert
Klein of doing.

Velázquez explained how the link between the latest victim,
Kurt Prall, and Arjan Gelens was that they were both Nazis. He
told about how Alfonso de la Torre had sympathised with the

Nazi cause, having been an ardent Franquista before the General died, and how the bullfighter and Gelens had also been involved in a homosexual relationship.

Sara Pérez wondered about Mohammed Haddad.

Velázquez shrugged and said all they knew for sure about Haddad was that he had given financial backing to a lot of bullfights. Although seeing he was an Arab, it was highly likely that he might have found common cause with the other three victims in their hatred of Jews.

Pérez didn't get it. Was the Inspector Jefe saying that a Nazi had killed two other Nazis, a Spaniard who sympathized with the Nazis, and an Arab they suspected of being anti-Semitic, simply because...of what...? Wasn't the only thing the victims had in common, according to this latest theory, *that all three of them hated Jews?*

Velázquez explained that Klein was a typical Nazi in his hatred of homosexuals, and how this would have given him a plausible motive for wanting to get rid of Arjan Gelens and Alfonso de la Torre. After the rise of Hitler in 1933, the Inspector Jefe reminded his team, the Nazis began killing all of the homosexuals in their party.

As for Kurt Prall, the man had been suffering with a bad conscience on account of certain atrocities he was forced to perpetrate under Klein's orders, back in their Mauthausen days. He suffered panic attacks and was seeing a lady psychotherapist in Bardino, and it so happened that Klein was romantically involved with the same woman.

Pérez wondered if she had understood this correctly. Was the Inspector Jefe making the assumption that Prall's shrink would've shared what he told her with Klein?

Velázquez told her he suspected that might well be so.

Jorge Serrano supposed they were talking about human rights abuses in the form of torture and so on?

Velázquez nodded and told the team how Mauthausen was one of the worst of the concentration camps because it was where the political prisoners were sent. Nobody was meant to leave the place alive. It was standard practice to lead prisoners, who were kept on a starvation diet, to their death by forcing them to perform pointless physical activities beyond the point of exhaustion.

Sara Pérez said she could see how Klein might have had a motive to want to kill Prall. Presumably he would have feared being linked to human rights abuses himself, if Prall had spilt the beans to the press.

She could also see that he might have had a motive to kill Gelens and de la Torre, given the fact they were both thought to be homosexuals. But she still couldn't understand why the man should have wanted to get rid of Mohammed Haddad.

Velázquez figured it was always possible Haddad might have got wind of what was happening. Or perhaps he had seen or overheard something that would have incriminated Klein.

Jorge Serrano said in any case it wasn't like they needed to link Klein to all four murders at this stage. Just one of them would be enough. Velázquez agreed. If they could tie Klein to one of the murders then with any luck the rest of what happened and why would come out in the wash.

The important thing now, the Inspector Jefe said, was to find Klein.

Javi Merino asked how they were supposed to do that.

Velázquez said they could start by calling the airports and ports.

Pérez wondered whether a man with his connections might be carrying a false passport.

Velázquez said that was also a possibility. They should give the people they were speaking to a physical description of the man. Klein was in his sixties, but was still surprisingly fit and athletic for his age. He had blond hair, and was tall and of powerful build. He spoke Spanish with a German accent. He also spoke English.

With any luck, he had not yet been successful in leaving the country.

They would have to divide the work up. Velázquez said he wanted Sara to concentrate on Málaga airport. Javi could help her. Jorge should call the port at Algeciras and José, Tarifa.

Any questions? No? In that case, get cracking everyone.

The officers all picked up their telephones and started making calls.

Velázquez sat at his desk and was about to pick up the phone when it rang. '*Hola?*' he said into the receiver. He felt his heart sink as Comisario Alonso started to bark down the line at him. He said that he had heard a 'silly rumour' to the effect that Alfonso de la Torre was *gay*.

What was more, the Mayor had to read about it in the morning newspapers, and he was furious. *Gay bullfighters*? What *tonterias!* Just think of the effect this could have on the bullfighting public. Not to mention the tourist industry. *Por cojones!*

The Comisario warned Velázquez that he'd better pull his finger out and arrest and charge the killer or else he was in for a 'rude awakening'. 'I don't take kindly to having top bullfighters murdered in the most brutal and unseemly fashion. Particularly when it's on my watch. Do you hear? And then to have them calumniated after they're dead is just too much, Inspector,' the man said. 'You're fast turning your Department and this entire city into a laughing stock.'

'But Comisario – '

'Everyone knows it's the victim's boyfriend that was behind the first murder,' Comisario Alonso said. 'The Mayor knows it, too. And he's just called me to ask why he's got to read what he and everyone else knows in the newspapers. Don't you read what they're all saying, *hombre*? Everyone is agreed that the vet's murder is an open and shut case if there ever was one. Yet you persist in refusing to charge the obvious suspect.'

And before the Inspector Jefe could say a word in response, Comisario Alonso slammed the phone down.

Gajardo looked over. 'Who was that, boss?'

'Just the Comisario calling to tell me how much he loves me.' Velázquez's craggy face creased in a rueful smile. 'Every now and then the man finds he just can't contain himself any more. So he gives in to the romantic urge to pick up the phone and warble a few sweet nothings down the line. Bless him.'

'Aren't you the lucky one, boss.'

Velázquez drove over to the Forensics lab on Avenida del

Doctor Fedriani, where his friend Juan Gómez was at work cutting up the body of Alfonso de la Torre. 'Take a good look, Luis,' he said, 'and see for yourself how we all end up.' He smiled. 'A sobering thought, isn't it?'

'Hopefully our own deaths won't be quite so messy, Juan.'

'What I meant was –'

'I know what you meant,' Velázquez cut the Médico Forense off. 'The lesson to be learned from mortality and all that. It's what you say when you haven't got anything else for me,' he said. 'I need to know whether Alfonso was killed where his body was found, or whether he was killed elsewhere and the body was moved to the crime scene.'

'I should have an answer to that by tomorrow,' Gómez said. 'How's Pe? I hope you're treating my favorite TV presenter well.'

'I'm doing my best, Juan.' Velázquez was making for the door. 'Call me if you turn anything up, okay?'

'Don't I always?'

Velázquez stopped off in a café, and had the waiter bring him the newspaper with his coffee in a glass and a ham roll. And the Inspector Jefe was disgusted to find that *Sevilla Hoy* had run yet another blistering attack on him and his team.

His reporter friend Tere Bernales had clearly failed to rein in the witch who was covering the investigation.

Velázquez figured Tere's editor must have spiked her piece. She had warned him that might happen.

The whole business stank to high heaven.

According to the crime reporter in *Sevilla Hoy*, Klaus Bloem was 'clearly responsible for the brutal murder of the famous *torero*, Alfonso de la Torre'. This, she argued, was 'made all the more obvious given that the killer had used the same *modus operandi* in killing both the bullfighter and Arjan Gelens'.

It was, the witch went on, 'greatly to be lamented that while the simple facts of the case were staring Inspector Jefe Velázque in the face, he was clearly incapable of discerning what was right under his own nose.' She went on to say that 'the city of Seville now found itself living in fear of a monster of the worst kind whose identity was known to all and sundry, with the single exception of the man whose job it was to investigate the murders'.

What was more, the reporter was able to inform her readers that she had 'exclusive information that went right to the heart of the workings of the local police force and the investigation itself'. A source of hers that was close to the Jefatura 'had revealed that the public of Seville were not the only ones to doubt Inspector Jefe Velázquez's professionalism, or indeed his sanity. Because the man's superior officer, Comisario Alonso, had insisted on having him attend a series of sessions with Police Psychologist, Ana Pelayo.'

To cut a story short, the reporter found it difficult to understand why Velázquez had not yet been relieved of his duties. What's more, she was sure that her readers shared her concern and dismay. Because only when Velázquez was replaced by someone who possessed the wherewithal to make an arrest, could the citizens of Seville sleep safely in their beds once more.

The reporter then spent the next couple of paragraphs talking about how serial killers liked to personalize their work by going in for highly individualised ways of murdering their victims.

These psychopaths, she went on, were every bit as intelligent as they were insane, and each one left his 'signature' on his work, much in the way that Goya or Picasso had personalized their paintings.

Velázquez ripped the pages that had so offended his sense of justice and personal honour from the newspaper and tore them up into tiny bits.

When he had finished, he folded what was left of the newspaper neatly and set it down on the vacant table next to his.

He saw that the waiter who was standing nearby had watched what he'd just done. Velázquez locked eyes with him and asked for the bill.

The man shrugged and went off to the bar to get it.

Chapter 53

Back at the Jefatura, Velázquez asked Gajardo if Juan Muñoz's prints had been sent off yet? The Subinspector said he would look into it and went off.

Some twenty minutes later, Agente Pérez came in looking excited about something or other. Before Velázquez could ask her what she was looking so cheerful about, the telephone on his desk rang. It was Gajardo, calling him to say he'd just had Juan Muñoz's prints sent over for analysis. They hung up, and the Inspector Jefe turned to look at Pérez. 'So what's new, Sara?'

'I've dug up something interesting, boss.' She reached into the pocket of her leather jacket and brought out a photograph.

Velázquez looked at it. The face didn't mean anything to him.

'His name's Javier Roman, or Javier to his friends,' Pérez said. 'He's from Macarena born and bred. And he has an interesting story that might just have a bearing on the investigation.'

'I'm all ears.'

'It turns out the man volunteered at the age of sixteen to fight with the Republicans in the Civil War,' Pérez said, 'and he ended up fighting in the Battle of the Ebro. Things went badly for his battalion and he was left with no alternative but to flee over the border into France along with his fellow soldiers, to escape from Franco's troops. The Vichy French got hold of him and before he knew it he was in Saint-Cyprien, a French concentration camp.

'As you probably know, a lot of the Republicans sent their children to France, thinking they were getting them out of harm's way, and they experienced a similar fate. They wouldn't necessarily have been treated badly there, but food would've been scarce. Most of the children were safely returned to their families in Spain after the war, even though some of them were perilously thin and perhaps close to starvation.

'But Javier Roman wasn't a child by that time. Or if he was

then he was one who'd fought in the Battle of the Ebro, which probably explains why he was treated differently. Because he was handed over to the Nazis, and moved on from one camp to another, until he finally ended up in Mauthausen, where he had the misfortune to come up against one Rainer Altenburg – otherwise known as Doctor Death. He injected Javier Roman, and others who were also used as guinea pigs, with Benzedrine.'

'What was the point of that?' Velázquez asked.

'None whatsoever, so far as I can make out,' Pérez said. 'Doctor Death just wanted to see if they could take it or not. Of course, many of them couldn't.'

'Some doctor.'

'But Javier Roman sounds like he must've been a pretty tough cookie. He was one of thirty people used as guinea pigs, and only he and six others survived.'

'How do you know all this?'

'I turned up an old newspaper article, boss, and it was all in there,' she said. 'There's even been a book written about him, although I've not yet had time to read it. Anyway, Javier Roman survives life in the camp, and things start to get really interesting after the war when he goes to Hamburg to work as a builder and comes across the doctor again.'

'Bit of a coincidence, wasn't it?'

'Altenburg had his own practice in Hamburg, and Javier Roman happened to've gone there to work.'

Velázquez pondered the matter a moment, and figured it probably wasn't necessarily such a big coincidence after all. Any number of Spaniards went to work in Germany after the Second World War ended, when Germany needed labourers and jobs were thin on the ground in Spain. Why, Velázquez had two uncles who had gone over to Hamburg to work at that time, and one of them was still living there. Practically everyone Velázquez knew had a family member or friend who'd worked somewhere in Germany. And it was in the big cities that workers were needed: places like Berlin and Hamburg...

'Apparently,' Pérez said, 'Javier Roman fell from a wall he'd been working on and sprained his wrist. That's why he needed to see a doctor.'

Velázquez nodded. 'So what happened when he saw who it was?'

'This is where the trail gets murky, boss. Javier Roman maintains that he saw the doctor and recognized him, and that he was so terrified he dashed from the surgery and never returned.'

'He must've told people who it was he'd seen, though, right?'

Pérez shook her head. 'Roman didn't tell anyone about what happened to him in the concentration camp, or about the fact that he'd seen the doctor in his surgery in Hamburg.'

'Bit odd, isn't it?' Velázquez said. 'You'd think he'd have screamed about it from the rooftops. I know I would have.'

'Perhaps he was traumatized.'

'Okay, so then what?'

'Javier Roman returns to Spain, where a journalist hears about his case and gets interested in him.'

Velázquez looked confused. 'But how would this journalist have heard about what happened to Roman at the hands of Doctor Death if the man never talked about it?'

'The journalist was writing a piece on the Battle of the Ebro, and he'd been talking to other survivors.'

'And one of them mentioned Javier Roman?'

'Exactly, so the journalist tracks him down. And when he talks to him he learns that he not only fought in the Battle of the Ebro, but also ended up being used as a guinea pig in Mauthausen.'

'So Roman finally broke his silence about the concentration camp?'

'That's right.'

'The poor man sounds like he must've been through a lot.'

'And some. So anyway, the journalist starts to get ideas about writing a book on our Javier, because there's too much material here for him to go wasting it on a single newspaper article. So the journalist has a contract drawn up, which he gets Javier to sign. And he tells him that the book's going to make them both rich. Who knows, it might even get made into a film. First, though, in order for him to be able to write it properly, he needs Javier to go back to Germany with him, to revisit some of his old haunts. That way, it will help the journalist to describe it all better and make it seem more lifelike.'

'So Javier goes there with him?'

'He sure does, in sixty-three – and all at the journalist's expense.'

'And don't tell me – he bumps into Doctor Death again while he's there?'

'Maybe he does and maybe he doesn't, that's the thing.'

'Huh?'

'Javier Roman denies having set eyes on the man during this second visit. But then he has good reason to do so.'

'Which is?'

'Doctor Death was brutally murdered while Javier Roman was visiting Hamburg with the journalist, and to cut a long story short Roman was accused of the murder. He claims he was stitched up, and says that the German police failed to investigate the case properly, once they learned of his being in the city.'

'I don't get it,' Velázquez said. 'How would the German police have known about him?'

'That he was there in Hamburg, you mean?'

'His being there, yes, for one thing. But not just that – how would they have made the connection between the doctor and Roman? How would they have known Roman had been one of the doctor's guinea pigs?'

'They wouldn't have, under normal circumstances. But the journalist was busy while they were in Hamburg trying to drum up a little advance publicity for the book.'

'Before he'd even written it?'

'This was a man who was used to dashing off stories quickly every day working as a journalist – and he knew a thing or two about how to generate publicity as well. Besides, time was of the essence. Anyway, he went on television and on the radio, and talked about it in interviews and basically appealed to anyone who'd known or ever met Javier Roman at Mauthausen to come forward, so that he could put their stories and recollections in the book, too.

'So the media appearances served a dual purpose, in that, as well as publicizing the book before he'd actually written it, he was also hoping that people might contact him with information and anecdotes that he could include in the work.'

'And while all this was going on, Doctor Death gets dead?'

'*Correcto.*'

'And everyone points the finger at Javier Roman?'

'That's right, and poor Javier was sent to prison for a ten year sentence before he knew what hit him.'

'And are you saying he still maintains he didn't kill the doctor?'

'Apparently.'

Velázquez straightened up. 'Where's Javier Roman now?'

'Unless I'm very much mistaken, it seems he's living quietly in Macarena.'

'Maybe we should go and talk to him.'

'That's just what I was thinking, boss.'

'Have you got his address, Sara?'

'I sure have.'

'Great work.' Velázquez was making for the door. 'We'll take my car.'

Chapter 54

They parked outside of the building where Javier Roman lived, on Rayo de Luna, then climbed out of the car and went over to the block of flats. Velázquez pushed the buzzer on the console. It took a while, but then a man's voice said, '*Hola*?'

'Are you Señor Roman?'

'That's right.'

'I'm Inspector Jefe Velázquez, Jefe de Homicidio in Seville.'

'Oh. What's happened?'

'I need to talk to you, *señor*,' Velázquez said. 'Can we come up?'

Roman buzzed them in, and they climbed the stairs to the third floor. Javier Roman was standing in the doorway to his flat, waiting for them. A man of slight build, his nose was ruddy with broken veins and a long scar ran down his cheek, ending just to the side of his left eye. He certainly looked like he'd lived a hard life, although it was difficult for Velázquez to imagine that this man standing before him had endured all the things that Pérez told him about. Perhaps that was only because it was difficult to imagine *anyone* going through all that. The man was wearing baggy grey trousers and a light-blue cotton shirt, the top button of which was undone. His cheeks were hollowed out, and he looked like he could have done with a shave. But whatever the Benzedrine that Doctor Death had injected him with did to him, Javier Roman appeared to have survived the ordeal with his faculties intact. Velázquez said, '*Buenas tardes*,' before he introduced himself and Sara Pérez. 'As I explained on the intercom, we would like to talk to you.' The Inspector Jefe produced his ID and held it out for the man to take a look at.

'I suppose you'd better come in.'

'*Gracias*.'

The man turned and they followed him into a narrow hallway and on through a door at the end, into a small living room. The television was on loud, some talk show, and Javier Roman turned it off.

The room was simple and bare, almost to the point of resembling a cell, but it was clean enough. There was a rug down over the tiled floor, and a couple of large black-and-white photographs had been mounted in glass on the wall: one of a man and the other of a woman. Seeing that Agente Pérez was looking at them, Javier Roman said, 'Those are of my mother and father.'

He came and sat in the imitation-leather easy chair. Over his shoulder, the sash window was open and the sun poured into the room, along with the sound of traffic and voices. 'I never married,' the man said. 'So they're the only family I've ever had, apart from my two brothers. And they're all dead now.'

'I'm sorry,' Pérez said.

'It's not your fault.' He waved a hand in the general direction of the sofa. 'Rest your legs, the pair of you.'

Velázquez and Pérez parked themselves.

'So,' Roman said. 'What's the purpose of your visit?'

'We happened to hear about what happened to you in Germany after the war,' Velázquez said. 'Actually it was my colleague here, Agente Pérez, who told me about it.'

'Yes,' Pérez said, 'I found some old newspaper articles about you.'

'Did you now?' Javier Roman's face creased in a smile that seemed to have a fair amount of sadness in it. 'They put me in prison for ten years for something I never did. But I served my time, and now it's all over and done with. So I don't see why you're wanting to talk to me.'

Velázquez smiled. 'You have no reason to be concerned, Señor Roman. We aren't here to cause any more trouble for you. We're investigating some Nazi revivalists who are living in the area, and we were wondering if you might be able to give us some background?'

'I'll do my best.'

'Good. So perhaps I can begin, then, with this man you were accused of murdering, Rainer Altenburg – or Doctor Death, as he was called,' Velázquez said. 'What do you know about him?'

'Apart from the fact that he was a vicious sadist, you mean?' Javier Roman frowned. 'Not a lot, really. But why do you ask?'

'Have you any idea who might have killed him?'

'None at all.' The old man shrugged. 'Why should I? I'm not a policeman,' he said. 'It was all a big mystery to me, and remains one to this day.'

'How old was the doctor when you were in the concentration camp?'

'He was a young man,' Roman said. 'I'd say he would've been around twenty-six or twenty-eight at most.' He shook his head. 'I should imagine he must have had a brilliant mind, to of been in the position he had at that age. It's so sad to think that a man with the ability to cure people should choose to behave as he did.'

'Did he ever talk to you?'

'No, we were no more than worthless objects so far as he was concerned…just things to be experimented on.' Javier Roman's face assumed an intense expression as he made an attempt to remember. 'He was a typical Nazi. You know, blond hair and blue eyes. Hitler would've loved him. He was tall and slim, but had quite broad shoulders, I remember. And he often used to hum tunes. I didn't know what the music was at the time, but I hummed it to someone who knew about German music years later and they told me it was Mozart.'

'Is there anything else that you remember about him?'

'No,' Roman said. 'I remember the injections and how terrible they'd make me feel each time. Most of the others who were injected along with me died, but somehow I managed to get through it all. Don't ask me how.'

Velázquez and Pérez exchanged glances, then the Inspector Jefe said, 'Does the name Kurt Prall mean anything to you?'

Roman shrugged. 'No, I can't say it does.'

'What about Arjan Gelens?'

The man shook his head. 'No…but what's all this about exactly?'

'Gelens was a vet,' Velázquez said. 'He used to look after the bulls at the Maestranza bullring, among other things.'

'I never was one for the *toros*.'

Velázquez reached into his pocket and brought out the photographs of Gelens and Prall. 'Perhaps if you wouldn't mind taking a look at these?'

Javier Roman took the photographs from the Inspector Jefe's outstretched hand. No sooner had he looked at them than a change came over him. He straightened in his chair, then squinted and brought first one photo then the other up closer to his face, to get a better look.

He studied the photographs for some time, and Velázquez had the feeling that the images were stirring up painful memories in Roman.

Finally he handed the photographs back. 'What did you say their names were again?'

'This one's Kurt Prall.' Velázquez held up one of the photographs. 'The other's Arjan Gelens, a Dutch vet.'

Javier Roman shook his head. 'I knew the one you're calling Prall as Hans Graf, and the other one's Franz Hauptmann. They were both guards at Mauthausen.'

Velázquez had already learned from Frau Prall that her husband was christened with the name of Hans Graf, but hearing Roman say the man's original name served as proof that he was able to identify the ex-camp guard.

The Inspector Jefe didn't know that Arjan Gelens had gone under the name of Franz Hauptmann during his time at Mauthausen, though. This was one of several details that Ans Gelens had omitted from her account of her brother's past.

'Are you quite sure?'

'Totally positive.' Roman nodded. 'Hauptmann wasn't too bad a man, as Nazis go. But Graf was a vicious sadist. He made us do all sorts of stupid exercises until we were fit to drop. If you stopped, he'd whip you.' He sighed. 'There's nothing like the threat of twenty lashes on your bare back to make you keep going.'

'When was the last time you saw these two men?'

'Just before the war ended.'

'They've both been murdered recently.'

'Have they now?' Roman shrugged. 'I can't say I'm sorry.'

'I don't suppose you'd know anything about it?'

'Not a thing…where were they killed?'

'Hauptmann was killed in his flat in Seville, and Graf was shot in his home outside of Bardino.'

Javier Roman looked stunned. 'You don't say those two bastards were living near here all this time?'

'You mean you didn't know?'

Roman shook his head. 'It's the first I've heard of it.'

Velázquez exchanged glances with Pérez. The Inspector Jefe got to his feet. 'Thank you so much for your time, Señor Roman,' he said. 'What you've told us has been most helpful.'

With that Velázquez and Pérez went out. The sun's rays were really beating down as they hurried back to the Inspector Jefe's Alfa Romeo and set off along Rayo de Luna. 'What did you make of Javier Roman?'

'He seemed like a nice chap to me, boss,' Pérez said. 'I feel sorry for him, I must say.'

'I know what you mean.' Velázquez stopped for a red light. 'It just shows that in this world you can go through what that poor man's endured, and end up living alone in a tiny flat on the third floor of a shoddy block of flats without a lift in Macarena.'

They drove in silence for a while. Then as they crossed the river, Pérez said, 'Now what, boss?'

'How do you fancy calling the police in Hamburg and seeing what you can find out about the case Javier Roman was involved in, Sara?'

'I can't speak German.'

'Speak English, don't you?'

'Reasonably well.'

'In that case, you know what you've got to do, then,' Velázquez said, as he turned into Juan Cruz.

Chapter 55

When he got back to the Jefatura, Velázquez called Ans Gelens and told her he'd just been speaking to one Javier Roman. 'I'm afraid the name means nothing to me, Inspector.'

'No, it probably wouldn't, Ans,' the Inspector Jefe said. 'But he knew your brother. And he knew his friend Kurt Prall – or Hans Graf, to give him his real name.'

He listened to her breathing down the line. 'He knew Arjan under a different name, too. Does the name Franz Hauptmann mean anything to you?'

Still Ans Gelens failed to say anything. 'Perhaps I can give your memory a jog. It was your brother's name back in the days he served as a guard at Mauthausen concentration camp.'

'I'm sorry, Inspector,' she said finally.

'Why didn't you tell me about this, Ans?'

'I told you as much as I felt you needed to know,' she said. 'You have to understand it's very painful for me to talk about these things. It's a shameful family secret that I have come to live with.'

'Was Arjan even Dutch?'

'He was one of many Dutchmen who served the Nazi cause,' Ans Gelens said. 'He got out of Europe at the end of the war with the help of a Catholic priest...Hulda or Hudal, I think the priest's name was. Arjan wasn't the only one to get out via the Vatican escape route. They dressed him in a monk's habit and took him to Rome, where they hid him in a monastery until such time as they were able to procure a passport for him from the International Red Cross.

'They even bought him his flight ticket to Buenos Aires and gave him some money to go with. Years passed and Arjan decided to come back to Europe. He'd changed his name to Franz Hauptmann when he joined the Nazis, but he took back his real name by birth – Arjan Gelens – on his return. He stayed in Holland for a while and then moved to fascist Spain, where he felt safe and happy – for a while, at any rate...'

'Thanks for your honesty, Ans,' Velázquez said and hung up.

Minutes later, Pérez called him. 'Hi, boss,' she said, 'I've struck gold in Germany.'

'Let's hear it.'

'I got onto the lawyer that represented Javier Roman in the murder case in Hamburg. He told me that Roman was convicted on what he considered at the time, and still considers to be, shaky circumstantial evidence.'

'I can't say I'm surprised about that.'

'No, but there's more,' Pérez said. 'It turns out that Doctor Death was gay, and had been living with a younger man for a couple of years, up until just before the time of his death. It seems he broke up with his younger lover and kicked him out, and the younger man was distraught and threatened to kill Altenburg if he didn't take him back.'

'So Javier Roman's lawyer tried without success to deflect suspicion onto Altenburg's spurned younger lover?'

'Exactly,' she said. 'But the really interesting part is the identity of the spurned younger lover. His name was Ernst Stachel, and he was twenty-seven at the time of the murder trial in sixty-three...But I did a little research, boss, and it turns out that Stachel changed his name and then moved to Spain.'

Velázquez said, 'Don't tell me he changed it to Klaus Bloem?'

'You got it in one.'

The Inspector Jefe was experiencing a rush of adrenaline. 'I'm going to Bloem's place now to arrest him.'

Chapter 56

Within forty minutes, they had Klaus Bloem back in Incident Room 1. Velázquez looked the man in the eye and said, 'I'm charging you, Klaus Bloem, with the murder of Arjan Gelens and Alfonso de la Torre.'

'But I didn't do it,' the German said.

'Anything you say may be used in evidence against you.'

'I didn't do it, I tell you. You've got the wrong person.'

'If you play ball with us now, Klaus, it will be better for you later,' Velázquez said. 'The Judge will take it into account when sentencing you.'

'I want to speak to my lawyer.'

'We've called him and he's on his way. But he won't be able to prevent us from charging you.'

'It's the widow, I tell you.'

'We know it was you, Klaus,' Velázquez said. 'We know rather a lot about you, as it happens... Or should we call you Ernst?' He saw the surprise in the German's eyes. 'Ernst Stachel is your real name, isn't it?'

'What?'

'Remember Rainer Altenburg?' Velázquez cranked out a false smile. 'Yes, of course you do. You loved him, too, didn't you?'

'That's got nothing to do with this,' Bloem said. 'I want my lawyer, and I'm not saying another word until you get him here.'

'He used people as guinea pigs during his time at Mauthausen.'

'Mauthausen?' Klaus Bloem looked confused. 'What's this all about?'

'The concentration camp.' The Inspector Jefe could see that what he was saying now was all news to Bloem. 'Didn't Rainer tell you about that? He was rather a star performer there, Klaus.'

Velázquez paused to allow what he had just said to sink in.

'Of course he would've been much younger then than he was when you knew him.'

'What are you talking about?'

'As I say, he used to do tests on people.'

Bloem looked like he was unsure whether to believe what he was being told. 'What sort of tests?'

'He injected Benzedrine into people, just to see what it did to them.'

'This is all bullshit.'

'We've been talking to a man who was one of your beloved Rainer Altenburg's guinea pigs, as it turns out. He's one of the lucky ones who survived and is currently living in Seville. Only a small number survived the ordeal.' Velázquez looked Bloem in the eye. 'So much for your beloved Rainer. I'm afraid I don't think Javier Roman, the man I was just telling you about, would be prepared to give him a very good character reference.'

Bloem's expression was a curious mixture of horror and disbelief. 'The man lied to you.'

'He was otherwise known as Doctor Death,' Velázquez said. 'But you loved him.'

'Rainer wouldn't have done anything like that – it's all lies.'

'We're talking about historical fact, Klaus. There were witnesses. And lots of them.'

Klaus Bloem dropped his face into his hands, and his shoulders began to judder as sobs racked his body.

Velázquez exchanged glances with Agente Pérez. 'It's okay, Klaus,' Sara said. 'Nobody's blaming you for Rainer Altenburg's war crimes.'

Bloem lifted his head. His eyes were wet and puffy with tears. 'He never told me about any of that.'

'No, well he wouldn't, would he?' Velázquez paused for a moment as he considered how best to proceed. 'You lived with him for a couple of years and you loved him, Klaus, isn't that right?'

'Yes, I loved him.'

'It would be difficult for most people to see what anyone could find so attractive in a man like that.'

'Rainer never showed me that side of his personality,' Bloem said. 'With me he was kind, considerate and sensitive – at least to begin with…until he began to lose interest in me.' Bloem dried his eyes with his hands. 'He was much older than me, which might've put some people off, but I was attracted to older men. I suppose I wanted a father figure. I needed someone who was mature and experienced, and Rainer had those qualities.

'Besides, he was what I suppose you'd call highborn – from an upper middle class family, you know. And he had all the airs and graces you'd expect from somebody of his background and position. He was cultured and knew lots of things, while I was young, working class and relatively ignorant. I suppose Rainer was attracted to me because of my youth and energy, while I was attracted to him for the reasons I've just described.'

'Then he dumped you?'

'Yes.'

'That must've been hard to bear.'

'Yes, it was.'

Velázquez nodded, then said, 'And the fact that he kicked you out of what had become your home must've rubbed salt into the wound.'

'I had a job at that time, so it wasn't as though I ended up on the streets.'

'But you loved him and he betrayed you.'

'Yes.'

'And so you killed him.'

'No.'

'How do you feel about the fact that another man was sent down for the crime you committed, Klaus?'

'I didn't kill him.'

'The man I'm telling you about served ten years in a German prison.'

'That's got nothing to do with me.'

'It should've been you that got sent down, not him.'

'I didn't do it, I tell you.'

'Another man was wrongly convicted of Altenburg's murder, just because he happened to be in Hamburg at the time. And because people found out that he was one of Altenburg's guinea pigs in Mauthausen.' Velázquez scratched his chin. 'How do you feel about that, Klaus?'

'I didn't kill Rainer. I loved him.'

'And then, years later, you fell in love with another older man, here in Seville, didn't you?'

'I loved Arjan, too, yes.'

'Once again you fell in love with a Nazi...'

'He never talked to me about politics,' Klaus Bloem said. 'But whatever his political ideas were, I can't see how it's got anything to do with this case.'

'Arjan was also a guard at Mauthausen concentration camp as it happens. Only he went under the name of Franz Hauptmann in those days.'

'You've got the wrong man.'

'I don't think so,' Velázquez said. 'What about Hans Graf?'

'Who?'

'He's been murdered, too.'

'I don't know any Hans Graf.'

'He changed his name to Kurt Prall.'

'I've never heard of him.'

'He knew your boyfriend from the time when they were guards at Mauthausen.'

'I don't believe a word of it.'

'I've got a witness.'

'Your witness is lying.'

'I don't think so,' Velázquez said. 'You thought you'd found someone you could trust in Franz or Arjan, and you loved him, didn't you? But he began to lose interest in you, just as Rainer Altenburg had years earlier.'

'I see where you're going with this, Inspector, but you're wrong,' Bloem said. 'You think I killed Rainer and Arjan for the same reason.'

'Why don't you confess now, Klaus, and save us all a lot of bother?'

'I'm not confessing to any crimes I didn't commit – and that's the last thing I'm going to say to you without my lawyer being present.'

'Okay, Klaus, your lawyer's on his way, as I've already told you. But he won't be able to help you this time.'

Bloem ran a hand through his tousled locks, as he appeared to consider the situation he found himself in. 'All right, you win,' he said finally, 'I'll tell you what really happened. All of it, okay?'

Velázquez nodded.

'The night when I was attacked, I was in bed at my flat when a man broke in. He was wearing a balaclava. That part of what I told you before was true. But what I didn't tell you is that I was in bed with Alfonso de la Torre at the time. Arjan and had a few threesomes with Alfonso making up the third person, as I've already told you in an earlier interview. After that Alfonso and I sort of splintered off and began to have a separate affair of our own.'

'You're lying, Klaus,' Velázquez said. 'Arjan left you for Alfonso, which is why you killed them both.'

'No, Inspector, I'm telling you the way it really was.' Bloem dried his eyes with his hand. 'Either you shut up and listen or I'm not going to say another word.'

'Okay, go on.'

'The truth is I'm a masochist and I was very attracted to Alfonso, because he had a cruel, sadistic streak in him. So did Arjan and Rainer, even though they could all be delightfully charming when they wanted to be. They all used to hit me about and I loved it. I'm sure this must all sound very odd to someone like you, Inspector Jefe, but that's the way I am, whether by nature or nurture. I didn't tell you the truth before, because I thought you'd jump to the conclusion I was lying and it would just make me look more guilty.'

'So why tell us now, then?'

'Because it's the truth, and because it occurs to me that I made a mistake in lying to you before.' Bloem shrugged. 'Maybe I should've told you the truth from the beginning. The fact is, I'm sick of all these lies.'

'Go on.'

'Okay, so the man in the balaclava's broken into my flat, like I was just saying, and he hit Alfonso on the head with a baseball bat. I jumped on his back, but he turned on me, and – well, that's how I got my arm broken. He knocked me out, and when I came round they were both gone.'

'You mean the man took Alfonso with him?'

'Yes.'

'Was Alfonso de la Torre dead by then?'

'I have no way of knowing the answer to that for certain,' Bloem said. 'But I should imagine he was. The man hit Alfonso on the head hard with a baseball bat. It made this awful cracking noise like his skull must've been smashed in.'

'Then what happened?'

'That's all I know.'

'So who was this man that attacked you both?'

'I couldn't see his face because he was wearing a balaclava,' Bloem said. 'But I already told you that before, Inspector. That part was true, but I didn't tell you all of it.' He blew out his cheeks. 'I was afraid that if I told you what really happened, you'd assume it was a lie and that I'd killed Alfonso. Admitting that I'd been in bed with him seemed like the last thing I ought to do.'

Just then, the door opened and a uniform ushered Klaus Bloem's lawyer into the room.

'*Hola*,' Fernando Belloso said. 'Before we proceed I'd like to have some time alone with my client, Inspector Jefe.'

After leaving the incident room, Velázquez went to find Agente Pérez, who was waiting for him up in the office.

'What do you make of it, boss?' she asked him.

'Hard do say, Sara.'

The telephone on Velázquez's desk rang and he picked it up. It was Gajardo. 'What's new, José?' the Inspector Jefe asked him.

'Juan Muñoz's prints have been found in the stolen Seat, boss. And there were also blood prints of his on Alfonso de la Torre's clothing,' Gajardo said.

'I'm heading over to arrest Juan Muñoz.'

'I'll see you at the man's flat, boss.'

Velázquez hung up.

Pérez said, 'What was all that about?'

'No time to explain,' Velázquez said, as he made for the door.

Pérez followed him out.

Juan Muñoz was at the flat on Joaquin Costa when Velázquez and Pérez got there. They handcuffed him and took him back to the Jefatura, then put him in Incident Room 2.

Velázquez told Muñoz they had prints that proved he'd killed Alfonso de la Torre.

'You're lying,' Juan Muñoz sneered.

The Inspector Jefe shook his head. 'We've got enough to put you away for a long time, Juan.'

Muñoz said, 'I'm not saying another word until I've got a lawyer here.'

When the lawyer arrived, he asked to see proof of the evidence Velázquez claimed to have. The Inspector Jefe showed him documentation the fingerprint experts had produced, and the lawyer studied it. Then he asked for some time to talk with his client alone. Velázquez told him he could have a quarter of an hour.

When they resumed, Juan Muñoz said he'd decided to make a full confession.

'It's your only chance of avoiding a murder one charge,' the Inspector Jefe advised him.

'I know. My lawyer has already explained all that.'

Chapter 57

'I killed them all. I killed the vet and the bullfighter, as well as Prall and Haddad,' Muñoz said. 'Yolanda de la Torre paid me to do it.'

'Was Monica Pacheco in on it?'

'No, she didn't know anything about it.'

'Go on.'

'For the first murder, I took the key Monica had to the front door of Arjan Gelens' place. I found it in her handbag and made a copy without her knowing. Then it was just a case of driving over there and letting myself in. I walked up the stairs and the guy was there, sitting up in his bed.

'He'd been reading a book, and he looked at me with a surprised expression, like he'd been expecting somebody else. I held him at gunpoint and said I'd heard he was into kinky sex and I wanted to try it.

'I actually think he half thought it was all just a kinky sex game we were playing at first. But of course that was just wishful thinking on his part. I mean, I had a gun and so there was nothing he could do.

'Anyway, I got him to turn round and knocked him out with a blow to the back of the head. After that...well, you know the rest.'

'Why did you have to kill the man in such an elaborate and sadistic fashion? Couldn't you just have shot him?'

'The bull's horn was Yolanda's idea. Her instructions were very specific.'

'And Alfonso de la Torre?'

'Yolanda told me I'd be able to find him at the German's flat.'

'At Klaus Bloem's place, you mean?'

'That's the guy.'

'How did she know he'd be there?'

'No idea.' Juan Muñoz shrugged.

'You never asked her?'

'It was none of my business. I was just doing what she paid

me for.'

Velázquez figured the widow might well have been having Alfonso followed. Or perhaps Yolanda de la Torre had overheard her husband arranging to visit the German over the telephone.

At the end of the day, it didn't really matter how she found out. 'Okay, so what were her instructions?'

'To kill the husband, and beat up the German and knock him out.'

'She didn't want you to kill Klaus Bloem?'

'No, she said something about him just being a bit-part player and a victim. She seemed to think he was pathetic more than anything. Apparently her husband had threatened to leave her for the vet. That's why she wanted the husband and the vet dead. But the other guy, Bloem, was just to have a warning. Break his arm and hit him about a bit but don't kill him, she said.'

'So what happened?'

'I did what she wanted done,' Muñoz said. 'I broke into the flat and found them both in bed, which made it a lot easier. The bullfighter was on top and they were both making so much noise, I don't think they even heard me enter.

'I killed the husband with a hard blow to the back of the head with the baseball bat I'd taken with me. I moved really quickly. He didn't even have time to react. The German tried to stop me, so I hit him a couple of times with the baseball bat. I heard his arm crack and then I knocked him out. After that, it was just a matter of having to put the husband's body over my shoulder, and carry him down and put him in the boot of the car.'

'Nobody saw you walk out carrying the body like that?'

'No, I went down in the lift. Luckily he was small and so wasn't too heavy to carry.'

'Taking a bit of a risk, weren't you?'

'If anyone had tried to challenge me on the way out, I'd have hit them with the baseball bat,' Muñoz said. 'But as it was, I didn't see anyone. To be honest, I didn't feel like I was taking much of a risk at the time. It was dark and there weren't any people about. It probably helped that I was high on coke at the time. I felt sort of invincible, you know? Besides, I was wearing a balaclava, so nobody could've identified me later even if someone did see me. But like I say, they didn't.

'Then what did you do?''

'I drove to the ranch and dumped the body there, like Yolanda told me to.''

'Why did she want you to do that, do you think?'

'To make it look like he'd been killed there, I suppose.'

'So you speared Alfonso de la Torre's body at the ranch, then?'

'That's right.'

'How did you get past the security gate?'

'Yolando said her husband had told her a heifer at the ranch was due to calve. Seeing as the old vet was no longer around, they had to look for a new one. So she told me if I just said I was the vet the chances were they would believe me and let me in.'

'What would you have done if they hadn't let you in?'

'I'd have driven off and called her to ask for further instructions.'

Velázquez nodded. 'But once they let you into the ranch, I'm assuming somebody would've had to show you to where the animal was?'

'A man said he'd take me to the heifer, but I knocked him out. Then I tied him up and gagged him, before I dragged him over to some bushes.'

Which was just what the ranch hand said had happened.

'Which car was it that you used?'

'The Seat that Monica stole.'

'So Monica was in on it?'

'No, she didn't know I'd taken it,' Muñoz said. 'In fact, it wasn't part of the plan to begin with. I was going to use my own car. That's why I left it parked a little way from the house and told Monica it was stolen. But then when she told me she'd nicked another car, the idea came to me to use that one.

'Looking back on it I suppose I shouldn't of done that, because I might've made it look like Monica was in on it. But she wasn't. I just figured if I used the car she'd stolen then it wouldn't be traceable, so I'd be able to dump it afterwards and there'd be nothing to tie it to either of us.'

'So your own car hadn't really been stolen at all?'

'I reported it as being stolen. But that was just to give me an alibi in case anybody remembered the number on the license plate. Because I was still planning to use it on the job at that time.'

'So why did Monica steal another car?'

'I'd left my car a little way from where we live, so Monica wouldn't see it, like I just explained. So she believed me when I told her it'd been stolen,' Muñoz said. 'Then she wanted to go down to the ranch to see her cousin. And seeing as she didn't have my car to drive and couldn't afford a taxi, she went out and nicked another one. She was a big fan of her cousin's, and liked to watch him work with the bulls. She stole another Seat, because that's the kind of car I've got and it's what she's used to driving. She was nervous about driving a different make of car.

'She once tried to drive a Porsche she nicked and ended up crashing it. So ever since then she's only ever driven a Seat. I've tried to tell her it's a daft way to carry on, but I can't get through to her.' Juan Muñoz shrugged. 'Her problem is, she lacks confidence in her driving.'

The Inspector Jefe was bothered by something. 'It doesn't add up, Juan,' he said. 'We'd already brought Monica in to talk to her about the theft of the Seat. So why would you then go out and use the same car knowing that we knew she'd taken it? Did you want to frame her? It's either that, or she had to be in on it. Which was it?'

'I didn't know about any of that. By the time Monica got back that night, I'd already gone out.'

'So you had no idea that we knew the car you were going to use that night was stolen by Monica?'

'That's right,' he said. 'I knew Monica had stolen it, but I didn't have any idea that you people knew about it. Obviously I wouldn't of used it that night if I'd known, would I?'

'What would you have done, then?'

'I prob'ly would've stuck to my original plan and used my own car. Then I'd have set it alight afterwards,' Muñoz said.

'That's why I'd reported it stolen in the first place, remember. As it was, what with it being a stolen car I was using, I didn't think it was necessary to burn it.' He shrugged. 'I didn't reckon there was any risk of me being linked to it.'

'But your prints and Alfonso's blood was in the car.'

Muñoz shrugged. 'Even so, there was nothing to make anyone think the car was linked to the murder.'

'You left blood prints on the body,' the Inspector Jefe said. 'I'm surprised you didn't wear gloves.'

'I did to begin with...but they soon got soaked through with the bullfighter's blood. I was having trouble gripping the horn properly, when I tried to ram it up into him. So I took them off and put them in my pocket.'

Velázquez played with his upper lip as he processed what he'd just been told. 'And what about the man down in Bardino, Kurt Prall – how did you kill him?'

'It was just a question of breaking in and shooting the man. Easy as pie.'

'Did Yolanda say why she wanted Prall killed?'

'She said something about wanting to throw the wool over your eyes by introducing a new angle. She'd found out that Gelens and this guy Prall were a pair of old Nazis.'

'You didn't use a bull's horn on Prall.'

'Yolanda just told me to kill the guy. She didn't care how I did it. Besides, the man's wife was there in bed with him.'

'And you came after me that time, too.'

'Yolanda wanted to put some pressure on you.'

'Then you broke into my flat some time after that...'

'When nobody was home, that's right.'

'What was the idea of leaving the bull's horn on the bed?'

'Again that was Yolanda's idea. She thought intimidating you and your wife might persuade you to end the investigation.'

'And what about Mohammed Haddad?'

'Yolanda told me to kill him to try and frame Bloem. She reckoned that way it would make you people think that Bloem believed Haddad killed Gelens or had him killed and so Bloem killed him in revenge,' Muñoz said. 'Thinking about it, that was probably the real reason why Yolando wanted Bloem to be kept alive.'

'Because she thought we would jump to the conclusion that Bloem figured Haddad was behind the tampering with the bulls,' Velázquez said. 'If she could get us to swallow that, then it would be logical for us to assume Haddad either killed Gelens or had him killed once he learned the vet had found out about him.'

'Exactly.'

Velázquez nodded slowly as he took what he'd just learned on board. It all added up. 'It sounds like Yolanda confided in you a fair bit?'

Muñoz shrugged. 'She likes to drink, and she'd sit down with me when her husband was down at the ranch and work things out in her head. And she'd sort of talk me through it. I suppose she figured she'd be bound to go down if I did, so there was no added danger in telling me what she was thinking. She's an intelligent woman – that was obvious from the way she thought it all out.'

'And a very unscrupulous and dangerous one.'

'Yeah, well that too. But she almost got away with it.'

Velázquez looked at Gajardo. 'We'll need a full written confession from him, José,' he said, and with that he left the room.

He took the lift down to the basement car park, found his car in its usual bay, and climbed in behind the wheel. Now all that remained for him to do was go and arrest the widow.

Chapter 58

Velázquez was heading south, with his foot on the floor, when a female voice came through on the radio. He took his hand off the wheel and answered it. '*Hola*?'

'*Hola*, Luis.'

'Who is this?'

'Can't you guess?'

'Yolanda?'

'Serrano was kind enough to let me use his radio.'

Velázquez had a terrible sinking feeling. 'Where's Serrano?'

'He had an accident.'

'Where are you?'

'That's not the issue here.'

'What?'

'It's where I'm going and how you're going to help me get there.'

'I don't follow.'

'I'll need a small plane with someone to pilot it.'

'And why would I help you, Yolanda?'

'Because you want to see your wife again, alive.'

'You're bluffing,' he said. 'You don't have her with you.'

'You know for a clever man, Inspector Jefe, it wasn't very bright of you to send Pe to her mother's like that where any old fool could find her. You really do surprise me at times. And then allowing Agente Serrano to drive her to the television studio. I can't say I'm impressed. All I had to do was wait outside for them to show up. And having the weapon of surprise on my side made things easy.'

Velázquez could see the crazy, twisted sense in the woman's words. 'If you harm Pe you'll only go away for an even longer time, Yolanda. They'll throw away the key. You'll never get out.'

'Oh come on, Luis. You and I both know that I'll never go to prison. Either I'll get away or I'll die trying. And if it's the latter then Pe's going with me.'

'Okay, I'll get you your plane.'

'That's more like it.'

'Where do you want it?'

'There's an old airfield ten kilometres north of Riogrande.'

'Okay…but you've got to let Pe go in return.'

'I'll keep my part of the deal, but only if you keep yours.'

'First I need to talk to Pe.'

'Sure, but keep it brief.'

Velázquez hit the brake hard, to avoid crashing into the back of the car in front, which had stopped for a light. At that moment, Pe came on. 'Luis?'

'Pe, are you all right?'

'Yes, but Yolanda's got me tied up and she's got a knife. She says she's going to cut my throat if you don't get her the plane she's asking for.'

'Don't worry about a thing, Pe. I'll see to it.'

'You'd better,' said Yolanda, who'd now come back on. 'And make it snappy. You've got an hour, tops. I'll be in touch.' And with that, she signed off.

The car in front began to move again, and Velázquez pulled over. He called his immediate superior, Comisario Alonso. The Comisario picked up and Velázquez quickly brought him up to speed. And for once Comisario Alonso showed that he had a human side and was sympathetic. He promised to get a plane to the airfield as fast as he could, and that was all that Velázquez cared about.

'If it's not there within the hour my wife will be murdered, Comisario,' the Inspector Jefe said. 'And she wants a pilot to fly her off to wherever she wants to go.

'Yes, I understand. I'll deal with it. Don't worry.'

They hung up and Velázquez set off again. He moved into the fast lane and headed for the airfield where Yolanda wanted the plane to be sent.

Sure enough, when he got there, he saw his wife and Yolanda. Pe was lying back on the bonnet of a blue BMW, which was parked on the runway, and Yolanda was holding what looked from a distance like it might be a kitchen knife across her windpipe.

Velázquez got out of his car and began to walk towards them. When he got to within twenty yards of the two women, Yolanda told him he was close enough.

Velázquez stopped in his tracks.

'Take out your gun and drop it on the ground. And do it real slow and easy, otherwise my hand might just slip a little. Which'd be a pity, because this knife's kinda sharp.'

Velázquez did as she said. He hated having to surrender his weapon, but right now he didn't see that he had any alternative.

'Now kick it as hard as you can.'

He sent it skidding over the tarmac runway, so that it was well beyond his reach.

Now he was no longer armed, he figured he had better try to keep the woman talking. 'So now what, Yolanda?'

'We wait for the plane to arrive.'

'You'll never get away with this.'

'You'd better hope I do for your wife's sake, Luis. Because if I go down then she's coming with me. But I already told you that. What's wrong with your memory, Inspector?'

'You're crazy.'

'On the contrary, I'm totally sane.'

'Crazy people always think that.'

'I never do anything without having a reason for it.'

'And what was all that business with the bulls' horns about?'

'Rather a nice touch, I thought, didn't you?'

'I can't say I agree.'

'You lack imagination, Luis.'

'You're sick, Yolanda,' Velázquez said. 'Having your husband killed is bad enough. But only someone who's crazy would want it done in the way you got Juan Muñoz to do it.'

'Didn't you just love the deviant macho sexuality of it all?'

'You need help, Yolanda. Stop this nonsense now and I'll be sure you get it.'

'The only help I need's for you to get me my plane and someone to pilot it.'

'I told you, it's on its way.'

'It had better be or your wife gets it.'

'I'm being straight with you.'

'So what's with all the talk about me needing help?'

'You can fly away and hide out someplace,' Velázquez said. 'Sure you can. But wherever you go, you'll be taking your problems with you.'

'Right now, I'd say you and your wife are the ones with the problems.'

'Leave Pe out of this. She never did anything to you.'

'She's in it up to her neck now, whether she likes it or not.'

Velázquez figured he'd better try to keep her talking, until the plane arrived. 'But tell me a little more about your *modus operandi*. Surely you must realize how cruel and vulgar all that business with the bulls' horns was?'

'On the contrary, the bull's horn has come to symbolise Spanish culture. When a woman's husband cheats on her, don't we say that he's *put a set of horns on her*?'

'But that's just a figure of speech.'

'It's a figure of speech that goes right to the heart of our culture,' Yolanda said. 'But you're Spanish, the same as me, so you hardly need me to explain all this to you.'

'Why didn't you just divorce your husband?'

'And lose half of everything?' she said. 'Then there was Alfonso's life insurance policy to consider.'

'So it was all about the money?'

'It always is, up to a point. But it was about other stuff, too. I'm a proud woman. Some women just sit idly by and let their men run around behind their backs and turn them into a laughing stock.' She shook her head. 'That just wasn't an option for someone like me.'

'So you preferred to pay a man to murder your husband and three other men.'

'That's right, Inspector. I'm what you might call a woman of character. I can assure you there's nothing the slightest bit crazy about me.'

'This is all over now, Yolanda. Can't you see that? You've reached the end of the line. Why don't you just let Pe go?'

Just then, as if on cue, they heard the drone of a light aeroplane's engine. They didn't see it at first, but then it came into view.

Moments later, the light aircraft began its descent, and they watched it as it landed on the runway and came to a halt a hundred metres or so from the BMW.

Yolanda pulled at Pe's arm and got her up off the bonnet of the car. Then she walked with her towards Velázquez. Pe was in front and Yolanda was right behind her, and she was holding the kitchen knife tight against Pe's throat, horizontally.

Velázquez realized that Yolanda was planning on picking up the gun she had forced him to kick away earlier. He took a step forward and Yolanda told him to stop right where he was or she'd kill his wife. Then she told Pe to kneel down on the tarmac, next to the gun.

Once Pe had done as she was told, Yolanda crouched forward and held the knife to her throat. Then she reached for Velázquez's Glock.

As she did so, Yolanda lost balance slightly for a fraction of a second and allowed the knife to move away from Pe's throat. Sensing her chance, Pe sprung off the ground.

She grabbed Yolanda's arm and pressed down on it, hard, to give herself traction. Yolando fell onto the tarmac and dropped the knife. But she had the gun in her other hand by now, and she tried to turn with it.

Seeing that Yolanda was about to try and shoot Pe, Velázquez dashed forward, then threw himself on top of Yolanda. They began to wrestle for the gun, and she sent it skidding over the tarmac with her free hand.

Yolanda tried to go after it, but Velázquez grabbed her round the waist and she found that she was unable to move.

The next thing the Inspector Jefe knew, a shot rang out and Yolanda's body fell onto the tarmac.

It took Velázquez a moment to realize what had happened. Then he saw blood running from Yolanda's mouth.

He turned his head and saw Pe, standing there with the gun in her hand.

Velázquez turned Yolanda over and felt for a pulse. There was nothing doing.

He gave her the kiss of life, but it was no good.

He looked at Pe and said, 'She's dead.'

Pe shrugged. 'What do you expect after what she did?'

Velázquez went over to his wife and wrested the gun from her hand. He took out his handkerchief and rubbed her prints from the handle. Then he put it in the holster he was wearing. 'You didn't shoot her,' he said. 'I did.'

'Who cares?' Pe said. 'Just so long as the bitch is dead.'

Turning his head, he saw that the pilot was making his way over. 'It's all right,' Velázquez told him. 'Your services won't be required after all. It was a false alarm.'

Chapter 59

In bed later that night Pe said, 'I suppose Yolanda must've reckoned she'd be set up for the rest of her life if she'd got away with it.'

'For sure,' Velázquez said. 'Alfonso had most of his money tied up in the USA. He'd taken sound advice and invested wisely. As his sole heir, Yolanda would have received five million US dollars from his life insurance policy alone. Add to that the three and a half million he was already worth, and she would have come out of it all sitting pretty.'

Pe dropped her head onto Velázquez's chest. 'Where does Kurt Prall fit into it all?'

'Yolanda got Muñoz to kill Prall to muddy the waters, after she discovered Prall and Gelens were both old Nazis. But there's more to it than that. Because it turns out that Prall took part in gay sex sessions with Alfonso de la Torre and the vet.'

'How did you find that out?'

'I talked to a contact I have down in Bardino this evening, a British private op. The man was keeping his cards a little too close to his chest for my liking to begin with, but I finally persuaded him to open up and play ball.'

'But how did this private dick know about Prall's sex life?'

'Prall's widow hired him to follow her husband.'

'Why did she do that?'

'She reckoned he'd been acting strangely…like he was frightened something was going to happen to him.'

'That makes sense, after what happened to Gelens and Alfonso.'

'Prall and Gelens were both guards at Mauthausen concentration camp in World War Two. So after the vet was killed, Prall might have figured it was someone from their past that had come back to get them.'

'A survivor from Mauthausen, you mean?'

'Those guys must have been looking over their shoulder all the time – especially after General Franco died. Although it seems Prall was also frightened that Albert Klein, who was the commandant at Mauthausen, had reason to want him out of the way.'

'And all the time it was a jealous wife that was behind it all,' Pe said. 'But there's one thing I still don't get. Why did Yolanda decide to spare Klaus Bloem?'

'There are two possibilities. One is that she might have figured he'd make a good fall guy.' Velázquez ran his fingers through Pe's hair. 'It's certainly true that the media wanted him to take the rap. If you recall, they were giving me a hard time because I refused to hurry up and charge him. And Comisario Alonso, Judge Bautista and the Mayor were of the same mind.'

'And the other theory?'

'Yolanda may have considered Bloem to be more of a victim than anything else.'

'Because Arjan Gelens dumped him?'

'That's right. Bloem was in love with the man. But it seems Gelens was only using him to entertain himself come the end.'

Pe kissed Velázquez's chest. 'Surely that horrible boss of yours has got to be happy with you now that you've solved the case?'

'Are you kidding? That man was *born* unhappy.'

Pe said, 'It's just struck me that there's a moral to the story.'
'Which is?'

'When you find someone you love and they love you then you'd better treat them right.'

Velázquez considered what Pe had said for a moment. 'What if one of the pair gets fed up?'

Pe ran a hand through the curly hair on Velázquez's chest and said, 'That's when all the trouble starts.'

Velázquez felt what, given his recent track record, was a rather unlikely stirring down below. 'You're right there,' he said. 'That *is* when all the trouble starts.'

After they had made love, for the first time in weeks, Velázquez fell into a deep sleep. He dreamed that he was in the office at the Jefatura, and that all of the officers in his team were smoking at the same time. Although he knew, somewhere in his mind, that Serrano and Gajardo were the only two smokers in the team, and that José was trying to give up. But such is the crazy logic of dreams.

And he told himself this as he slept.

Don't expect any of this to make too much sense, because it's only a dream.

Finally, the smell of smoke in his nostrils was so intense that he woke up…and he realized that the flat was on fire. He tried to wake Pe up. She mumbled something, without opening her eyes.

Velázquez lifted his wife onto his back and carried her to the door. But when he opened it, huge flames licked at him. He slammed the door and recrossed the smoke-filled room, still with Pe on his back. He struggled to get air into his lungs as he opened the French windows, then stepped out onto the balcony. He set Pe down on her feet. She was still groggy, so he held her arms as she gasped for air.

'What's going on?' she said, once she realized where she was.

'The place is on fire.'

Velázquez knew he had to think of something fast. The fire would soon consume the bedroom and they would be burned alive. And jumping from this height would be suicidal. He dashed back into the bedroom, grabbed the sheet from the bed, then tied it to the rail on the verandah. 'Watch what I do, Pe,' he said. 'Then you follow me. ' He stepped over the verandah, and used the sheet as a rope to climb down to the balcony directly below.

Pe climbed down after him and, once Velázquez had caught her in his arms, he banged on the window. He had to keep banging for a while, but eventually Boris, the man that lived in the flat, came and opened the window. 'What the devil's up, Luis?'

'Our flat is on fire,' Velázquez said. 'What's it like on your floor?'

'There's no smoke as yet.'

'Even so, we need to evacuate the building.'

Boris let them in, before he went and roused his wife. Meanwhile, Velázquez and Pe crossed the bedroom, then went into the hallway. Finding there was no fire there, they went out and began knocking on the doors of the neighbouring flats, and telling everyone to leave the building.

Then Velázquez remembered his neighbour, Señora Tejado. He ran up the stairs, and began to choke on the smoke that was coming out from under the door of his own flat. Fortunately, the fire had not yet spread to the hallway.

Señora Tejado took a while to come to the door, but she did so eventually and Velázquez was able to help her down to the street without any problem.

With that, Velázquez and Boris began to talk to the other neighbours, to ensure that nobody was still inside the building. And no sooner had they satisfied themselves that the building had been safely evacuated than someone tapped Velázquez on the shoulder.

The Inspector Jefe turned, and who should he find himself face to face with other than Art Blakey, the private dick. 'Hi, Luis,' he said. 'I'm glad to hear everyone's got out in time.'

'But what are *you* doing here, Arthur?'

'Oscar, the programme manager for your wife's breakfast show, was worried that somebody's been out to do her harm. So he hired me to keep an eye on your place.'

'And why would he have called someone like you, a dick that's based down in Bardino, instead of getting a local guy?'

'He told me he asked Pe if she'd ever heard you mention any private investigators that you reckoned you could trust.'

'Pe never mentioned it.'

'Oscar didn't tell her what it was about, so she probably forgot about it.'

'But it was Yolanda de la Torre, the bullfighter's wife, that was behind all the murders,' Velázquez said. 'She paid a man by the name of Juan Muñoz to do her dirty work for her.'

'Oscar was concerned that it might be somebody else who had it in for your wife…somebody who was close to the politician, Pedro Villalonga.'

'But Juan Muñoz confessed to breaking into our flat and leaving the bull's horn on our bed.'

'Maybe so…only it wasn't him that burned down the

television studio.'

'How did you know about that?' Velázquez said. 'And if you knew something about it then why didn't you tell me, when I was with you down in Bardino?'

'I didn't know about it then.'

'Huh?'

'This chap Oscar only contacted me after he'd seen the report on television about how the bullfighter's wife was killed in a shootout. He was concerned that you would think Pe was out of danger.'

'And what made him believe she *wasn't*?'

'He was convinced the person that attacked her at the studio before setting the building alight was linked to Pedro Villalonga, as I said.'

'You're saying this person's not linked to Yolanda de la Torre?'

'You got it.'

'So you mean to say you were out here, keeping an eye on the building tonight while we slept?'

'I was indeed.'

'In that case I'm afraid you didn't make a very good job of protecting us, Arthur,' Velázquez said. 'I woke up to find my flat in flames. We were lucky to get out of there alive.'

'Yes, I'm sorry about that, Luis. I was about to go in and get you out. But I see you're both alive and in one piece.'

'Yes, by the grace of God – and no thanks to you.'

'I'm afraid I was taken up with chasing the man that broke into your flat.'

'You what…?'

'I caught up with him all right in the end, though.'

'Come again…?'

'If you'd like to come with me.'

Velázquez followed the private dick over to his Porsche, and watched him open what the Inspector Jefe at first took to be the lid on the engine. But then he remembered that the 911 had the boot at the front…and there was a man lying in it, bound and gagged.

Art Blakey ripped the tape from the man's mouth and said,

'Who sent you?'

The man told him to go and take a jump.

Art Blakey put the tape back over the man's mouth and slammed the boot shut. Then he looked at Velázquez and asked him how he fancied the idea of going for a spin. Velázquez said he couldn't think of anything he'd like more.

The two men climbed into the car and headed out of the city, then joined the motorway.

Velázquez asked the dick where he was taking him.

'It's not so much where I'm taking *you*, Luis,' Blakey said. 'But rather where we're taking *our friend* in front.'

'Okay, so where are you planning on taking our friend in front?'

'Somewhere nice and dark, where nobody will be around to see us.'

'That sounds like a good place,' Velázquez said.

Chapter 60

They drove for a few more minutes on the motorway, then Blakey turned off and headed up a B road. Minutes later, they turned off into a dusty track. There were some trees up ahead. The private dick asked Velázquez if he didn't think this might be a good place to stop.

Velázquez said it would be as good a place as any.

Blakey drove off the track and into the trees and pulled up. The two men climbed out of the car and Blakey opened the bonnet. They lifted the man out and dropped him onto the ground.

Velázquez had the idea of sitting the man up and tying him to one of the birch trees.

When they had finished tying him, Velázquez took the tape from the man's mouth and asked who had sent him.

The man spat in the Inspector Jefe's face.

Velázquez kicked the man in the stomach.

Then he asked him again.

They went on like this for a little while, until the man eventually broke down and confessed that Pedro Villalonga had sent him.

Blakey untied the man's hands and gave him a pen and a letter-writing pad. He explained to the man that he could either write a short confession, stating that he had set the Inspector Jefe's flat alight under instructions from the cabinet minister, Pedro Villalonga, or he could expect to be kicked and beaten until he did so.

The man complained that he couldn't see to write in the dark.

Blakey produced a torch and shone its light on the page, and the man began to write.

When he had finished, Velázquez told him to put his signature at the bottom and then print his name and national insurance number under it.

The man did as he was told.

Velázquez took the confession from him and read it.

Next he reached into the man's pocket and took out his wallet. He found the man's ID card in it, and checked the number on it against the one the man had written under his confession to see if they matched. They did.

Velázquez asked the man where Pedro Villalonga lived.

The man said he didn't know.

Blakey asked the Inspector Jefe whether he was prepared to accept the man's confession and let him go, or whether he would prefer to throw him in the river.

Velázquez said, 'What river?'

The man began to sob and beg for his life.

'There's got to be a river somewhere near here,' Blakey said. 'Or we could drive down to the coast. I've got a little yacht moored there, and we could take him a way out and give him a proper sea burial.'

The man was still sobbing and begging for his life.

Velázquez told Blakey to cut the rope that bound the man's ankles. As soon as the private dick had done that, the man tried to make a run for it. But Velázquez tripped him and he fell. The man tried to get up, but Velázquez kicked him hard in the privates. He made a yelping noise and fell back down to the ground.

'Now you're going to take us to Pedro Villalonga,' Velázquez said.

The man said he didn't know where Villalonga lived.

The Inspector Jefe told Art Blakey he was beginning to favour his idea of giving the man a sea burial.

The man began to beg for his life once more.

Velázquez told him to shut up and kicked him. 'Now this is your last chance,' he said. 'Either you take us to Pedro Villalonga or you go to sleep with the fishes tonight. Which is it going to be?'

'Okay,' the man sobbed. 'I'll take you to him.'

'We need an address,' Velázquez said. 'And if it turns out you're lying to us, we'll turn the car round and take a drive down to the coast. How does that sound?'

'Okay,' the man said. 'He lives in number seven, Calle San Vicente.'

Velázquez knew the street.

They tied the man's hands and feet again, and put him in the boot of the car. Then they drove back the way they had come. Once they reached the city, they headed for the exclusive area in which Calle San Vicente was situated.

The minister's home turned out to be an elegant old palace. Blakey pulled over and took a pair of handguns from the glove compartment. He handed one to Velázquez. 'I hope you're not averse to using a Beretta, old boy,' he said in English. Velázquez asked him whether it was loaded. Blakey assured him it was, then the two men climbed out of the car and went over to the house.

As Velázquez was still wearing his pyjamas he stood to the side, out of sight, while Blakey rang the doorbell.

It was Villalonga himself that came to the door. Blakey showed him his gun and said they were going for a drive.

'What is this?' Villalonga wanted to know. 'Are you kidnapping me?'

'Just get out here before I change my mind and shoot you.'

Villalonga stepped outside and found himself looking at Velázquez, standing there in his pyjamas. 'What is this?'

'Señor Villalonga,' Velázquez said, 'it's my duty to inform you that you are under arrest.'

He read the man his rights.

'But what are you talking about?'

'We've got your man,' Velázquez said.

'My *man*?' Villalonga was playing it dumb. 'What the *devil* are you talking about?'

'Get in the car.'

Villalonga realized that he had no alternative other than to do as he was told.

Velázquez would later tell friends and colleagues that the arrest marked a double first in his career. It was the first time he had ever arrested a cabinet minister, just as it was also the first time he had made an arrest in his pyjamas.

Printed in Great Britain
by Amazon

78363559R00162